EACH
PERFECT
*Gift*

*Also by Alicia G. Ruggieri:*

A TIME OF GRACE series
> *The Fragrance of Geraniums*
> *All Our Empty Places*
> *A Love to Come Home To*

*A Holy Passion: A Novel of David Brainerd and Jerusha Edwards*

*The House of Mercy*

*Jemima Sudbury and the Mystery of the Missing Cufflinks*

*Mr. Portly Finds His Purpose*

*For you, "Annie":*
*Whoever and wherever you are, the Father God*
*knows your name.*

God sets the solitary in families;
He brings out those who are bound into
prosperity;
But the rebellious dwell in a dry land.
*Psalm 68:6*

## Chapter One

*November 15, 1937 – Monday*

The night burdened him; the darkness troubled him. The scent of stale smoke and cheap booze filled Ben's nostrils, burning his throat. Had he been drinking as well? It was not possible, was it? He had been free of alcohol's chains for months now... hadn't he?

Yet, as he let his eyes fall to trail the smoke that spewed from his nostrils, he found that a cigarette, half-smoked already, balanced nimbly between his thumb and index finger. The taste of nicotine sweetened and then bittered in his mouth. Disbelief fell over him. It was a feeling of discomfort, as of a too-tight collar, one made for another man's neck.

Ben let his eyes wander over his surroundings, eerily

familiar. How had he gotten here? Hadn't he taken Betty on a date tonight? They'd made plans... plans to... The alcohol he'd already consumed mixed with the smoky atmosphere. His thoughts muddled. He shook his head to clear it. Oh, yeah, he'd planned to bring Betty to the hayride that the church's young people's group had planned.

Why, then, was he here, sitting in the old loose box stall he and Aldo and the boys used to play cards in, far from Chetham, Rhode Island? Why had he abandoned his plans with sweet Betty? And how had he gotten here?

And this was no longer the life he'd chosen to live.

He was redeemed. Restored. Forgiven. The old had passed away...

"Your move, buddy," Aldo's voice sliced through Ben's jumbled thoughts like a sharp blade through soft cheese.

Or had it? At this moment, his past seemed as close as it ever had. In fact, it seemed to be his present.

Ben's gaze connected with Aldo's dark eyes, shadowed and hooded even more by the dim lighting of the single kerosene lantern set on the makeshift table.

He looked down at his cigarette-free hand and saw that one card remained. Reaffirming his eye contact with Aldo, Ben set the card down, a feeling of dread circling through his gullet and spiraling up through his chest. Somehow, he knew he'd lost – even before he set down the card.

Sure enough, a thin smile snaked along Aldo's lips. "You're done. Pay up, Benji-boy." The man leaned across the table, so close that Ben swung his head back to avoid the garlic-and-unbrushed-teeth aroma emanating from his fellow card-player's mouth.

Aldo must have thought Ben was shaking his head, refusing to pay. Eyes narrowing, the smile dropped from his lips. "I said, you pay up, buddy."

Ben's head felt water-logged. It must be from the booze. "Hold on, hold on a minute! Lemme get my money." He tried to stand so that he could access his wallet. As he did so, his leg twisted in the wooden folding chair somehow, and he felt his body flip out of the chair.

His head hit the straw-strewn floor of the stall. The impact disoriented but didn't hurt him, and he tried to get his feet untangled from the chair legs. Yet his limbs seemed unwilling to cooperate.

"Don't wanna fork over the dough now that you've lost, huh?" Aldo hovered over him like a turkey vulture, his face shadowed by the increasing darkness of the stall. "Don't have it, after all?"

"No, it ain't that. I got the money. Lemme... Gimme a minute to get up."

But Aldo either didn't understand or merely wanted to take advantage of a man when he was down because, the next thing that Ben knew, thick hands wrapped around his throat, elbows dug into his ribs, and that terrible, no-good-thing-about-it breath clouded the air around his head. For a moment, Ben couldn't figure out which one strangled the air from his lungs: Aldo's hands or his halitosis.

As his windpipe closed, he knew, though, that for some reason, this time was different than any other time Aldo and he had scrapped. Usually, one or both emerged with some bruises. This time, Ben sensed that, if he could, Aldo wanted to choke Ben to death.

*And such were some of you...*

The scraps of the Bible verse Reverend Cloud had

given Ben recently flickered through his head.

*And so am I still.* The despair that flooded, that filled his soul at the realization nearly made Ben give up the struggle against his attacker. The cigarette dangling from his fingers, apparently standing Betty up tonight in favor of playing cards and drinking with his old buddies, and now, grappling on the floor like an animal.

*I never changed. I never was different.*

*But I want to be! Oh, Lord, help me!*

With a sudden shove of desperation, he threw Aldo from him. He heard a crack, followed by a groan. Then silence. Ben rose, rubbing at the place where Aldo's hands had bruised his neck, and peered over at the unconscious man lying a few feet away. It appeared that he'd hit his head on a brick; a scarlet rivulet threaded its way down Aldo's forehead, between his closed eyes. Staring at the dark-haired man's head, lying there on the dirty straw, fear flew over and settled upon Ben. What if Aldo was…?

He swallowed hard. He had to escape. He had to get back home, back to Chetham, back to Betty, back…

He was no longer a part of this scene, of this life. Was he?

If he wasn't, if he had left it all behind months ago, why then was he here? Terror seized him, and sweat broke out on his skin, dampening his shirt.

*I've gotta get out of here.*

His mind focused only on escape, Ben whirled toward the open door of the stall and rushed through the dark aisle, paying no heed to the nickering of his beloved horses.

*Run! Run as far as you can. Escape!*

He nearly tripped over his own feet as his boots finally met the threshold of the stable's main door and slid into the black night. Pausing for a moment, he let his eyes travel up to the sky, taking in the cold brilliance of the stars. It came back to him, what he'd once read in a book and passed along to his sister, Grace: *We're all in the gutter, but some of us are looking at the stars.*

Bitterness crawled up his belly and into his throat, strangling even the fear he'd felt moments before. What good did it do you to look at the stars when there was no way to reach their light? Ben glanced down at his hand, the same hand that had thrown Aldo, maybe killed him, just moments ago. Ben had thought Christ had washed him clean, made a new man of him. *But no, I'm the same ol' Ben as ever.*

How could he go back? Back to Chetham and Betty? Could he pretend that he'd never come back to his old life?

*But maybe you returned here because this is what you really want.* The thought slid through the crevices of his panic.

He shook his head with violence. *No! No!*

He would forget all of this night. He would forget it all. He would get back to Chetham somehow – though he couldn't remember how he'd arrived at the stables in the first place.

The night looked darker, but he strode forward into it. He could catch a ride, surely.

"Ben? Is that really you?"

The voice came from behind him. He recognized its soft lilt. How long had it been since he'd heard that sound, sweet as fresh honey drizzled over homemade bread?

His gut twisted with a new emotion: desire that pierced all his bones, laced with guilt. Dread fell over him, yet he felt forced to turn around, to meet the siren who owned that voice.

She stepped out of the shadows near the stable door. At the sight of her, even in the dark, memories flooded Ben's brain: memories he'd worked hard to bury forever.

Stepping toward him, the young woman spoke again. "Ben. I knew it. I knew you'd come back for me." Her heavy-lashed eyes met his, and he saw that hope had made them glisten, made the greens and browns that swirled together in them even more captivating.

He couldn't speak. With her, he had always been at a loss for words. When he'd done anything that he knew she'd dislike, or if he wanted to leave, he'd just up and go, without a word to her. He could never take her tears or the disappointment that would fill her face. He could never take it before... and he knew that he could not take it now.

*Run.*

But though the word filled his mind, though his heart beat faster in anticipation of the exertion his mind demanded, Ben found that his feet could not move from their spot in the stable yard. Her presence paralyzed his will.

She stepped closer to him, and he saw that her beauty was undiminished by the time he had been out of her company. She had always been like a rose to him – He'd called her that, his wild Irish rose, just like the song – when they'd gotten along, that is.

Which wasn't often, as she had the temper of a bobcat whenever something or someone displeased her. And Ben had done that often.

And yet, when they had gotten along, it had been wonderful...

Now the girl's lips parted with the beginning of a tender smile, and she reached up a small pale hand to touch his cheek. Her fingers glided over his skin, and his heart began to beat more quickly. As she raised her face toward him, Ben couldn't have run if he'd tried.

Yet just before the girl's lips touched his, the remembrance of Betty came to mind. Sweet Betty, whose heart he'd determined to win. He could not break her trust. He could not go back to his old ways, not even for…

Desperation rose in his chest, the desire to flee battling with the desire of his flesh. Then he heard, as though from far away, as though it came from someone other than himself, a shout for mercy.

Ben jolted awake, limbs trembling and stiff. After a moment, he forced himself to relax, letting his muscles sink into the mattress. He listened to the silence of the night embracing the old brick house, empty except for his own presence there. *It was a dream. Only a dream.* Beneath him, the linens felt moist with sweat, despite the chilly air outside his bedcovers.

He rose, lifting his pounding head from the pillow and swinging his legs over the edge of the bed. Relief flooded him as the solidity of the cool wooden floor met his bare feet. He smoothed a hand over the sheets, glad – oh, so glad! – that he truly was in Chetham, among his family, with Betty, for good. His old life – the old Ben Picoletti – was as dead and buried as was the physical body of his father, Charlie.

*"Buried with Him in baptism…"*

Closing his eyes, he brought the memory to mind of his baptism, held just this past September, in Mill Pond, past the edge of town. The brownish-yellow water had swirled around Ben's pant legs as he'd waded out to where Reverend Cloud, Betty's father, stood, submerged to his chest and smiling that serious but joy-filled smile of his.

The plump, middle-aged minister's strength had surprised Ben when he'd dunked him beneath the murky water. Ben had been afraid that Reverend Cloud – who admitted to being overfond of his wife's homemade doughnuts – wouldn't be able to lower and raise up a sturdy, hard-muscled young man like himself. But no sooner had the water closed over his head than Ben felt the liquid part again over his head. The sweetness of the blue sky on an early autumn day met his eyes, equally filled with both lake water and tears.

*"Raised with Him in newness of life!"*

The baptism hadn't saved him; Ben knew that. Only Jesus Christ could save a man – not a dunking in Mill Pond. But he'd known that it was a step of obedience that God wanted him to take at the start of his new life as a born-again Christian – telling people out-loud by his action that he was indeed on a new path in life.

*Raised in newness of life.* How could there be so much hope – real, sure hope – in three words? Strange though it might seem to some, there was.

Now, standing up from his bed, Ben sucked in a breath. "Thank You, Father. Thank You that it was all just a dream." Picking up the flashlight from his bedside table – the same rickety, chipped one he'd had during all his growing-up years – Ben made his way from the bedroom and down the stairs. Dreams like that called for a tall glass of cold milk and four or five of those molasses cookies Mama had handed to him the last time he'd gone over to the Giorgi home.

### *November 16, 1937 – Tuesday*

"You ain't staying here, girl." Her father's voice rubbed her ears like large-grain sandpaper. "Noooo, siree, you ain't. Left before, didn't ya? Told me that ya needed no place here." Daddy's coffee cup slammed down on the scratched and sticky countertop. A little wave of liquid, weighed down with heavy cream, splashed over the rim, trickled down his beefy hand, and puddled in the tiny crevices of his oil-stained cuticles. At this, he wrinkled his wide, flat nose and wiped his paw across his bleach-spotted overalls. "Sheesh-Louise...."

Annie swallowed down the panic that crawled up her throat. Visible panic would only block her way back in the door of 438 Buckley Road. Daddy would sniff out fear quicker than a hound on the trail of a coon. He would relish the fact that she was desperate for a place to stay and that he could fulfill her need... but wouldn't. He would teach her a lesson, as he'd always said she needed to learn. *Don't panic, Annie. Don't show him that you're desperate.*

She breathed slowly, refusing to allow her chest to shake with fear. Fear that she'd be on the dark street tonight. She had no more money to secure a room. She'd used the last of it for bus fare to get home.

Letting her eyes travel around the diner, she held back a bitter wave that threatened to overwhelm her. *Home?* Is that what this was? Daddy, his face carved into an unvarying expression of scorn whenever his eyes fell on her, reminding her without words that she was no true daughter of his. Mama... gone. Still gone.

Annie hadn't even tried to go to the house when the bus dropped her off in a cloud of dust this morning. She'd turned from the nearly-empty drop-off point near the center of the dead-end town – if a town as tiny as Rulls Landing could be said to have a center – and gone straight to the garage her father had worked at for the past twenty years.

That was one good thing that could be said about Daddy, Annie considered as she let her eyes glance at him now: He was consistent.

Sometimes mercilessly so.

When she'd showed up at the garage, he'd just pulled himself out from beneath a silver Ford. When he saw her for the first time in two years, his eyes hadn't widened in surprise, his mouth hadn't dropped open in joy, and his arms hadn't received her in a wide hug of welcome.

Nope. He'd remained consistent.

He'd just looked at her with that same yet ever-deepening expression of I-told-ya-so-ness, wiped off his huge hands with an old rag, and strode through the open door into the street. She'd known where he was headed: to the same place he'd gone for the past twenty years, five days a week, every morning at ten o'clock. Keeping her ratty purse tucked beneath her arm, Annie had scurried after him. She had to get him to take her back. There was no Mama any longer to go crying to, to sympathize with her, to wipe her tears away with the edge of a worn apron.

Mama'd been gone ten years this March. And Daddy's treatment of her had worsened ever since that day.

"Ya know, you've got some nerve, girl." Daddy didn't make any attempt to keep his voice down. He seemed glad for the few ears of those customers in the diner pretending to be completely absorbed in drinking their mid-morning cup whilst chowing down on scrambled eggs with ketchup and thin-cut toast smeared with grape jelly. "Coming back home now, like this. Ain't right. Ya should know bettah. I taught ya bettah, didn't I?"

Annie suppressed the shudder that ran through her as she remembered that Daddy's teaching, as far back as she could remember, had involved being sat down on a hard chair while listening to him lecture her about whatever terrible deed she had done... for hours. By the age of twelve, she had become very good at adjusting the radio dial of her mind to another station entirely.

But now he was looking at her, waiting expectantly for her answer. She licked her dry lips. "Yeah, Daddy, ya did."

He leaned back on his wooden stool, the pleasure apparent on his face that she had affirmed him publicly, before all the customers in Joe's. "Well, then, ya know exactly what I'm gonna say now to ya, girl, don'tcha?"

She opened her mouth to speak again, but the words wouldn't come out of her throat: *Yeah, Daddy, I know.*

"Ya reap what ya sow." Satisfaction laced the words that came easily from his mouth. He raised his cup to his lips and slurped, not taking his gaze off his only daughter – if daughter he considered her still – or ever had. "Your road leads to hell, Annie, not to Rulls Landing." With one last hard glare, he turned his back on her.

Annie stood for a long moment, unable to find the will to move. But a giggle from one of the two waitresses – a girl Annie'd gone to school with – finally gave movement to her legs.

Dropping her eyes to the ground, she turned, face hot as a boiling kettle, and quickly stepped out of the coffee shop's door.

She had gone only a few feet down the dusty brown street when her feet slowed, weighed down by the crushing anxiety and hopelessness she felt. Lifting her gaze for a moment, she saw that the general storekeeper's wife, Mrs. Hanson, had stopped sweeping her store's porch across the way. The woman wore a look of pity but not of help. When her eyes met Annie's, Mrs. Hanson turned and hurried inside her store, as if she'd not seen her in the first place.

The seriousness of the situation – no home, no job, no family, no security – pressed down on Annie's shoulders. She hugged her threadbare coat around her body. And winter was well on its way. *What am I gonna do?*

# Chapter Two

*November 17, 1937 – Wednesday*

Annie let her gaze drift over the stableyard, taking in the way the leafless trees bowed and shook in the stiff November wind. The emptiness of the place in the late afternoon chill, after the morning business had finished and before the evening business began, seeped into her bones. The owner, Gerald Bousquet, had gone away on a trip – Annie had heard that from the gas station man in the small town nearby. A weight had lifted from her shoulders when the grizzled man had informed her of it. She wouldn't have dared to step across the stableyard openly if Gerald had been at home. He had a nasty temper and no patience, and he wouldn't care for riff-raff crowding his stable yard. No matter that she'd worked for him as a maid for a full year. Nope, Mr. Bousquet was out for his own gain.

But then, weren't all men?

The wind whipped her hair into her face, and Annie's body gave an involuntary shiver at the cold. Immediately, she stiffened herself against the weakness showing itself and set her jaw. At the age of eighteen, this world had already taught her very thoroughly a necessary lesson: To survive, Annie Cartwright must harden herself against blows from the outside, whether they were physical or emotional.

Letting her one-buttoned coat flap open to spite the wind, she took fast, determined steps toward the stable. At the threshold, where the gray, late-November day met the stable's darkened interior, she paused again, the doubts flooding her mind, threatening to sweep her under the tide of anxiety.

*Why did I come back here, anyway? This place is no better than home.*

Home. As if the town in which her father lived could be called "home." If home merely meant a place to be born, well, then, Annie guessed that Rulls Landing was that. Yet, despite Daddy's rejection, which had stung but which she had expected, something deep in Annie's heart craved a tie to something, to someone, who might help her figure out the mess she was in, who might provide her with safety, at least. She dared not hope for love; she didn't believe in that.

Which is why she had found herself back at Bousquet's, peering into the sweetly-hay-scented dimness, wondering if her cousin Aldo still worked here. Aldo wouldn't throw her out, would he? Though, what sort of accommodations did he have but an empty stall fixed up for sleeping? Of course, she couldn't stay with Aldo once Bousquet and his family returned.

But he was smart, Aldo was. *Street-smart* is what Daddy called Mama's older brother's stepson. If anybody would know what to do, it'd be he. Hadn't he gotten her the job as one of Mr. Bousquet's maids in the first place? He'd told her it'd be his pleasure to help her become gainfully employed after she'd run away from Rulls Landing nearly two years ago… if she'd be willing to sneak him a few things from their employer's home, that was. Who could count the number of fine cigars, leftover kitchen delicacies, measures of bootleg alcohol, and more that Annie had slipped from the towering brick residence, transferring it to a hidden spot in the stable for Aldo's gratification?

Annie smiled without joy. Aldo would help her, all right. *As long as there's something in it for him.*

Shoving away her fear, Annie plunged forward, not letting herself dwell on what he'd demand from her this time around.

Aldo leaned back against the haybale, smoke draining from his nostrils. His expression – calm, half-hooded eyes, his lips slightly curving upward – told Annie that he was more than happy about her visit. He was thrilled.

"So, Cuz, looks like your pop threw ya out on your backside, huh." It was a statement, not a question.

How had he known before she'd told him? He wasn't in contact with Daddy; Annie knew that for certain. Yet Aldo seemed to have eyes everywhere – like God, but worse because, while God didn't care much to get involved, even though He knew everything, Aldo took pleasure in scanning every detail of others' lives to see what benefit he could extract from their happiness or their pain.

But Annie didn't speak her thoughts aloud. She simply nodded, perching on the edge of a bale herself, glad to take a load off her swollen, aching feet and legs. She'd walked much of the way from Rulls Landing, nearly thirty miles. "Mr. Bousquet will have your head on a silver platter if he finds you smoking in here," she couldn't resist adding. She'd never seen a stable go up in flames... and she didn't want to. The way the men smoked in here on the sly had always made her nervous.

Aldo shrugged, one dark, shaggy eyebrow raised. "How's he gonna find out? He's gone on a trip with his mistress while the wife is off visiting her sister."

Another stablehand – a new one whom Annie didn't know – passed by, giving Aldo's cigarette a second, alarmed glance. "He could tell on ya," Annie pointed out once the young man strode out of earshot.

Aldo grunted a laugh. "Yeah, but he won't. I got so much dirt on Jimmy already, ya wouldn't believe it, Annie-girl."

Annie let it drop. What did it matter to her, as long as the stable didn't burn down with her inside it? *Though maybe even that'd be for the best.* Then, at least, she wouldn't have to deal with this inescapable situation she'd gotten herself into.

"So..." Aldo drew the word out, "whatcha gonna do, Annie? Ya know ya can't stay here. No work for ya here at Bousquet's. And nobody out in town's gonna want– "

"I know that," she cut in, not wanting to hear how

he'd choose to describe her. "But I didn't know where else to go. And you can always think of something."

Silence fell on them for a few moments, punctuated only by the faint nickering of the horses and the audible blowing out of smoke through Aldo's nostrils.

"What about Ben?"

Annie's pulse picked up at the name. She tried to drop her eyes from the hold Aldo's had on them but found that she couldn't. "What about him?" she tried to ask nonchalantly, her fingers playing with the sole button dangling from her coat. She'd not wanted to bring Ben into this at all. She'd never wanted to see Ben again, not after how he'd betrayed her with Maggie.

"Is he the father?"

Her stomach crunched at the question, pushing the air from her lungs. For a moment, she couldn't answer, her tongue sticking behind her teeth.

"Come on, Annie. I know you," Aldo coaxed in that slimy-smooth way of his. "You ain't the type to run around. You ain't no floozy."

He let the silence linger for another few seconds and then sighed. "Well, you don't gotta say nothing. No matter, I got the answer to your problem."

Problem… Annie looked down at her stomach, swollen out like an early watermelon. It was a big problem.

And yet, sometimes, as she lay in bed – wherever she'd found herself a bed, that is, after Mr. Bousquet had given her the boot last month, when she'd been unable to hide her pregnancy any longer – Annie didn't see the baby as a problem but as the one thing in life that she still possessed, the one thing that still gave her any spark of joy. The baby didn't move as much as she'd been told babies in their mothers' wombs usually did; sometimes she wondered if that was its way of apologizing for its existence, of trying to make itself as unobtrusive as possible so that she would let it continue as it was.

Sometimes, truth be told, Annie waited for those movements from the baby within her. Waited with her heart in her throat, wondering if they would come at all, or if the bad parentage had finally poisoned the child. Had finally terminated its life.

A cloud of smoke, puffed straight toward her face, rattled Annie out of her thoughts. Coughing, she glared at Aldo, who leaned back, satisfied that he had her full attention again. He was a mean one, that Aldo, when he wanted to be. A mean one with no conscience at all, it seemed, nor guilt.

"Go on," she bit out.

"Well, my plan'll take a little courage on your part, that's certain. I sure as heck wouldn't wanna be in your shoes to do it. But, if I were you, that baby would've been a thing of the past by now, so…"

Annie clenched her jaw, unable to tell him that she'd tried to halt the pregnancy but something inside her – some last softness – had begun to die every time she'd considered it in those first months. She'd felt her very heart dying, it had seemed. Ultimately, she had feared more greatly what she would become without that last, locked-away vestige of softness than she had feared the consequences of carrying this child to term. *Though every day until it moved, I prayed that I might lose it.*

"What is your plan, Aldo?" The question came out with every word clipped by the scissor of her tongue. How it irked her to be under the thumb of a man like Aldo… or the thumb of any man, for that matter. How she wished she could wipe the smirk off his face with a burst of temper and a slug in the face, as she'd done with Ben more than once!

But Aldo was the first person to offer her help — really offer it, other than one of the other maids, who had suggested that she get rid of the child way back in the summer and had offered to help her find someone to do it. Too, Aldo's plans usually did work; just look at how Annie had gotten the job as a housemaid through his scheming. So now she gritted her teeth and waited for her cousin's solution.

But a plan didn't come out of Aldo's mouth. A question did, though. "You hear what happened to old Benji-boy Picoletti?"

She swallowed down the memories that came with Ben's name spoken aloud and nodded. "'Course I know what happened to Ben, but what does that have to do with anything? He's gone."

Just saying it aloud brought a sting of pain to her heart. How she hated him for what he'd done… and yet could not forget him either.

"Whelp, I tried to get him into serious trouble here."

She despised the smile on her cousin's face. "I already know about that, Aldo. I worked here then."

He dropped the half-smoked cigarette onto the dirt floor and crushed it beneath the heel of his boot, taking his time. *Probably happy that I'm at his mercy.* Annie raised her chin and let all emotion drop from her face. She would *not* show him that she really needed him to get her out of this fix. She would not let him think she was groveling, begging…

*But who am I kidding? Ain't that what I'm doing?*

Annie clenched her teeth and straightened her shoulders. She still had her dignity to uphold, didn't she?

Though, as her hands rested on her rounded stomach, she had a hard time believing that to be the case.

Aldo struck another match on the sole of his boot and lit the fresh cigarette held lightly between his smooth lips. "So, Benji was all locked-up tight in a box stall, with dear ol' Bousquet believing that he was responsible for ruining a prize horse," he continued, apparently oblivious to Annie's comment that she knew what had happened to her old boyfriend. As always, Aldo was determined to get to his point his way. "They were set to call the cops and all, but then... out of the stark blue... comes Benji's savior." Through the smoky haze, Aldo smiled at her, and she shivered compulsively.

"Yeah, his mama had out and married some rich doctor, who, against all odds, decided to bail Benji out with a load of dough. Bousquet's greedy, and he took the money quicker than a fox with its tail on fire. Dropped the charges. Took Benji home with him down to Rhode Island. And that's the last, hide or hair, I seen of Benji-boy Picoletti." He pinned Annie with a sharp look. "Unless you got fresher dibs on the situation?"

Wordlessly, Annie shook her head. She'd barely spoken two words to Ben since they'd broken up – or, rather, since she'd broken up with him late last spring – and definitely not since he'd left his employment at Bousquet's stables.

"So here's what you're gonna do, Annie."

She bristled at his commanding tone. "Who are you to tell me what I'm gonna do, Aldo?" she hissed. "Specially when it involves... involves Ben." Her voice dropped low as she spoke his name; she couldn't help that it twisted sharp as a boning knife in her chest. *I don't never want to see Ben again.* Not after he'd hurt her as he had... not after she'd loved him so fierce… with nothing to show for it.

Aldo sat back, humor glinting in his eyes. "Ain't that why you come to me? For me to tell ya what to do?"

She didn't need to nod this time. She clenched her jaw, pursed her lips, dropped her eyes to her torn-up cuticles. He already knew her answer was a *yeah*. No one else would help her – effectively, at least.

"Well, then. You sit there, and I'll tell you. But," he paused significantly, "A'course ya know I'm gonna need to get something out of this deal as well."

## November 23, 1937 – Tuesday
## Providence, RI

"You haven't said what you're planning to give Betty yet." Ben could hear the smile in Paulie's voice, though he didn't turn his head to look at his stepbrother.

Better to sidestep that statement. "Have ya decided on what you're getting Grace?" Maybe asking that question would distract Paulie from further prying into Ben's concerns. Paulie always liked to talk about Grace, Ben's sister and the one whose relationship with Paulie had brought their parents together in marriage.

However, Paulie wouldn't be dissuaded. He ducked his head as they passed near a low-slung Christmas wreath hanging from one of the streetlamp poles. "It's rude to answer a question with a question, you know." Now laughter had joined the grin in Paulie's words. With Paulie's fiancée Grace home for her holiday break, Ben had noticed that his stepbrother was even more jovial than usual. Paulie had been the one to suggest that the two of them head out to do some shopping in the city while Mama, Grace, and some of their friends gathered to bake pies this evening in preparation for Thanksgiving, just two days away.

"I didn't think ya'd asked a question," Ben shot back. He kept his voice playful, knowing that Paulie didn't mean no harm, but his neck heated at the very thought of having to answer. He shoved his hands deeper into the pockets of his jacket. Though it hadn't snowed yet, the temperature had sure dropped enough for white flakes to start coming out of the smoke-tinged Providence sky. He shoulda worn mittens, but he'd done so rarely over the past few winters working in Gerald Bouquet's stables. Mittens got in the way of tending to the horses. *Time to adjust to your new way of life, Ben.* Would that ever happen, fully?

Just then, Paulie sprang in front of him, facing him, and Ben nearly slipped on the slick sidewalk as he stopped fast to avoid the collision. "Well, let me ask it as a question, then: Have you decided on what you'll be giving Betty Cloud for Christmas, Mr. Picoletti?" With mock seriousness, Paulie looked up into the night sky, his brown eyes glinting with fun in the light thrown by the street lamps. "Let's see: You could get her a monogrammed handkerchief – I hear that they're very popular this year – or perhaps a leather dictionary. Though perhaps all she requires is a kiss on her fair hand, with which I am quite sure you'd be happy to oblige her."

Ben stared silently at Paulie, discomfort crawling up his spine. He knew he could trust Paulie, but did he want to tell anyone at all what he was thinking of getting his girlfriend for Christmas 1937?

"Come on. Tell me. I promise I won't tell Grace or… or anybody."

Nope.

"Nothing doing." He shoved past Paulie, keeping his head down in the sharp wind that whipped around the corners of the brightly-lit shops and dove into Ben's collar. His skin prickled with cold. "Tell me first what you're getting for Grace," he called over his shoulder.

Long-legged Paulie caught up with him in a couple of steps. His breath puffed out, a cloud of whiteness. He flipped the loose end of his red cabled scarf – made by Mama – back over his shoulder. "All right. I've got nothing to hide."

Of course he wouldn't. Paulie never seemed to, did he? *Well, when you've lived such a clean life as he has, of course you're all set.* Ben, on the other hand, had many things he wished he could forget – memories that he hid even from himself.

"I'm giving Grace a first-edition of Tennyson. I found it in the used bookstore on Thayer Street. He was one of the first poets we found out that we both liked."

Ben nodded. His sister – and Paulie's fiancée as of last summer – would love that gift.

"Alright, now your turn," Paulie urged. "Spill it, Ben."

Ben grimaced. How could he tell Paulie what he was getting Betty – that truly special girl – when he wasn't sure himself? Wasn't sure if it was the *right* gift, that is? If it was too soon to give it? He turned his light eyes away from Paulie's probing dark ones – only to see the shop right across the street – the shop that surely held the gift he wanted to give his Betty this Christmas.

"Hey, I'm just teasing you, you know." Paulie's mittened hand came down on Ben's shoulder. He could feel the gentle pressure right through the gray wool of his coat. "You don't have to tell me. If you want to keep it just between you two, I understand."

"Ain't that. It's just… I'm not sure if it's the right gift. If it's the right time, either," he mumbled, looking down at the darkening cobblestones and then up at Paulie's face. "And I ain't so sure that I'm the right one to give it to her, ya know?"

For a second, Paulie looked confused, but then Ben saw his gaze go over to the shop Ben himself had been staring at a moment before. When Paulie's eyes turned back to him, Ben could see that he'd guessed.

"You want to get Betty an engagement ring," Paulie stated. All kidding had disappeared from his eyes. Did he disapprove? Did he agree that maybe Ben wasn't good enough for the likes of Betty Cloud, a reverend's daughter, the sweetest girl, and the prettiest thing he'd ever clapped eyes on?

Paulie was waiting.

Ben hesitated just a second, then nodded. "Yeah."

"You want to ask her to marry you."

Ben raised his eyebrows. If he'd not known better, he'd be thinking at this point that Paulie Giorgi was not the brightest bulb on the Christmas tree. "Yeah. Yeah, I do."

Inwardly, Ben cringed, waiting for the disapproval sure to flow from Paulie's mouth. How could it not, when Paulie, of all people in Chetham, knew the worst that Ben had been capable of, before he'd come to know Christ as His Savior and Lord?

But no condemnation came from Paulie. Instead, shock filled Ben as Paulie reacted not with the frown he'd expected and steeled himself against, but with a grin as warm as hot cocoa right off the stove. Then the Giorgi kid further surprised him by grabbing Ben around the shoulders and bear-hugging him, right there in the middle of the Providence sidewalk! Ben felt his cheeks redden as a passing woman glanced at the two of them, surely wondering what had lit a fire under the grinning young man with curly brown hair tucked beneath his cap. Ben pulled back a bit from Paulie's hug. He'd always felt uncomfortable with physical affection, and to be hugged in public was even worse.

Paulie didn't seem to notice Ben's embarrassment and only drew more attention to them by giving a loud whoop of joy. "That's great! That is just terrific, Ben. Betty's a wonderful girl. I'm so happy for you, truly I am."

Ben glanced from side-to-side, tense from the curious looks of those who passed by them. "Save the congratulations for after Christmas, Paulie. She hasn't said yes yet." *And probably won't when I do.* There was a sinking, clutching feeling in his gullet at the thought.

Paulie laughed. Apparently, he had no problem with everyone on the avenue staring. "No, but she will. You just wait and see. She will."

He grabbed Ben by the shoulders again and pulled him toward the street. "Come on, we'll look at rings right now–"

The trolley bell cut Paulie off, and Ben grabbed his friend by the coat-sleeve to stop him from walking right out in front of the passing red vehicle, its nose bedecked with a green wreath.

"If we don't get hit by a trolley first, that is," Paulie added. Once the trolley had passed by them, he grinned and dashed through the traffic, earning some exasperated honks along the way.

Ben followed more cautiously, waiting to see if the cars would actually stop. He'd taken too many risks already in life to act as carefree as Paulie could afford to be.

# Chapter Three

*November 26, 1937 – Friday*

The whole house smelled like lasagna, and the kind only his mama could make at that. Ben paused at the threshold, sucking in a deep lungful of the combined scents of sausage, ground beef, heavily-flavored marinara, sautéed onions, garlic, and lots of melted cheese – not just one kind, but three. Alongside that heavenly aroma, another wafted through the air: fresh bread from Filangieri's, the town bakery. Ben could practically taste its buttery flavor and feel the crispness of a crust that had been overbaked on purpose. Mama would surely serve a green salad alongside it, sprinkled with olive oil and vinegar and certainly some oregano.

"Ben, come inside and shut the door!" Mama called

out from the dining room. "And wipe off your shoes."

He grinned and shuffled his work boots across the mat. "How'd ya know it was me, Mama?" he called back as he shrugged off his jacket and then held his hands over the radiator that warmed the foyer. The November wind was sure getting nippy.

Mama came to the doorway of the dining room. Sure enough, she held a big salad bowl in her hands. "I always know my boys." Her blue eyes echoed the smile on her lips.

Ben reached for Mama, enveloping her rounded body in a hug and dropping a kiss on her graying brown hair. "Somethin' smells good. I'm starved."

"Is that what this hug is for?" Mama gave a playful push at his chest and shook her head. "No wonder they say the way to a man's heart is through his stomach."

He grinned back. "Then you must have a permanent road to mine, Mama. You're the best cook I know."

Mama rolled her eyes and turned back to the dining room, where Tabitha, the Giorgi's part-time cook, helped to set the table. "Is Betty coming for supper?" she called over her shoulder as she set the salad bowl down.

Ben shook his head. "Naw, she couldn't make it. Has tryouts for that Christmas play at the church."

Recognition lit up Mama's face. "Oh, that's right, that is tonight. Betty must be looking forward to it."

Ben snitched an olive from the salad bowl. "Yeah, but I think she's a little nervous, too." He popped it into his mouth, delighting in the salty brine.

"Betty, nervous? I'm surprised."

Ben shrugged. He'd been surprised as well. It wasn't like the pastor's normally unable-to-be-ruffled daughter to become nervous about anything at all. Other than smart and beautiful, *self-assured* would be exactly how Ben'd describe his girlfriend. "She kept saying that she wasn't sure if it was somethin' she'd be good at. She's never directed a play before, ya know." Even as he reported Betty's explanation, Ben recalled how it had seemed to him that she was hiding her real reason.

"But she's very musical," Mama commented as she straightened a chair. "Don't – I mean, doesn't the Christmas play have music in it?"

"Yeah, she'll do swell. I don't know what's bothering her about it." And the knowledge that he didn't know bothered Ben. Sure, he'd asked Betty, but all she'd said was that she didn't know if she could do it right. Yet it was clear as day to Ben that Betty Cloud could do anything she set her mind to doing, and do it well, too. It had been one of the things to which he'd been attracted in Betty – her confidence and the sense that she knew exactly where she was going in life.

So often, for himself, Ben hadn't a clue.

Betty straightened the music on the piano one more time, hoping that the shakiness of her hands didn't show. Her eyes ran to the clock perched right below the small balcony that provided additional seating for the sanctuary of First Baptist.

6:30.

*Time to start.* Betty had never been late to anything – not for a single day of her four years at high school, not to one of her music lessons, and never to church. Now, not even her silly nervousness – if she admitted herself to be nervous, which she didn't like to – would make her tardy at this point in her life.

She rose from the piano bench, insides in a tizzy, hands gripping the typed script. What seemed like a sea of children – but which was in reality more like a couple dozen – filled the pews before her. She remembered again why she'd gotten stuck with this job. *Not a job, Betty, a ministry.* One that she could easily fit in-between her part-time day job as a receptionist and her several piano students, couldn't she? At least, everyone else seemed to think so.

"Besides," her mother had said, after getting off the phone with the usual Christmas-play director, elderly Joanna Lambert, whose husband had broken his hip, "we live next door to the church, anyway, Betty, dear. I was sure that you wouldn't mind. Mrs. Lambert feels it necessary to put aside any distractions so that she can nurse poor Tom. And she says it won't be difficult for you at all; you already play the piano for the play every year, anyway."

After Mrs. Lambert had said it that way, Betty felt that she couldn't refuse. It would make her appear incompetent. People would think that she wasn't able to take on the flock of children, that she didn't want to pull her fair share of the church's ministry, that she was uninterested in the Christmas message.

Nope, far better to grit her teeth and endure the few weeks of Christmas-play preparation and hope against hope that she would be able to pull off an at-least-nearly-perfect program on December twenty-third. The thought of her already-full calendar and carefully-outlined holiday plans made her blood pressure rise… and her irritation.

She swallowed hard against it as she plastered on the

smile she knew the two dozen children expected to see. Excited by the prospect of a play's fun, all of them sat in four rows near the front. A few parents stood near the back of the sanctuary, hats and coats still on, waiting for Betty to begin.

"Welcome, children," she said aloud. Or tried to say. Her throat felt so full of cotton-balls that she nearly choked on the words. She made another attempt, this time pairing it with that smile, hopefully one not too false-looking. "Welcome, children. We are so glad that you could come. We are going to do something very special together: We are going to put on a play about–"

"Christmas!" Toby Fenelon, a black-haired butterball of a boy, age six, squealed from his place on the thin-cushioned pew. His excitement apparently had created springs in his body, as Betty observed him bouncing like a tennis ball gone out-of-control.

She managed to nod and, pushing back her frustration, forced herself to continue. "Yes, Christmas."

A little girl with nutmeg-hued pigtails thrust her hand up, but she didn't wait for Betty to call on her before she spoke. "You got a sore throat, Miss Betty?"

"Remember, Jennifer," Betty responded, refusing to answer the child's question (for how could she answer it honestly?), "to wait to speak until I call on you."

Jennifer – to whom Betty taught weekly piano lessons – raised her hand again immediately, but Betty ignored it. "Now, can anyone tell me what Christmas is all about?"

"Jesus!" answered Toby again, without a raised hand. He bounced so hard on the pew that Betty heard its old joints wince. She cringed in sympathy.

In despair, she ignored the fact that Toby hadn't listened to her instruction regarding raising hands. "And what about Jesus? Someone raise their hand and tell me."

A hand shot up in the second row, followed by a few others around it. Betty called on the first one she'd seen, belonging to eleven-year-old Lily O'Brien, another one of Betty's own piano students… and the one she'd secretly already cast as Mary, the mother of Jesus.

"He was God's Son. God gave Him as a gift to the world." Lily bit her lip, obviously thinking, and Betty was tempted to finish the thought herself. "He wasn't what everybody thought they needed, but He was what God knew that they needed. We needed," the little girl finished, correcting herself.

"Yeah, they thought they needed a king, like King David from the Old Testament," piped up Bob, Lily's twin brother, never to be outdone by his sister.

"Jesus *is* a king." Beside him, ten-year-old Skippy gave him an elbow-jab.

Bob rolled his eyes at his friend. "I know that, but the people wanted a different kind of king, like a warrior. They wanted to get rid of the Romanovs," he finished with an air of superior knowledge.

Betty opened her mouth to help the children along and bring them back to the speech she'd planned out. But Lily, not to be outdone by Bob or Skippy, burst out, "The Romans, you dumbbell! The Romanovs were the king and queen of Russia. 'Til they got killed, that is."

"Romanovs. That's what I said," huffed Bob, folding his arms across his scrawny chest.

Lily sighed loudly. "Anyway, they thought God was going to send them the perfect way out of all their problems, but they didn't know that they had a bigger problem than the Romans."

Betty started to relax. Maybe this wasn't going to be

so bad after all. The children had reminded her that they already knew the story. "And what was that, Lily?"

"Sin." The little girl's eyes widened with seriousness. "All the bad stuff we are and the bad way we are."

"That's right." Betty felt a small-but-natural smile come to her own lips. She had a future Sunday-School teacher here before her. She plunged on. "And when God sent Jesus as His gift to us, how did Jesus come? Already grown-up?"

All being church kids, the children didn't even need to look at each other for confirmation. "No," they chorused.

"How did He come, then?" Betty egged them on, even enjoying herself a little. Maybe she could be good at this.

Jennifer's hand shot up, but once again, she didn't wait for Betty to call on her. "As a baby!"

Betty sighed. "That's right, Jennifer, but please raise your hand. Yes, Jesus came as a baby in a manger. And the Christmas story we are going to act out – and sing about – tells all about it."

Some of the tension had drained from her as the children had talked. She took a few papers from the stack on the wooden podium. One sheet slipped out from between the others and floated beneath the pew. Toby bent over and nearly flipped from top to bottom in his effort to secure it for her, finally bouncing up with a sneeze and the paper in his hand.

She took it from his pudgy hand with a genuine smile. "Thank you, Toby. Now, children, I'm going to read the names of the characters in the play so that you will know what part you would like to audition for. Some of you may want to have a speaking part."

"What's a speaking part?" stage-whispered six-year-old Carol to her older sister, Bernice, who sat beside her.

"Shh. It's a part that speaks," Bernice answered in an equally-loud whisper.

"That's right." Betty realized that she would simply need to explain every technical term, though many of the children had been in the play in previous years. She felt her small store of patience draining away again. "Any character who says something is called a *speaking part*. Now, there are lots of non-speaking parts for those of you who might be feeling a little nervous or shy about –"

"I ain't shy, Miss Betty!" announced Toby. "I wanna be Joseph. He's in this story, right?"

*Toby as Joseph.* Betty opened her mouth to tell him that he would do very well as a sheep but then decided against it. She was the one making the casting decisions, after all. Let Toby try out for Joseph; what harm could it do if she didn't cast him in the role? Joseph needed to be someone very un-Toby-like. Someone who would cause her as little trouble as possible and make this play run smoothly from start to finish.

"Let me read to you the parts we have." Betty lowered her gaze to the papers she held in her hand and saw that the one that had dropped, the one that Toby had retrieved for her, remained on top. And it wasn't part of her own papers at all, but something written by someone else. She recognized Ben's painful penmanship and bristled ever-so-slightly. What right did he have to interfere with her paperwork? What if he had messed something up? For a moment, she let her eyes rest on the brief note, torn carefully from a Big Chief tablet, most likely:

*Hey, Betty. I'm praying for you and the try-outs tonight. I'll see you tomorrow. Love, Ben.*

*Love?* He never signed his notes *love*, not until this one. What did it mean? Her mind froze for a single moment as she tried to figure out something – anything – that he could have meant... besides the obvious.

*He loves me.*

The sound of a thud met her ears and jolted Betty out of her trance. Toby had flipped off the pew entirely, like an Olympian gymnast, hanging on upside-down by his chubby hands; all she could see of him was his corduroy-clad calves and his brown oxfords flailing wildly in the air.

She was starting to get the feeling that this was going to be a night, and a Christmas, to remember in so many ways.

"You think there's leftover pie for dessert?" Cliff's crackling adolescent voice cut into Ben's thoughts... and his kid brother's elbow to Ben's ribs made him spill water across his own scraped-clean plate.

"Watch it, kid." Irritation edged Ben's voice like Mama's flower beds edged the lawn, come springtime. The minute he heard it – and saw the hurt, guarded look come over Cliff's face, Ben regretted letting himself lose self-control over his emotions. "Sorry, Cliff. I shouldn't've snapped at you like that."

Cliff shrugged it off, and Ben felt the guilt grip him even more tightly. *I sure as heck know what it's like growing up with a man snarling at me, being kind only when it made him happy.* He could still remember the way he himself had shrugged off the hurts Papa had thrown at him, acting like they didn't matter, when all the while he was bleeding inside.

Pretended indifference had seemed like the only way to staunch the wound, to numb the pain. Gradually, he'd built up callouses around his heart, so that nobody – *nobody* – could reach him.

Until Jesus had, through the love and truth and forgiveness offered by the Giorgi family to him – undeserving Ben Picoletti.

Now, though, as he watched Cliff scooping up his leftover lasagna with a scrap of bread, suffering from the emotional cut he'd just been dealt, Ben wondered if he'd really been changed at all. *Would a changed man act as I do sometimes? Would someone who had been saved by Jesus Christ still hurt his kid brother like I do?*

Mama certainly had changed, and Grace, too, after they'd come to know Jesus in a personal way. Right now, he could hear Mama in the kitchen, singing a hymn in harmony with Doctor Giorgi, her voice lilting with joy – and not just the happiness that came from having a good man for her husband or a refrigerator full of food, though Ben knew that Mama sure was thankful for those blessings, too.

"Hey, Cliff, you wanna play checkers after supper?" It was a poor substitute for doing the right thing in the first place, but Ben had to do something to ease his conscience and win back his brother's trust. *Funny, even now, I'm more concerned with how I feel, than how Cliff does!* What a selfish guy he was.

His sixteen-year-old brother's eyes took on a reserved but excited light. "Ain'tcha gonna go see Betty? By the time we finish, it'll be too late to visit her."

Oh, he wanted to, all right, even though he'd told Betty in that note that he'd see her tomorrow, but he owed this to Cliff now. "I can see her tomorrow," he said casually, as if it didn't matter at all. *It's not as if you're gonna propose to Betty tonight.* He could spare an hour to play a board-game with one of the several siblings he'd neglected all his life.

"Paulie, you gonna play, too?" Cliff asked.

Across the table, Paulie glanced up from winding his wristwatch. "Sure, why not?"

Feeling every bit the responsible older brother, Ben cut off Cliff's whoop of joy. "Paulie probably wants to spend some time with Grace tonight, Cliff. She's heading back to school tomorrow, you know."

But Paulie shook his head. "She went over to the Kinners to watch David for them. Won't be home 'til later." He gave Cliff a grin. "I'll play the winner."

"Swell!" Cliff leaped from the supper table, all thought of dessert forgotten.

The feeling of concentration filled the living room so much so that Sarah could practically feel it as she peeked her head around the door. The three "boys", as she liked to call and think of them, despite the fact that the youngest was now sprouting whiskers, crouched around the checkerboard spread out on the oak table near the bookcases. Their heads bent, their eyes riveted on the black-and-red game pieces.

"Your move, Paulie," Ben announced after he slid his piece forward. A grin whispered on his lips.

Paulie sat back and stared, hands pressed to the sides of his face, as Sarah knew he did whenever he was deep in thought and somewhat perplexed. Cliff glanced at the board, looked up at Ben's good-natured smirk, and then leaned toward Paulie to whisper in his ear.

Paulie listened, nodded, and moved his piece.

Ben's smirk turned into a full-blown grin. "King me," he announced, moving his checker forward.

"Ah!" Paulie slapped his forehead. "I didn't see that one coming. How come you didn't warn me, Cliff?" he asked jokingly. "Or are you working for the enemy?" He narrowed his brown eyes as he looked playfully from Cliff to Ben and back again.

Cliff's eyes grew wide at that remark, and Sarah saw the Picoletti defensiveness rise sharp and earnest in them. "Naw! Honest, I didn't see it. I wasn't playing you, Paulie. Honest. I would've told you if I'da seen it."

Paulie's face relaxed into a smile. He reached up a hand to ruffle Cliff's already-mussed hair. "I know that, Cliff. I'm just pulling your leg."

Sarah's heart warmed at the sight of her sons, both the two born of her body and the one given to her through marriage. "Cliff, got any homework?" she asked, as Paulie contemplated his next move.

He swiveled from where he leaned on the back of Paulie's chair and faced her with a slightly guilty expression. "Not too much, Mama."

"Well, you'd better get to it, hadn't you? Monday's going to come soon, and you don't like doing homework on Saturdays," Sarah reminded him, marveling once more at how she cared about her children in a new and deeper way these days than she ever had in the past. Oh, she had loved them before, but something had been missing. She had been blind in some way, groping in the darkness. How she wished that so much of her life was not already behind her. She had made so many mistakes, so many things that she wished she could rectify but now never could. *I wish I could have started fresh, from the beginning. Even before I married Charlie.*

The thought slithered through her mind as it often did, and she had to stiffen her back to fight against it, to remind herself of all that God had done for her, how He had given her a new start, a new beginning that she could never have dreamed that she would possess. Did He really want her to continually grieve over past mistakes she could not alter?

She forced herself to press past the oppressive gloom and spoke words of thanksgiving in her heart. *Thank You, Lord for the new start You have given to me. You resurrected the past and breathed new life into it in ways I could never have looked for. You know what is best for me. You will work Your perfect plans together for my life. I trust You.*

Her eyes drifted from Cliff to Ben to Paulie. *And for them. You will work all the errors of the past together for good, for those who love You, who are called according to Your purpose.* The words from the book of Romans that Reverend Cloud had spoken last Sunday echoed in her mind and became her prayer.

"Come on, Cliff. Let's go," she urged again when her youngest son continued to dawdle at the game board.

"Aw, Mama. I don't even get the homework Mr. Simmons gave us, though," grumbled Cliff, dragging himself away, slow as cold molasses.

"You'll figure it out. Just try your best," Sarah advised. She couldn't give him any practical help with it, that was for sure. Mr. Simmons had taught mathematics at Chetham High School for the past thirty years, and Sarah remembered failing his geometry tests repeatedly twenty-five years ago.

"Need some help with it, Cliff?" Paulie offered. "I'm okay with mathematics."

Cliff turned back to the two older boys sitting across from each other, the game board between them. "Naw, you're in the middle of the game."

Paulie laughed. "This game was over before it began. I'm no match for Ben at checkers. I concede."

*Concede.* Whatever that fancy word meant, Sarah figured that Paulie was giving up the game to Ben.

"You sure?" her oldest, auburn-haired son asked, a grin playing at the corners of his lips again. "You still got a chance to win it. Ain't over yet, you know."

"Yeah, who're you kidding? It's over." Paulie grinned back. "You win. And I'm going to help Cliff with geometry so you can telephone Betty, like I know you've been wanting to all night."

Sarah watched, amused, as Ben's face flushed like a schoolboy's. "Oh, go on."

Paulie and Cliff headed out of the room, toward the staircase that mounted upward from the tiled foyer, and Sarah turned to leave as well. She had some laundry to put away yet before she could turn in for the night. Ever since they had let go of their old housekeeper, Mrs. McCusker, last summer, Sarah had taken on more of the household tasks. The Giorgi household employed a part-time maid to help with heavy cleaning as well as with serving when they hosted occasional dinner parties. But, to her own surprise, Sarah found herself much more comfortable when she had an active hand in the running of their home, and so she and Sam had decided that, at least for the time being, they would put off hiring a new housekeeper.

"Ma," Ben's voice reached her ears, just above a whisper. She could hear the hesitancy in it and turned back to him, curious.

His eyes were glued to the game board before him. "What... What d'ya think of Betty and me?"

The question surprised her. She had gotten so used to her eldest son's relationship with the pastor's daughter – a relationship that made her glad, knowing Betty was such a good, sweet girl and knowing that Ben wanted so to follow Christ now – that she had not thought that anyone, least of all Ben, questioned it in any way. The only thing that bothered Sarah about Ben and Betty's relationship was, well, her own discomfort in the presence of such a girl; sometimes, Sarah had the feeling that Betty's eyes were always taking Sarah's spiritual measurements.

But still, she couldn't have asked for a nicer, more virtuous girl for her son.

"What do you mean?" she stalled.

He hesitated, his rough fingers skimming over the tops of some of the checkers, lining them up in a pattern. "Do you... Do you think I'm right for her? For Betty?" he finally asked.

Sarah frowned in her confusion. Ben and Betty seemed to get along well whenever they were at the Giorgis' house for supper or when Sarah saw them together at church. The Clouds appeared content with their daughter's relationship with Sarah's former bad-boy son, seeing the truth of his conversion in how Ben's character had slowly but surely changed in the months following Paulie's accident last summer. "I don't know what you mean, Ben," she finally stated, her heart troubled at the anxious expression that had come over his face, handsome like that of her own daddy, deceased years ago.

He began to stack the checkers now – one red, one black, one red. "I mean," he spoke quietly but forcefully, "am I good enough for her? Am I... Am I....I don't know... I know she's right for me – I couldn't ask for anything better – but am I right for her?"

Motherly pride flared up in Sarah's chest. *"Good enough" for Betty Cloud? I should say so!* But she didn't let the words pass her tightened lips.

"I mean, look at all the stuff I've done. Who I've been, Mama," he went on before she could answer him. "And you, honestly, don't know the half of it. There are ways I've acted, things I've done, that I couldn't say 'em aloud to you, Mama, because I don't wanna have to relive them in my memory."

Silence stretched long and painful between them.

"It's not about what you've done or not done, Ben," Sarah finally found the words to say, "or what Betty has done or not. It's about what Christ has done for you, for Betty, in your places, at Calvary. About you and about Betty accepting the free gift of God's love toward you." *Mercy, I sound like Emmeline Kinner or Bertha Cloud.* "That's where any good enough-ness comes from. The rest – that's all what He does through you, not of you, yourselves."

Ben's lips turned up in response, but to Sarah the smile appeared a bit forced. *You're imagining things,* she scolded herself, especially when Ben rose from his chair and came to give her a clumsy hug. Though short of stature himself, Ben towered over his little mother. "Thanks, Mama." He bent to brush her cheek with a kiss, and she smelled the woodsy cologne he sometimes wore.

"Are you going to go call Betty?" The question came out before she could stop herself. Ben was in his twenties; he didn't need his mama trailing behind him all the time.

"Naw, it'll be kind of late by the time I get home.

Reverend Cloud don't – doesn't – like it when I call after nine o'clock." He moved toward the foyer, where his coat hung in the closet.

Sarah stopped herself from telling him to feel free to call Betty from their house; then he would be able to do it before the clock struck nine. *He already knows that.* Something else was stopping him from wanting to call his girl tonight. And what that something else was troubled Sarah.

## Chapter Four

Ben stepped outside into the November darkness and closed Mama's front door behind him with a decisive click before letting the smile slide off his face. Relieved, he sucked in a deep draught of air, crisp with the late-autumn coolness, fragrant with the earthy scent of fallen leaves, and let his shoulders relax. He loved his family, both old and new, but sometimes a man needed time apart, away, by himself, to think, to reason, to try to understand and sort through the confusion that hampered him.

*I love Betty. I know I do.* He moved down the front steps and felt the corduroy material of his trousers tighten against the jewelry box. Pushing a hand into the pocket, Ben pulled out the little case, letting his eyes caress the gold lettering on the top. With slow, careful fingers, he raised the lid, hearing the hinge's delicate snap, and gazed at the ring inside. The small but precise diamond glittered in the moonlight.

It was perfect, transparent, flawless. *Just like Betty.*

With work-scarred fingers, Ben removed the jewel from its nest of deep-blue velvet, closed his eyes, and tried to imagine putting it on his sweetheart's smooth hand.

But instead of Betty's face, memories of the dream he'd had over a week ago – that nightmare of his past life – surged into his mind. He sucked in a trembling breath.

"Going home, son?"

His stepfather's voice broke into Ben's thoughts: a welcome intrusion, though Ben hurried to hide the ring from the older man's sight. Why, he wasn't sure. But something in him felt embarrassed – awkward – vulnerable – at the notion of Paulie's dad knowing what Ben had in mind for the near future. What if... What if he thought Ben wasn't worthy of what he hoped for?

Jamming the ring into the box, he shoved the whole thing into his pocket as he looked for the source of Sam's voice. The man stepped out from beneath the canopy of pine trees that lined the lawn. "I was just taking a walk to relax before heading up to bed," Sam explained as he walked toward Ben.

Ben nodded. "I'm going home now." He hadn't been able to stuff the box deep enough and knew that it was sticking out a little from his pocket. Had Sam seen the ring, glimmering?

Maybe, because the tall man's dark eyes darted to the bulge on Ben's hip. "Well, goodnight, Ben. See you tomorrow for supper?"

"Uh, yeah, sure. 'Night."

Sam clapped Ben's shoulder gently as he passed.

*What would he think if he knew I'm getting ready to ask Betty's dad for his permission to marry his daughter?*

Suddenly, the need to know the answer to that overcame Ben's awkwardness and desire for secrecy. Sam had become – well, maybe not a father to him yet, but certainly the man whom Ben most admired. If Sam thought Ben wasn't acting with wisdom, then…

"Sam."

The older man turned quickly, surely at the note of urgency that even Ben could hear in his own voice. Hopefully, Sam couldn't hear the pounding of his heart as well, banging through his ribcage like a bass drum. "Yes, Ben?"

Ben searched his stepfather's face for a half-moment. Was he too busy? Too much in a hurry to get inside and spend time with Mama? Would he wish to waste time hearing his stepson's troubles, a stepson who had caused Sam more than his fair-share of pain, worry, and money already?

But Sam's face looked patient and open, though tired, most likely from a long day at the hospital, where he performed surgery a couple of days a week. The moonlight showed Sam's graying curls and face as an older version of Paulie's, his only biological son.

"What d'ya think of me and Betty?" Ben sputtered out before he lost his nerve.

Sam shifted on his feet, and something in his face relaxed, though Ben hadn't noticed it as being tense before. He smiled. "Well, now, from what I see, I'm glad to see God blessing your relationship with Betty. It seems to me – and to Reverend Cloud, when I talk to him – that the two of you are striving to put Christ first in your relationship with one another, that you want to please

God. And it seems to me, whenever I see you together, that you enjoy each other's company; that's pretty clear, I think."

Ben felt his heart slow its racing beat as Sam's well-thought-out approval registered in his mind. "That's good. Because..." He took a breath and looked away, unable to meet Sam's eyes completely when he told him, "because I'm thinking of asking Betty to marry me." He risked a glance back at Sam, who, as usual, didn't show what he was thinking straight out on his face. *Thinking? You already bought the ring!*

Sam shoved his hands into his pockets and stepped across the few ambling paces that lay between them before he responded. "When?" he finally said.

"Huh?"

"When are you thinking of asking her?"

Ben swallowed, trying to rid his throat of the large clot that had taken residence there. "Christmas, I was thinking. I've got to ask her father first." Which was almost more nerve-wracking than asking Betty The Question.

Almost.

Sam was quiet for a long moment, his gaze set on the frosty ground beneath his feet. At last, he looked up and met Ben's gaze with his. "You two have only been going together for a few months. Are you sure that you shouldn't wait awhile before moving forward?"

Ben stiffened inwardly, though he tried to hide it. Something inside him rankled at the thought that Sam disapproved. And disapproved why? *Because he doesn't think that you're good enough for Betty, for the preacher's daughter.*

*Maybe he thinks that you might go back to your old ways.*

He shoved away the frightening whispers and asked a

question instead. "Why? If I know it's Betty that I want to marry, why should I wait?"

"It's a pretty big step, that's all. You want to make sure that this is what both of you want, how God is leading you both, and not just act out of passion and emotion. If it's the real thing, if you really both love one another, you don't have to rush into anything." Sam met his eyes with a steady gaze.

"But if it's the real thing, like you say, we don't gotta put it off, either," asserted Ben, knowing that the defensiveness showed itself in his voice. "You put off your engagement to my mother, and see where that got you."

Oh. He hadn't meant to say that last bit. Had those words really come out of his mouth, out of his heart?

Sam's eyes widened in surprise, hurt glimmering in them. And no wonder. Never, since his conversion, had Ben brought up the errors of the far past – Sam's abandonment of Mama, his once-fiancée, when they were both young, due to his family's desires that he finish college and medical school… and marry a girl from a "better family."

"We both weren't Christians then," Sam said, his voice quiet but strong, "and God was merciful to both your mother and me, I believe, Ben. Despite our mistakes, we've had the joy of seeing her children come into a saving relationship with Christ, one-by-one. Including you. And if not for my first wife, I myself wouldn't have become a Christian and Paulie would not have existed. God has been gracious. But, yes, I regret my own actions because they were wrong; they were dishonorable."

Ben stayed quiet. He knew he should apologize to this man who had taken him under his fatherly wing, who had unofficially adopted him, but a frustrated and hard lump inside Ben's chest stopped him from humbling himself immediately.

"With you and Betty, I'm advising you to make sure that this is the way God is leading you and Betty before you make a hasty decision that you end up regretting. Partially as a result of what occurred between me and Sarah all those years ago and what I've learned since, my belief is that once a man promises marriage to a woman, he cannot renege honorably, unless she wishes to break the engagement herself."

Ben raised his eyebrows. "Renege?" All these big words.

"Back out."

His lips tightened. "Well, in that case, I'm good. I wouldn't want to back out on it. My mind's made up where it concerns Betty."

"All right."

His old defiance having taken hold of him, Ben stood facing the doctor, unwilling to be the first to back away from this conversation. Something within Ben desperately wanted something: *His blessing.* Not just Sam's reluctant assent.

But Sam didn't give it. "Good night, Ben." With the same loving smile as usual, Sam turned to go toward the house, its lit-up windows welcoming in the darkness.

"You let Paulie and Grace get engaged." The sentence burst out of Ben's lips. He hadn't realized until that moment how desperate he was to keep the doctor there until he affirmed that Ben was right to go forward with Betty.

Sam turned again, his face hidden by the shadows cast by the trees. "I did. Eventually. What Paulie might not have told you is that I made him and Grace wait to become involved with one another romantically for quite a while."

"Yeah, he told me." He'd probably regret it later, but Ben let his tongue loose. "He also told me that you wished you hadn't done that, though. It almost drove them apart for good. Grace was ready to marry that Haverland guy."

Sam hesitated. "Yes… and no. I should have been clearer with them both about what I meant. I didn't intend for them to completely cut off their affection for each other. And I didn't intend for my housekeeper to take Paulie and Grace's letters and destroy them, unread each by the other." He paused another moment, as if making sure that he was saying exactly what he meant. "But I don't think Paulie, if he's honest, had his heart and mind in the right place that year he and Grace graduated high school. And that was part of my hesitation with their relationship then."

"Paulie loves my sister," Ben said, almost defensively.

Sam's face showed his surprise again. "I know that," he hastened to agree, "and I think he loved Grace even then, when he was in high school. I know my son, though, and Paulie wasn't thinking clearly about their future; he was only thinking of the moment at hand and what he wanted, which was to deepen his romantic relationship with your sister. And, to be honest, Ben, I was responsible for Grace. I had just married your mother. You were out-of-the-picture at the time. I felt a love and responsibility for Grace, the same as if she was the daughter of my flesh, and not merely my wife's daughter. I still do. I wanted her to make her own decisions, guided by the Lord. I wanted her – I still want her – to have the kinds of opportunities your mother never had, if Grace so wishes, and not to be limited by a hasty promise made in the passion of a possibly shallow, youthful love. It was for Grace's good, believe me, that I put the brakes on their relationship back then. So I think you can go a little easy on me if I erred on the side of caution. I would think that's what you would want for your sister, anyway."

Ben turned his gaze away, ashamed. "Of course, yeah." So was that what the doctor thought? That Betty would say yes in the moment, but then she would regret it when she realized the other choices life could give her? The other, more suitable men who might offer her their hand in time to come?

Is that what Sam meant?

*Or maybe that I myself might fall away from the faith I've professed?*

His head swirled. Where had that thought come from? Did it slither into his mind out of the swampy mists of that dream that haunted him? *Nightmare is more like it.*

Silence hung heavy between them. There was nothing more to say, it seemed. And yet, so much left unsaid, unexplained, to Ben's mind at least. He wanted to take Sam by the shoulders and shake him, force him to tell Ben that, yes, he was good enough for Betty Cloud. *Even though I know I'm not.* To tell Ben that Sam knew that his faith would stand the test of time. *Though I myself doubt myself so much.* Sam's approval of their engagement – of Ben's proposal at least – well, it felt like the stamp of authenticity that Ben craved.

But he wouldn't – couldn't do that. What good would a forced approval from Sam be, anyway? And, knowing Sam even for less than a year, Ben knew that the older man had too much integrity to give such, even if Ben did shake him.

So Ben simply said, "It's getting late. I gotta get back

to my place. Gotta get an early start." Lifting a hand halfway in farewell, he left the leaf-strewn lawn.

With a new weariness added to the physical tiredness of his body, Sam trudged up the wide brick steps that led to the front door. *Lord, how do I handle this now?*

Sometimes, the unusual structure of his family brought joy to Sam's heart – the beauty of how his son Paulie had fallen in love with sweet-yet-determined Grace Picoletti several years ago, not knowing that his classmate was the daughter of Sarah, the woman to whom Sam, now a widower, had been engaged many years before; the restoration of his own relationship with, and ultimately marriage to, Sarah herself; and the unexpected blessing of suddenly becoming a stepfather to her numerous half-grown and grown children, after having only one child himself.

Yet, other times, the challenges of this new life he'd been given drained him: when he'd feared that Paulie had been rushing things with Grace and he'd erred on the side of zealous caution with them; when his stepson Ben had gotten into trouble with the law and Sam had bailed him out, only for the young man to brutally harm Paulie before finally turning to Christ in repentance and finding in Him both forgiveness and a fresh beginning; and when Sarah had encountered such difficulties in trusting him and finding her place in his life when they first married.

Sam turned the brass knob of his front door and pushed it open. *Yet, through it all, You have sustained me. Your right hand held me up.* With the statement, with the praise, his heart took hold of a little courage, though his legs felt as weary as ever.

He shrugged out of his light jacket and put it in the coat closet before taking the stairs with a steady gait. In the master bedroom, Sam found Sarah already cozily lying in bed, the lamp casting its rosy glow on her face and providing light for the book she held on her lap. She'd taken her soft brown hair down from its usual low chignon, and it traveled down the shoulders of her white nightgown.

Sarah lifted her eyes toward him. "Have a nice walk?"

Shutting the door behind him, Sam leaned against it for a moment and looked at his beloved wife. Should he tell her his concerns about Ben and Betty? Was it silly of him to see it as such a serious issue? Perhaps he should back off.

He must have paused for too long, because Sarah closed her book and gave him her full attention. "What is it, Sam? Something's happened, or you're worried about something. Or both."

He smiled sheepishly. His wife knew him too well. "Nothing's happened. Not yet, anyway. And maybe it never will. I'm probably worrying for nothing, as usual."

"Probably."

He heard the teasing in her voice and shook his head as he unknotted his tie and pulled it off.

"But you might as well tell me anyway."

Opening the bureau drawer, Sam drew out a pair of striped pajamas. "I think it's nothing," he insisted. Why should Sarah worry about Ben and Betty? She was so happy that her eldest, rebellious son had become a Christian, so delighted that he was settled within walking distance, that God had blessed his carpentry business with plenty of customers, that he was involved with their church, and that he'd hit it off so well with Betty, a nice, sweet girl. Sam pulled off his button-down shirt and pushed first one arm and then the other into the sleeves of his pajama top. *For all I know, Sarah's been encouraging Ben toward this.*

"Have you been encouraging Ben to ask Betty to marry him?" the question came out abruptly as he turned to face his wife again.

Her eyebrows rose in surprise, and her eyes widened a bit. "I... Well, not encouraging, but I think that's the direction they're heading in. Hasn't it seemed that way to you? They've been dating..."

"Only since September," Sam hastened to remind her. "And even then, it was just dinner at her house once a week and maybe a soda at the drugstore afterward. Or going to a youth outing together. Casual dating more than anything, I thought."

Her eyebrows scrunched, Sarah opened her mouth to reply, but Sam continued quickly. "I'm not really sure that they're ready for marriage, Sarah. It's a lifelong commitment. Does Ben realize that? Does he even know Betty well enough? Or is she just the first young woman he's come across that's garnered his attention? Is he mature enough in his walk with the Lord to be a good husband to her? Or is this just his flesh speaking?"

He had to suck in a deep breath when all the words had made their way into the vanilla-scented air of their bedroom. He felt no better for having spoken all his worries aloud.

Sarah sat, waiting for any more that he wanted to say, but Sam sighed and shuffled over to the bed, clicking on the lamp on his side and sitting down on the mattress, more weary than ever. Where had the peace gone that he'd experienced when he'd spoken to the Lord immediately after talking with Ben?

He shut his eyes, anxious to escape, and a moment later, felt Sarah's hand on his back. The mattress sprang down beneath them as she scooted over to sit near him, her legs curled up beneath her. "First off, knowing my son, Betty is not the first girl to catch his interest. Maybe as a Christian, she is, but not otherwise. And we've both seen Ben's walk with the Lord these past few months, Sam. He's not faking it. He's got a lot of growing up to do, but he's on the right path." Sarah paused, her finger drawing patterns on Sam's back as she thought. "Betty's a Christian, like you said, and I'm sure that she'll be a good wife and mother. If the Clouds are all right with it, and Ben believes it's from God, then why should we stop them?"

He glanced at her over his shoulder, and she smiled. Sarah made it all seem and sound so easy.

"Well, if they do marry soon," he said in an attempt at a lightheartedness that he didn't feel, "we might have news of a coming grandchild at this time next year."

She smiled, but there was a sadness there.

"What is it?" he forced himself to ask.

"Nothing."

He turned now completely to face her, trying to push away his tiredness, to give one-hundred-percent of the one-percent he had left. He picked up her plump, soft hands. "What is it, dear?"

She dropped her eyes from his down to their joined hands. "It's just... I wish sometimes that I hadn't given David to Emmeline." She paused. "Is that terrible? That's terrible, I know."

Sam waited, speechless. He'd never had imagined that Sarah felt that way at all. She never showed it, to his mind at least.

"I… I just sometimes wish that I could have had one more opportunity to bring up a child in the right way, in a godly way, now that I know better. And I see Emmeline with David, and I wonder if I did the right thing." She shook her head as if to clear it. "But I know. I know it was the right thing. I'm being silly. Forgive me, darling."

She bent near and touched her lips to Sam's cheek, feather-light.

"I love you, Sarah," he said, unable to think of what else to say, how else to comfort his wife.

She forced a smile. "I love you, too, Sam."

## Chapter Five

**Saturday, November 27, 1937**

*"You go there, you get the money, and you get out of there. Then you meet me. That last part's the most important, Annie."*

Clinging to the metal trolley-car pole with one cold hand, Annie shuddered as she remembered Aldo's determined smile.

*"Ya know, we might've lucked out with you getting pregnant just when Benji-boy hightails it to his rich old man. We can really make some dough outta this. You wait and see."*

But some part of her didn't want to wait and see. Some small part of her still revolted at the thought of using her child as a chip on the gambling table of life.

*"I don't care what you do with it afterward. Leave it with them if you want. Listen, you can get a new start on your life, Annie, this*

*time with money in your pocket. Take it from me, though, no guy's gonna want you with that in tow, so don't take it with you when you split."*

*It.*

That's how Aldo had referred to the baby she carried. But Annie knew differently. She'd felt the child move at night when she tried to sleep. Could nearly trace the outline of a foot sometimes in the skin of her stomach. Had endured months of sickness that had proved and yet kept his or her existence concealed for months because she had not gained the amount of weight the time of her pregnancy dictated – until her pregnancy was too far advanced for her body to conceal it any longer.

*"Get rid of it early."* That's what one of her fellow maids had advised her. *"I know a doctor in town who'll do it, no problem. Won't say nothing to nobody, either."*

But she hadn't been able to give in to the maid's pressure then.

How could she do as Aldo dictated now? How could she give birth to this child and then abandon him or her, as though the baby was refuse?

Yet even now, riding on a public street-car, she felt glad for the gloves that covered her hands. No one else on the crowded car – not the off-duty policeman nor the housewife with her two sticky-faced children nor the several blue-collared workmen would know that her left hand bore no wedding ring, despite her protruding stomach. Instead, they must think that she was the legitimate wife of a fellow New Englander, albeit obviously impoverished, given the state of her clothing. Though, with this Depression lingering on so, that was to be expected.

*"And what happens after I leave? What if Ben comes after me*

*with the police?"*

*"He'll have no proof, Tootsie Roll, that you took anything. And besides, you and me are going to disappear. They won't be able to track you."*

She closed her eyes, desperate to escape the fear, the desperation, the dread that clouded her heart every time she thought about going through with Aldo's plan.

*"It'll work. You'll see."*

Yeah, it would work all right. That was what she feared.

But what else could she do?

She gulped and placed a shaking hand on her bulging stomach.

*Nothing.*

"On the twelfth day of Christmas, my true love came to me..."

Paulie's tenor voice floated through the air from the staircase, and Sarah couldn't keep – and didn't want to keep – the smile from spreading across her mouth like soft butter across a warm slice of the pumpkin bread she had pulled from the oven a half-hour ago.

"Ain't it supposed to be, *my true love gave to me?*" Cliff called from the living room.

Paulie's laugh bubbled through the foyer and into the kitchen ahead of him. "Not in my version," he said over his shoulder as he ambled into the kitchen. "Grace'll be here for Christmas, and that's gift enough for me."

"But she's going back to school today, ain't she?" Cliff called again.

"Yeah, that's the sad truth."

Sarah glanced up to see the smile drop off her stepson's face at the thought. Just as quickly, though, his face lit up again when he caught sight of her drizzling icing over the plump breads that rested on the cooling racks.

"Is that pumpkin bread I smell?" Paulie sidled up to her and dropped his nose to within inches of the tops of the baked goods.

"Out of the way, Paulie," Sarah scolded, her spoon poised and ready to ladle more of the thick sweet whiteness. Despite the no-nonsense words, though, she couldn't help the affection that warmed her voice.

Paulie sucked in an audible breath. "Is that... cinnamon?"

Sarah pursed her lips to keep them from curving up again. "Yes, and maple syrup and nutmeg."

Paulie stood upright and put a hand to his heart as if he was John Barrymore himself. "Maple syrup *and* cinnamon *and* nutmeg? And you would deny me one little, itsy-bitsy slice of heaven on earth?"

"Yes." Sarah crossed her arms to show him that she meant business. "If I give you a slice, you know Cliff'll be in here in an instant, wanting one, too."

Paulie opened his mouth to protest, but Sarah continued before he could. "You can wait until tonight after supper."

"That long?" Paulie looked so pitiful that Sarah felt her determination give way.

"Alright," she said, glancing toward the door and keeping her voice down. "One little sliver. But you'll have to eat it in here."

Paulie's face burst into a grin of thankfulness, and then Sarah felt his enthusiastic embrace around her shoulders. "You're the best."

"Mmmm." Sarah raised her eyebrows and lifted a knife to cut him a slice without another word.

"Did you say we could have a slice of bread, Mama?" Cliff trotted into the room, head quirked in question, a comic book in hand.

Her younger son had the hearing ability of a rabbit. Sarah lifted her eyes to give an I-told-you-so look to Paulie, but he only gazed back with complete innocence and held out his hands for the promised slice. She sighed. "Yes, Cliff. But just a small one. I need enough for everyone tonight."

"Who's coming for supper?" Cliff asked, receiving the chunk of cinnamony bread. "Other than us?"

The smile dropped off Paulie's face. "Grace won't be here. She's leaving this afternoon for school."

"I know that. But who *is* coming?"

Sarah wondered if Cliff really wanted to know or if he just wanted to ascertain whether there really was a need to conserve the rest of the bread – or if he could beg for another slice with a reasonable chance of success. "Ben'll be here, I'm sure, and maybe Betty."

"Lou's coming?" Cliff licked a drip of white icing off the back of his hand.

"I think so." *I hope so.* Her older daughter – the twin of Nancy, who had moved out-of-state with her husband last year – seemed to go through phases of wanting to join in the joy of the Picoletti-Giorgi household and wanting to avoid it as much as possible. Right now, with Christmas coming in a few weeks, Sarah wasn't sure which way the wind would blow for Lou, her little daughter, and her husband. "I told them they were welcome."

"Are the Clouds coming, too?" Paulie popped the last

bite of his slice into his mouth and reached across the cutting board for another piece, his eyes dancing in fun.

Sarah slapped his hand with hers. "No more!" She softened her sternness with a smile, something she wished she'd learned to do earlier on with her children. "And, no, they're not coming." And what a relief, though she and Bertha, Betty's mother, got along very well. Too many people crowding her all at once made Sarah want to escape, even if they were people she loved and knew. "Don't you need to leave for the train station soon?" she asked Paulie.

"Yes, ma'am, I do. I'll see if Grace is all packed." Paulie bent to peck her cheek. "Thanks for the bread, Mother." The title lifted Sarah's lips into a smile.

"Hey, can I come along for the ride?" Cliff asked as Paulie headed out of the kitchen.

Paulie turned and gave him a grin. "Not today, kid."

Sarah watched him depart, warmth filling her heart as she pondered the ever-growing affection between her daughter Grace and Paulie. Yet, a sigh expanded her chest at the same time. *All my children have grown up so fast. The years flew by while I was busy worrying about other things.*

"Can I have another piece? I won't tell Paulie you gave it to me."

Sarah didn't tell Cliff that another piece of pumpkin bread was probably the last thing on Paulie's mind right now. She eyed her younger son as if in serious thought, and then relented, picking up the knife again and slicing off a sliver, fragrant with spices. "Here you go." She passed it into his hand. "But that's it. Scoot. Don't you have homework?"

"Finished it last night, Ma. Dontcha remember?" Cliff took a giant bite of the bread, as if he ate rarely in this house, instead of getting three square meals a day... plus snacks.

Paulie scanned the train platform, teeming with every variety of people, from grandmothers clutching the hands of small children, wrapped up well against the November chill in their thick woolen coats to station employees, smartly dressed in their starched uniforms, to travelers coming home for Thanksgiving. He and Grace had arrived just as the whistle blew, announcing that a train had come into the station and passengers were disembarking. Grace had needed to use the ladies' room, so now he waited for her to return so that they could make sure that she had everything in order for her short ride to Gladstone Conservatory.

There she was.

Though they'd just spent nearly a week together, Paulie's heart picked up its beat as he watched for a long moment. Her back to him, Grace scanned the crowded platform, looking for him, her brown leather weekend bag clutched by her side. The diamond-and-pearl engagement ring sparkled on her finger as she touched her left hand to the small olive-green hat resting atop her golden hair, which was neatly pulled into some kind of twist at the base of her neck. She'd been growing out her hair for months, despite the trend toward shorter styles among most women, and Paulie rather liked it. Her petite form was dwarfed by the swarm of people around her; he could tell that she couldn't find him in the crowd.

"Grace!" Paulie shot a hand up into the air and waved

as he made his way across the platform, excusing himself as he pushed through the crowd. "Grace, over here!"

She turned at the sound of his voice, a smile lifting her lips, but as she turned, she must not have noticed the person right behind her – one of the disembarking passengers. With a jolt, they collided. Grace's bag flew from her hand, and the other young woman stumbled backward, her back still to Paulie.

Quick as a fox, Paulie darted forward and grasped the young woman's elbow to prevent her from toppling backwards onto the hard cement platform. The heaviness of her body surprised him, and Paulie had to brace himself in order to keep her and him upright. Regaining her balance clumsily, the girl turned, fixing the cheap little hat on her head. Paulie saw that she was heavily pregnant.

"Are you all right?" he inquired, releasing her scrawny arm as she yanked it out of his grasp.

Unlike he knew Grace would have in a similar circumstance, this young woman did not appear shaken but rather straightened up her spine as she met his gaze with a steely one of her own. "Yeah I'm all right," she said, "if this dame here would've watched where she was going." She darted a fierce glance at Grace.

A defense of his sweetheart was on Paulie's tongue, but Grace spoke before he could say anything else. "I'm really very sorry," she said, gentleness on her tongue. "I should have been watching where I was going. You're right."

The defensiveness in the other young woman's eyes melted just a little at Grace's admission. She brushed her hands over her worn skirt and nearly-buttonless coat, as if to arrange her garments in an orderly fashion. "Yeah, well, it's all right. No harm done," she said after a moment.

And with that, the young woman gave a tug to her hat and brushed by them, barely slowed by the heavy burden at her waist. Both Paulie and Grace's eyes followed her as she disappeared into the crowd.

Sarah put the last cookie on the tray. It was a beautiful almond cut, perfectly crunchy on the outside and soft on the inside. She knew because she had already tasted more than one. Perfect cookies for dunking into the hot mug of cocoa, the makings for which simmered in a pot on the stove, complete with a cinnamon stick to impart a wonderful spicy flavor. On another burner, Sarah had placed her teakettle, already well-heated and ready to pour out its contents in a steaming stream. Lovely teacups waited for the teakettle on the table in the living room just beyond the kitchen. Whirling around on stocking feet – she'd slid her heels off hours ago – Sarah popped open a cupboard overhead. She had to stand on her tiptoes to reach deep within and grasped the candy canes that she had put away, hiding them from Cliff's ever-searching sweet tooth... and her own.

"I think everything is ready," she said aloud to herself. To Sarah's disappointment, Lou had called and said that she could not make it. Sarah's heart felt a little heavy at the thought of how many of her children were not here tonight: *Lou and Nancy.* Add to that her once-favored daughter Mary Evelyn, named after Sarah's own sister, with whom she now lived as an adopted child.

*And David.* Sarah's mind drifted to the Kinners' home. She could picture the scene: Emmaline and Geoff

Kinner sitting with the small boy – *my boy* – on their laps, reading aloud to him. *The last child of my body…* Was that why the thought of giving him up still wrenched her, years afterward? Sometimes, she had to remind herself why she had given him – had to remind herself that it was all for the best, wasn't it? He had been the best gift she could give barren Emmaline, who had given her so much, and, too, Sarah had come into a difficult time in her own life after Charlie's death. She'd barely been able to keep herself, Cliff, and Grace alive and had thought for a time that they'd be homeless. *Giving away David was the best thing for all three of us.* Sarah nudged one of the cherry winks with her finger, tucking it under a sugar cookie cut-out on the tray. Ultimately, despite the lingering sorrow, she was glad that she had given David to the Kinners. She was thankful, too, for the children that God had given to her, not only all of those who came from her body, but also for Paulie.

Yet something within her heart grieved and longed for the many years she had wasted – the years that the locusts had eaten, as the Scriptures said – the years that she had lived outside the light of Christ, enslaved to her fears and chained by her own self-centered decisions.

*You have given me so much, O Lord,* her spirit breathed, *and yet I wish… I wish that I could go back and do things differently. I wish that I could be Emmeline Kinner, starting fresh, instead sometimes feeling like I'm just trying to put the broken pieces of our lives together in a way that makes sense. I wish I had one more child, just one more…*

Almost as soon as she'd thought it, the wish deflated like a spent balloon. *But I know that this won't be.* Her last child had been a surprise, little David, born a decade after Evelyn. She was nearly in her mid-forties now and knew that she should be thankful for what she had. She and Sam had so much. She shut her eyes and then opened them deliberately. *I will rejoice.* Picking up the tray, loaded with holiday goodies, she set her heart and her mind resolutely toward contentment in this season of the coming of the Child-Christ.

## Chapter Six

Despite Grace's recent departure, Paulie felt light of foot when he bounded down the staircase two steps at a time into the brightly-lit foyer of his family home. After all, Grace would be home again in less than three weeks, and Christmas was coming – one of his favorite holidays. Who could be grumpy at such a time?

Just as Paulie's feet touched the tiled floor of the foyer, a knock sounded on the front door. "I've got it, Mother!" he called over his shoulder, heading straight for the front door. Betty must have decided to come after all. Ben had said something about her having rescheduled a piano lesson for this evening, but maybe the student had canceled again. Having Betty here would be a great treat for Ben. He worked so hard that he barely saw his girlfriend much at all.

He swung open the door without looking through the peephole. "Hiya, Betty!"

But it wasn't Betty standing on the wide front stoop. Instead, a young woman stood there, her reddish hair brushing against her shoulders, her profile to him. Upon hearing Paulie's voice, she turned toward him.

It was the girl from the train station, the one Grace had bumped into, the one Paulie had caught and heaved back to her feet. He stood there and stared, confused and at a loss for words. If she had been a stranger whom he had never seen before, he would have politely asked what she needed. But the coincidence of having met her – bumped into her, quite literally – less than an hour before left Paulie speechless.

His silence, however, was apparently a mistake. The girl's sharp little chin lifted and her eyes, in which he thought he had caught a sliver of fear and vulnerability just a moment before, hardened.

Paulie tripped over his words as he tried to make up for his rudeness. "I'm sorry," he said. "Where are my manners? Can I help you?" Paulie saw that she was very young indeed, perhaps no more than sixteen. His heart turned over in pity as everything clicked together. Somehow, some way, for some reason, this obviously-impoverished girl must have been sent to visit Dad, an eminent obstetrician and surgeon. It was unusual, sure, for this young woman to come straight to the house, rather than to Dad's office or to the hospital, but it must be all right. *Dad must have a reason for it.*

She opened her mouth to reply, but Paulie hurried on. "Why don't you come on in? It's freezing out here. Almost feels like we may get some snow, doesn't it? And still in November! Early for that, don't you think?" A little embarrassed from the silly way that he had acted when he opened the door – Why in the world had he answered with greeting Betty, anyway? – Paulie stepped back and held the door open wide, gesturing with his other hand for the girl to enter. "Come on in, come on in,"

Her expression softened for a split second, and her eyes grew wide with surprise. But she did just as Paulie asked, stepping into the house on floppy shoes, clutching a holey carpet bag with one bony, blue-veined hand.

"Can I take your coat?" Paulie asked, trying to make the young woman feel welcome. Her shoulders, already straight-angled as a scrub-board, had grown even stiffer when she had stepped into their nicely-appointed home, which Paulie knew from Grace's past experience, could feel a little intimidating if you weren't used to it.

The young woman shook her head. *She can't be more than sixteen. Maybe seventeen.* She wore no makeup, and the skin ringing her eyes bore such an intense shade of yellowish-brown that, if Paulie had passed her on the street, he would have taken a second glance out of surprise. *She doesn't look so good.* "Well, hold on a second here, and I'll see if Dad is able to come down. I'm sure he's expecting you." Without waiting for her to answer, Paulie turned and started toward his father's office located in the rear of the first floor of the house.

"I'm not here to see your father." The voice, its edges trembling yet strong, like a china teacup set down too hard on its saucer, stopped Paulie in his tracks.

He turned, bewildered. His assumption had been wrong? He waited for her to continue, the silence stretching out between them.

"I'm here to see Ben Picoletti," she stated at last, her jaw set. "He lives here... don't he?"

*What?* Uneasiness prickled up Paulie's spine as he realized that he had completely misjudged this situation. "Well, no. No, he doesn't," Paulie stumbled over the words. "He lives in his own home across town, but he comes here a lot. For meals and such, you know. We're his family, so..."

Why was he telling her all of this? *Be quiet until you know more, Paulie.* He swallowed back more words, the ones he'd already let out making his stomach churn. "Uh, wait here just a second."

He turned from the visitor but then hesitated, undecided. Should he go and tell Dad? Or Mother, who was putting the finishing touches on a cookie tray in the kitchen? Or, maybe, just maybe, Ben himself?

Paulie decided to take his chance on that last option. With one final glance at the girl, he strode through the barely-cracked-open door into the living room. His anxiety fell away a little, and he breathed a deep sigh of relief when he saw his stepbrother sitting on the sofa near the fireplace. Ben's head lay propped on his arms as he dozed, resting his eyes. Knowing that Ben woke early every morning to start work, Paulie felt a little pang of regret as he poked his stepbrother's arm. "Ben. Ben."

Ben shifted, and his eyelids fluttered. "Huh?" Opening his eyes, he blinked at Paulie. "What is it?"

Paulie glanced over his shoulder. "There's a girl here who wants to talk to you," he said, keeping his voice hushed. "I don't know what she wants. I met her earlier at the train station."

Ben's eyebrows scrunched as he straightened up on the sofa. "You know her?" he asked, his sleepiness showing.

Paulie shook his head, impatience nibbling at him.

"No, I don't know her from Eve. But she says she knows you. She came here to –"

The door swung open with a crash against the wall beside it. "I came 'cuz I gotta talk to ya, Ben Picoletti."

Paulie whipped around to see the young woman standing in the frame, her face smile-less. Her eyes met his. "I couldn't wait no longer."

He glanced at Ben, who had jolted from the sofa at the girl's entrance. The appearance of their visitor had bleached Ben's face and seemed to have torn every word from his throat.

These few days before, during, and after Thanksgiving, Sam had trouble concentrating, period. What man could keep his mind on writing a journal article for the American Medical Association when the scent of roasting chestnuts mingled with that of baking almond cuts and anisette biscuits? True, Sarah had offered to bring him a plate of samples earlier, but he'd refused, knowing his enjoyment would be truer if he waited. Besides, he'd already enjoyed a very adequate evening meal of scrumptious holiday leftovers.

He checked his watch. Ten more minutes until eight o'clock. Then he would break from his work – unless an emergency call came in – until Monday. Just the thought of spending that time with his family stretched his lips into a smile and inspired him to pick up his pen with renewed energy.

*Bang.* The sound of what had to be a door crashing against a wall a room away distracted him. *What in the world?* The only one young enough to do that was Cliff, and Sam knew for a fact that the teenaged boy had headed upstairs after dinner to work on a model airplane. Frowning, Sam tossed his pen down and rose from the desk chair, not stopping to stretch the kinks out of his back. He grasped the handle of the door that separated his study from the sitting room and opened it, ready to give a word of rebuke to one of his older sons.

But the sight that met his eyes surprised him, and he hesitated with uncertainty. A young woman whom Sam had never before seen stood just a couple of steps within the room, her arms crossed defiantly across her middle, clenching the ratty coat closed. Evidently, she was the door-banger. At Sam's entrance, she spared him a long, narrow look that ended with a glare.

A few feet away, Paulie stood in front of Ben as though he was his stepbrother's guard. Both young men wore wary expressions, with Ben's face drained of color, his eyes unblinking.

"What's going on here?" Sam asked, trying to keep his tone as neutral as possible until he found out what had turned his two sons into garden statues.

After a moment, Paulie tore his eyes off the visitor and met Sam's gaze. "This... This girl says that she knows Ben."

Dread swirled and sank straight to the pit of Ben's stomach. He found himself unable to move.

*"She says she knows Ben."* Knew him? Annie sure did. Seeing her again – here, in his stepfather's house, in his

new life – felt like waking up in the morning to discover you'd had a tick sucking behind your ear all night.

Ben tried to move his lips, to form some coherent sentence to add to Paulie's, but he couldn't. His legs and arms became as liquid as hot jelly. In a second, he might need to sit down. *Unless this is a nightmare. Then I just gotta wake up.*

Sam must have mistaken Ben's horror for mere awkwardness at the sight of a friend from his old life because the older man suddenly shook off his uncertain expression and gave the young woman one of his openhearted smiles. "Well," he began with little bow, "any friend of my son Ben is welcome here."

Annie seemed to gather courage from that statement. "I'm real glad to hear ya say that, sir. 'Specially since your son and me, we're more than just friends."

*Oh, no. No, no, no, no.* Panic joined the horror. What was her point in coming here and embarrassing him in front of his entire family by telling them of their illicit relationship? A relationship of which Ben was now heartily ashamed. He opened his mouth to say something – anything – that would stop her. *Why is she doing this? Why is she here now?*

But she was too quick for him. The young woman stepped toward Sam, her petite height dwarfed by his stature. "Ya see, sir, your son and me – well," and here, even she had the decency to fumble for the proper words – if there were proper words. From the corner of his eye, Ben saw Cliff and Mama enter the room, curiosity sketched over their features.

*Good. Let her fumble.* If she was going to humiliate them both – for some reason known only to herself, apparently – then let her suffer at least a little, too. Anger steamed through Ben as he watched her lower her eyes — eyes with which he had once been entranced.

Then, as if with a burst of bravery, she threw open the immensely baggy, torn coat she wore.

Ben choked on his own saliva. As he coughed with the force of a TB victim, one thought ran over and over through his mind: *She's pregnant.*

She raised defiant eyes to Sam's face. *She doesn't dare look at me.* "As ya can see, sir, I'm going to have your grandkid. I'm nearly nine months along."

All the eyes in the room — from his baby brother Cliff's innocently surprised ones to Mama's deeply troubled ones — turned from the girl to Ben. And everyone's gaze asked a question. A question Ben couldn't bring himself to answer: *Is it true?*

The panic took over completely and finally solidified Ben's legs. Still hacking, he stumbled to his feet and fled from the room like a guilty Joseph.

Ben only stood outside in the cold, alone, for a few moments before he heard the backporch door open behind him. Rigid against the dark night, he didn't turn to see who had arrived to condemn him.

"Here. It's cold tonight." Sam's voice reached out to him as he felt the soft drape of wool over his shoulders. With a glance, he saw that Sam had brought him his overcoat.

"Thanks," he mumbled without looking at his stepfather — a man whom he had once hated and now loved and admired perhaps more than any other. The man whom he would least wish to disappoint.

As he surely had now. *I've humiliated this family. My family. Just like Papa always did.* He could barely breathe at the thought. *And Betty...* His mind failed him as he let himself think for just a moment of how she would take this news.

For several minutes, they stood quietly beneath the velvet sky, looking at the cold stars tossing glitter as they danced silently around the moon.

Sam broke the silence. "Is she... That is, do you know if the young woman is telling the truth?"

Would Ben be out here if there was a shred of a chance that she wasn't? He would've stayed in there and fought, not run like a coward. But he knew Annie – knew her well. He'd broken up with her a month or so before Aldo and he had fought like the dickens, last spring. *And she's not a cheater.* He knew that.

"I-I'm sure that she is." Ben hung his head. *Oh, God, why did You let this happen?* And yet, even as he asked the question, how could he blame God when this was a natural, God-designed consequence to his actions? His shoulders slumped, all rebellion gone.

Ben swallowed hard, past the rock wedged deep in his throat. "I'm sorry I brought this all on your family," he muttered. "I didn't know... Annie and I broke up weeks before everything happened at Bousquet's. Then I came here. I never thought... I haven't heard from her since I left the stable."

"Annie? Is that the young woman's name?"

He nodded, remembering how he'd found the sound of it so appealing at one time. Now it struck his ear with dissonance, wildly out-of-tune with the new life he had begun in Chetham. "I'm so ashamed." The words tumbled from his mouth. "Ya must think…"

Immediately Sam's arm stretched around his rigid shoulders and gripped him in a sideways embrace. "I think nothing. What you've done in the past – we knew all that – and all of it is forgiven by God. How could I hold it against you? You're my son, Ben, and there is nothing you could ever do that would interfere with my love for you."

At those words, Ben dared to look up into Sam's dark eyes and found grace there, rather than the condemnation he deserved. "You are a new creation in Christ. Old things have gone forever. All things have become new." Sam released him.

Ben nodded, a lump pressing his throat. "But I still got the consequences."

Sam pulled in a deep breath. "Yes," he answered in the truthful way Ben had come to expect from his stepfather. "You do."

Ben could not bear to leave the question unasked – the question that had pounded through his mind since Annie had thrown open her coat. "What'll I tell Betty?"

Sam paused, the cold air clouding white before his slightly-opened mouth. "You'll have to tell her the truth."

*The truth.* Ben's eyes slid shut in dread.

"Without the gory details, but the truth," Sam repeated, then added more gently, "There's no way around it, Ben."

Ben nodded and opened his eyes. "Yeah." He swallowed. "I know." In a town the size of Chetham, everyone would know within days, anyway. *Oh, dear God, help me.*

The house felt quiet and tense when they walked back inside. Or maybe the tension pulsed so heavily through Ben's body that he felt it in every step he took. He steeled himself to face his former girlfriend – to see the familiarity they'd once shared gleaming from her eyes.

But Annie wasn't there in the sitting room. Pausing in the doorway, Ben shot a questioning glance at Mama, who sat on the sofa with some knitting work in her hands. Paulie and Cliff faced each other in a game of checkers, cross-legged on the rug.

Mama rose and met Ben and Sam near the doorway, out of earshot of Cliff. "She was exhausted," Mama spoke quietly, her face strained. "I gave her a guestroom on the second floor – your old room, Ben."

Even as the words left her mouth, Mama winced, and Ben realized afresh the awkwardness of the situation in which the foolish sins of his youth had placed the family.

Mama glanced from Sam to Ben. She licked her lips. "Is she telling… That is, do you think –?"

But Ben couldn't allow her to finish the question. "Yeah, Mama, I'm one-hundred-percent sure that she's telling the truth." He couldn't meet her eyes. "I'm sorry." What a way to spoil the holidays for his mama. What a way!

"There's nothing more or less to be sorry for now than there was before, Ben. Just because you've got to deal with the consequences now doesn't mean that what you did in the past is any better or worse."

He raised his eyes and met his Mama's gaze. The no-nonsense love he saw there gave him courage.

"If I'm honest, I do wish that you didn't have to go through all this." She sucked in a breath. "But you won't face it alone, you know."

"And we should start with prayer together," interjected Sam.

Mama nodded.

"Paulie, we're going to my study, all right?" Sam turned toward his son.

Paulie looked up, and his eyes landed on Ben. "Sure, Dad. Cliff and I are just going to finish this game and then turn in."

Ben looked away, wanting to look anywhere rather than to face virtuous Paulie, who, Ben suspected, had probably not even kissed Grace yet. Turning to trail after Sam and Mama, Ben suddenly felt the hard hug of his stepbrother from behind. He stopped, and Paulie stood before him.

"Hey, don't worry about all this, Ben," he said, his voice firm. "It's in the past. It doesn't change anything, you know."

Forcing a wobbly smile, Ben let his shoulders lift and fall. For Paulie, maybe it didn't. And there was relief in knowing that Paulie would stick by him, no matter what.

*But Betty...* The ring-box pressed uncomfortably into his thigh. This *would* change things with her. And no one – not Paulie, not Mama, not even Sam – could say that it wouldn't.

Sleep eluded him that night. When he'd moved into the old Picoletti place this past autumn, he'd placed the old bed from his childhood beneath the huge, curtainless picture window in the former sitting room. He'd always enjoyed watching the moon shining high at night and had wanted to wake with the sunlight on his face. Usually, the light comforted him. But now the moon's searching beams only enflamed the turmoil in his soul. Oddly, he found himself craving darkness. He longed to hide from the situation, from the young woman lying in the guest room at Sam and Mama's house, from the memory of his own foolish sins, from tomorrow itself.

But there was a life growing inside Annie – permanent, living evidence that Ben had done wrong – that perhaps the Ben Picoletti that others saw was not the real Ben.

That perhaps he was just like his father.

*That's what folks in town will say.* He knew it.

*Couldn't You have let her lose it?*

The thought sparked through his heart, leaving a burn of guilty feelings behind it. Yet, in all honesty, could he repent of it? If Annie'd lost the baby, all traces of his sin, of his guilt, would be gone. Neither she nor he nor Betty Cloud nor any of his family would have to bear the consequences of his past actions.

# Chapter Seven

Annie pulled the curtain back, letting the exquisite lace trail through her fingertips. *Will he come back this morning?* If he did come, what would he say? Last night, he'd run from her. This morning, she wondered if she should go downstairs or if she should wait for someone to come fetch her. She'd been up and dressed by the time the sun's rays had just touched her windowpane – sitting here in this rocking chair, warm blanket pulled over her legs, waiting.

Ben's mama seemed nice enough. At least she'd given Annie a place to sleep – and a troubled but kind, "Goodnight." When Annie had asked, she'd explained that Ben lived elsewhere – in his own house. Annie had not been sure if she should feel disappointed that Ben was at arms-length or if she should feel relieved that he was financially well-off enough to afford a house of his own.

It was no wonder that the lady appeared troubled, though. For not the first time that morning, Annie peered at her comfortable surroundings while her hand stroked the soft blanket on her lap. These people lived a swell life; that was for sure. And Annie's entrance into it – bearing such a shocking announcement – surely would put a damper on their holiday celebrations.

*If I'd had anywhere else to head to, I woulda gone.*

But there was nowhere. There was no one. Aldo had made that clear – though she'd known it herself from the moment of Daddy's rejection.

No one, except for Ben Picoletti. Nowhere, except for his family's home here in Chetham.

She glanced at the little fold-out alarm clock that perched on the bedside table. Seven-thirty. Gathering her courage once more – *How much more of that do I got left?* – Annie braced her legs and heaved all four feet and eleven inches of herself to her feet. She'd made up her mind. Never one to run away from confrontation, she was going downstairs.

"Mama, I gotta get to work." Ben pushed himself away from the table and stood. He'd been here bright-and-early, ready to hash it out, get the worst of it over with, but Annie had stayed upstairs. What time was it anyway? Nearly eight o'clock? He'd woken before dawn… well, if he'd even really slept. And with the sun's rising a new layer of feelings had surfaced in Ben's heart – one that he couldn't call by any name but resentment. Desperate to get away from his thoughts, Ben had not stopped to really pray or read his Bible this morning. What good would it have done? *I'm reaping what I've sown.*

Mama took a quiet sip of her coffee. "On a Sunday, Ben? You never work on Sundays." She set the cup down on her saucer.

Ben's jaw pulsed, but he sat back down. "I can't go to church today, Mama. I can't face Betty or anybody else."

Mama caught his eyes. "I'm not saying you have to go to church this morning." She paused. "The girl – Annie – was so tired last night, she could barely walk up the stairs. I think we can let her sleep a little longer."

Ben shifted from foot-to-foot and let his gaze fall to the floor, to the walls, to the leftover breakfast food still on the table – anywhere but Mama's eyes. If only there was some way to turn back the clock so many months and re-work his life. *Why, Lord God? Why didn't You have me come to You sooner? You are in control; You can do everything. Why did You allow this to happen?*

He looked at the clock. Irritation sparked inside him. "I gotta go, Mama. I'll be back later." Without meeting her eyes again, he whipped around the table, pecked her cheek, and turned on his heel to exit the room.

And came face-to-face with Annie. Well, face-to-shoulder, at least. Ben wasn't a tall man, by any standard, but Annie's head still only came up to his collarbone. He stepped back and almost fell backwards across the chair that Cliff had probably neglected to push in when he'd left the kitchen after a midnight snack last night.

"Sorry!" Annie reached out a hand to his arm to steady him. "I didn't mean to startle ya."

His skin crawled at the touch of her fingers on his

skin. "I'm okay," he muttered, pulling away and righting himself and the chair in one clumsy, loud movement.

"Good morning, Annie." Mama's greeting clanged against Ben's unsettled spirit. Why was Mama being so friendly?

*Why shouldn't she be friendly? Isn't that what Christians are supposed to be like?*

He gritted his teeth against the mental reminder. *Yeah, but most Christians don't have to deal with such a past rearing up and taking its pound of flesh, so to speak.*

But Annie wasn't privy to his feelings, and she responded to Mama's kindness with a surprised, unsteady smile. "Uh, good morning, ma'am."

"Would you like some coffee? There's toast and eggs, too, if you're hungry," Mama offered. "Some of it might be a little cold, but our cook Tabitha can warm it up in the oven for you."

*What is this? One big, happy family reunion?* Didn't Mama realize what Annie's announcement meant for everyone's future? No, it wasn't all Annie's fault – the pang of guilt in his heart told him that – but did they have to welcome her like a long-lost relative?

Before Annie could accept or decline, Ben sent a glare Mama's way that he hoped might shed a little rain on her parade of thoughtfulness. "We don't have time for that, Mama. Annie and me have gotta talk before I leave, remember? Isn't that what ya wanted?" He cringed at the savagery he could hear in his own voice.

He turned toward Annie but would not – could not – look her in the eye. "We can go into the sitting room," he directed, gesturing her toward the threshold.

She turned and shuffled out, bearing that burden before her, a burden he couldn't bear to face, for it only allowed the memories of his past sins to dig their claws deeper into his soul. And yet, his eyes fell to her swollen stomach continually, as if drawn by fascination. The idea that a child – his child – grew in Annie's body staggered him – bewildered him.

He turned to follow her but felt Mama's fingers close around his forearm with jolting firmness. "What is wrong with you?" she whispered. "Don't you be rude in my house."

He looked down into Mama's eyes, turned from soft-as-a-lamb's to fierce-as-a-tiger's in seconds. For a few moments, her gaze held onto his – surely to let him know that she meant business – before she reached for the teapot on the table.

"Take her some tea," Mama ordered, pushing a newly-filled cup-and-saucer into Ben's unwilling hands. As he moved from the room without another word, he thought that he heard Mama mutter, "It's the least you can do."

She felt his anger striding behind her all the way through the entryway. It made her afraid, but she refused to shorten her step or let him know that it numbed her from head-to-toe.

*What if he throws me out? I got nowhere else to go.*

He couldn't throw her out. Not if she carried his child. Right?

*That's what Aldo said. "He's responsible, before the law, ya know."*

She walked toward one of the doors that opened into

the entryway. It seemed like the right one, the one she'd gone into last night, wearing all the confidence she could muster to cover her exhaustion and her terror.

"Not that one." Ben's voice sliced the air. It was quiet – a sure indication with Ben that all was not well. "Over here."

She lifted her gaze to meet his but just as quickly looked away again. His eyes burned with the fire of hurt and anger – a dangerous combination, she knew – as he indicated the door to his right with a nod of his head. She saw that he carried a cup-and-saucer in one hand.

"And here," he held it out to her. "Mama said to give this to ya."

Wordlessly, she took it from him, nearly dropping the delicate china. She wasn't used to handling such fine things – not since she'd left Bousquet's service.

He led the way through the door he'd indicated a moment before. When she followed him, Annie found herself in that same sitting room as she'd been in last evening. A giant Christmas tree, decked in gold and blue splendor, hunched in the corner, as if it didn't want to participate in whatever conversation would ensue, either. Ben planted his feet with his back to Annie, looking out the window at the autumn-brown landscape.

He stayed silent for a long time. Annie felt her heart beating so hard that she looked down to see if the thundering was visible. Her feet ached, and she shifted from foot-to-foot to relieve the pressure from them.

Finally, he looked over his shoulder, an inscrutable expression on his face. "Ain't you gonna sit?"

"Are ya?" she asked, unsure of where to take her place on the battlefield – if this was going to be a battlefield.

"No." He turned and walked toward her. She retreated toward the sofa and gave into her feet's wish, perching on the edge of it and keeping her gaze focused on the floor.

Silence.

When she stole a glance up, he just stood there, staring down at the floor, his jaw pulsing as it did whenever he was angry.

Well, they had to start somewhere. And Annie figured that maybe she was the one who had to start. "Ain't ya gonna ask me what I'm doing here?" The words sounded loud as a lunch-bell in the silence between them.

"Nope. I know why you're here." And when he asked it, his eyes narrowed at the corners, like a police investigator's in the picture-shows. "What I wanna know is, why are you here *now*, Annie?"

She swallowed down her fear. "Whatdaya mean, *now*?"

"I mean, what took ya so long? The baby's obviously coming any day now. Ain't it?"

She swallowed. "Middle of December, far as I can figure it."

"So… What gives? Why'd it take ya nearly nine months to come to tell me about this?"

Should she tell him the truth? The preacher's words from her Sunday-School days whirled through her mind: *And the truth will set you free*. But this kind of truth – it was the kind that would harm her, the kind that killed, not the kind that brought freedom. Annie ran her tongue over her teeth, feeling each grooved surface before she pulled up enough courage in her heart to answer. "I wasn't sure if I was gonna keep it," she heard herself whisper. It wasn't the real reason why she'd not come earlier, but one of the many reasons why she sat here in this lovely room now. "But I waited too long, and then it moved." She dropped her eyes at the admission: that she had considered getting rid of the child at some back-alley place. After a long moment, she looked up.

Ben's face showed the full extent of his shock.

*She was gonna kill it.* The thought sickened him... and hardened his resolve. He wanted nothing – *nothing* – more to do with this girl who sat before him. She was his past; not his future. And yet... that child in her body – the very one whose extinction she had thought of ensuring – tied the two of them, Annie and Ben, together as surely as any cord of steel. "How can a woman kill her own baby?" The words crawled out of his throat. They slid toward her, meant to shame her.

And yet... was there some small, guilty corner of his heart that wished just the tiniest bit that she had sinned in that way, too? Then this wouldn't be a problem that he needed to deal with, that he needed to face. His conscience burned as he remembered his own thoughts during the previous restless night: *If only she had lost the baby!* Then there would have been no consequences for anyone. How was his thought any different, then, from her own? Both had wished for that little life to be extinguished, hadn't they?

Annie lowered her head. But instead of feeling the salve of satisfaction, as he had in the old days when he'd held power over her, he experienced the burn of shame. *Oh, dear God, what are we supposed to do?* What a mess he'd made of his life – of Betty's – of Annie's.

"The baby needs a father."

Annie's words startled him – drove the stake of panic deeper. He strained at the rope that held him to that stake, desperate to run, to be free of those words.

To be free of the past. Not to be forgiven only, but to be free of the consequences of his past. *Is that so wrong?*

Was she asking the impossible? The one thing he had hoped with desperation that she did not want? His heart raced in his chest. His tongue grew numb. His legs shook.

Annie waited for him to respond, perched on the couch like a mute parakeet with a stomach tumor.

Unsure how long his legs would hold up, Ben took a seat beside her. Well, if beside her was a full foot away, that was.

She turned surprised eyes to him – softened but a little wary, too.

"Look, Ansy," he began and then stopped, his eyes catching on hers, like a wool sweater on a nail. How easy it had been to go back to using his pet name for her – the nickname he'd called her for the whole year they'd dated – right up until the day that she'd told him that she'd had enough with his cheating on her. He cleared his throat at the memory. "Can ya stop pussyfootin' around? Just tell me what you want from me."

"I want ya to marry me. Give the baby a real father."

The numbness spread. He tried to swallow the lump in his throat to no avail. "Dontcha know ya can put the baby up for adoption, Annie? There are lots of couples who can't have kids of their own, lots of 'em who'd be glad to have your baby."

"I thought about that." She pulled her lips together. "But I don't want *our* baby to go to strangers. It don't seem right, giving it away like a Christmas present ya don't like."

And yet, wasn't that exactly what this baby was? Did either of them really want it? He closed his eyes and then forced them back open, forced them to face the young woman before him. "Look, Annie, I've changed. I'm not the guy I was before. I don't think you'd be happy with this kind of life I live. It ain't fast or fun, not in the way you're used to. I don't drink anymore or play cards or none of that stuff no more."

She stayed quiet for a moment, picking at the ragged cuticles on her fingernails. "I heard you'd changed. Aldo said that ya sent back the money ya stole from him."

Ben nodded stiffly. "Yeah. Yeah, I did." This fall, he'd estimated what he'd taken by cheating his old rival at the stable and sent it to him – disregarding any debts Aldo himself might owe Ben. Ben had never gotten a reply, so he'd not known whether or not the money had made it to him. Apparently, it had... and the news of it had made its way through the grapevine right to Annie's ears.

"What happened?" she asked. "What made ya change, I mean?"

For some reason, it was hard to make the words come this time. The eagerness he usually experienced when telling others of his conversion... well, it just wasn't there. Nonetheless, he pushed out the story. "I guess I finally realized how rotten I really was. I... I asked God to forgive me. He... He made me new inside." But right now, he felt anything but new. He felt dirty in his soul, as though he was right back to cheating Aldo at cards and chasing women and swigging a bottle and...

He eyed the girl sitting next to him. It was her fault. Why'd she have to come here now, when his pocket bulged with the box containing Betty's ring? Why'd she have to come bearing the physical sign of his past errors? Couldn't she have just hushed it up, hid herself in a home for unwed mothers or something until she had the kid, and then gone back to the life she loved – leaving his new one untouched, pristine?

Ignorance here truly would have been bliss.

Yet, even as the thoughts filtered through his mind, the conviction came sharp. *That's not who ya are anymore, either, Ben... Someone who always runs away from the consequences, someone who doesn't make right what's wrong...*

But couldn't there be a middle ground somewhere, a compromise between what Annie was asking – humiliation, a loveless marriage, and the end of all his hopes and dreams of a life with Betty Cloud – and what his old man longed to do?

Though, did Annie really *want* to marry him? Well, he might as well find out. "Look, I know that ya need some money. It can't have been easy, these past months. I bet Bousquet let ya go and –"

But she cut him off, her backbone straightening. Her eyes flashed at him, blinding sunlight on spring grass. "I ain't a money-grubber, so don't try to paint me as one, Ben Picoletti."

And she wasn't. Ben knew that. She never had been one to stick with him for what little cash he had. Oh, she'd been happy to help him spend his measly earnings, but he knew that wasn't what had kept her with him for the better part of a year. *She really did love me.* In a strange and worldly, selfish way, she had loved him much more than he had her. *I used her.* Guilt clenched at his heart at the realization. He knew that now, maybe had always known it. "How do I even know this... kid is mine? Maybe it's someone else's," he lashed out in desperation, knowing the impossibility of it even as he suggested it. She'd always been faithful to him; it was he who had been the unfaithful one, so often. The guilt of the memories cinched his neck, a too-tight bowtie threatening to cut off his breathing.

Annie met his eyes, the hurt his suggestion had inflicted shining there.

And something else, too: a fear...

"It's yours," she stated after a moment. "And I'm not leaving until I know how ya plan to provide for us. This baby," and here she laid her hand upon the mound resting on her lap, straining against a cheap, worn-out dress, "is as much yours as it is mine, Ben."

The anger boiled up again. She couldn't force him to do whatever she wanted like that! His spirit strained, a live butterfly, held down to a board and pinned in place, while everything inside it wanted to fly free on the wind of grace.

He sucked in a deep breath to calm himself. There was only one way out of this situation that he could see – only one way that would take care of everything, that would wreak the least damage. *Thank You, God.* "I just thought of something, Annie," he said, his voice quiet and calm, the kind he'd use with a hurt horse that he was trying to catch. "There's a home in Providence. A place for unwed mothers. You could go there. Mama would take ya, today even. Ya could get on with your life after that, ya know, and –"

"Oh, you'd like that, wouldn'tcha, Ben Picoletti? Tuck me away in some charity place so's ya wouldn't have to fork over your dime – so's that *your* life wouldn't be interrupted." Her eyes flashed again. "Ya don't care about me getting on with my life. It's all about you. It always has been." She smirked without joy. "Ya haven't changed one iota, have ya? Not really." She lifted a finger and poked it at his chest. "Same Ben Picoletti, right inside there. Selfish as ever." As she shook her head, her overgrown fringe fell into her eyes, and she brushed it back. "Well, ya ain't getting away from it now. Not this time." Angry satisfaction surfaced in her expression.

For the first time, Ben felt himself intimidated by her. With a lurch to his feet, he broke away. "I'm going," he stammered, the doorway open before him, urging him to escape. "We'll figure this out later."

He spent about seven hours down at Tom Gibson's place, reframing the old grocer's windows, before his shaking hand couldn't hold the hammer any longer. As he put away his tools, Ben's mind kept wandering to the house on River Avenue. What was Annie doing there today? Talking to Mama? Figuring out a plan?

He unhitched his tool belt and laid it on top of his wooden box. Had Betty heard anything? Had Cliff kept his mouth quiet? Probably. After all, what kid brother wanted to expose his family to humiliation? And Ben knew that Paulie wouldn't say anything, nor would Mama or Sam.

But Betty would have to know sooner or later.

Ben's jaw couldn't have been set tighter if it'd been sewn shut. Even just knowing about this… could she still love him? A pastor's daughter, pure and undefiled – could such a one really love Charlie Picoletti's son, pocked by sin of his own choosing, complete with the blemish of an illegitimate child to his name?

He locked the grocery store behind him with the key

Gibson had given him. Even doing that gave him pause. Because of the evident change in his character shown over the past months, the grocer had trusted Ben with entering his store unaccompanied. What would Annie's arrival – and the news she carried – do to his hard-earned new reputation?

In the twilight, Ben found his feet speeding not toward his own house but once more toward the Giorgi home, desperate to bring this to a conclusion. *If I could just give her a little money, maybe she'd leave...* He didn't have much. Sure, the house was his as a gift from Mama and Sam, but everything else – his clothes and food, most of his tools – he'd earned all of it by the sweat of his brow. Above him, the sky hovered low and gray, oppressive – echoing Ben's own feelings much better than the gaily-lit store fronts that lined Main Street.

But Annie said that she wanted the baby to have a father. Sending her off wouldn't accomplish that, even if Ben gave her all the dough he had in his pockets.

He approached the Giorgi home, tucked away from the center of town on River Avenue. He saw that Sam's car was absent; his stepfather must be working late at the hospital, called in to attend an emergency, perhaps. But light shone from both the sitting room and the dining room, the windows of which stretched out from both sides of the entryway. As he climbed the brick steps, the faint sound of orchestral Christmas music greeted him from inside. A newly-hung wreath rested against the red-painted door, touching the crisp air with its balsam fragrance.

Out of courtesy, Ben tapped on the door but didn't wait for anyone to answer before pushing it open. "Mama?" Leaving his toolbox on the porch, he raised his voice to be heard over an arrangement of "O Little Town of Bethlehem" as he stepped into the entryway. "Paulie?"

No one answered him, but he could hear activity in the sitting room. Shedding his coat and cap, Ben made his way to the room on his left. He peeked through the open doorway before announcing his presence again. His heart slowed its pounding as he realized that Mama was alone.

Body relaxing, he entered the room and watched Mama as she garlanded the tree with ropes of popcorn and cranberries. She arranged one loop here, fluffed up a branch there, and then finally stood back to admire her work.

Ben finally cleared his throat. "Looks real nice, Mama."

She startled and turned. "Ben. I didn't know if you'd be coming here tonight."

When he stayed silent, Mama picked up a small hatbox brimming with golden balls and turned back to working on the tree.

He had to know. "Where's Annie?" Had she taken his suggestion? Maybe she was actually gone! Maybe he was free...

"She's upstairs."

"Did she tell you about the idea I had of...?"

"I heard." Mama turned to face him, disappointment clouding her brown-lashed eyes. She set the box of baubles carefully down on the coffee table and stepped near enough to him so that he could smell the sugar-cookie scent that clung to her red cardigan. "To you, Annie – and the baby she's carrying - are only a problem. Nothing more. Send her to the home for unwed mothers, isn't that right? Let someone else handle the problem, even though you are more than capable of handling it. You just don't want to."

He shifted to rid himself of the discomfort her words brought him as they crawled up his neck.

"You would rather get on with your own plans, your own life, than do the right thing," Mama went on, her face as stern as Ben had ever seen it.

Against his will, tears tensed his throat. "And what is the right thing, Mama? You tell me. I don't wanna live in the past – where I did all those terrible things. I wanna have a future. I – Betty…" The emotion choked and embarrassed him.

Mama's face softened. "You don't have to live in the past, Ben. That's not what I'm asking," she replied softly. "But you have to trust God for the grace to bring you through the present, to give you a hope and a future that is worth having."

He snorted dismally. What kind of future would be worth having now? Illegitimate children were not the sort of thing that went away eventually. And Annie was asking for marriage! Did Mama understand that?

Mama paused. "Annie carrying that baby – and you finding out about it – is a sign of God's love, Ben." She gave him a rueful smile. "Though I know that it doesn't seem like it right now."

She took a breath and looked away, toward the fire burning low in the hearth. "I don't know what the future looks like for you and Betty, but usually the only way to any future worth having is by dealing with – not living in, but dealing with – the past. And Annie is part of your past. And the child that she carries – well, that's part of your future, son, whether you like it or not."

Ben ground his teeth but stayed silent. He didn't like it. Not one bit.

## Chapter Eight

When Ben opened his eyes the next morning, a grief clung to his heart. It took him a moment to remember why.

*Annie.* She was here in Chetham, a memory of his past come to life, bringing with her a piece of his unlooked-for future, as Mama said.

Once, he had loved that girl... well, loved her as best he could before the Holy Spirit had come into his heart and had opened his eyes to a sacrificial kind of love, the love of the Cross. But when he closed his eyes, as when he had dreamed those few days ago, he could still remember the softness of Annie's skin, the feel of her lips under his, the way her eyes had glistened with yearning as they had looked into his. The memories, when they first surfaced, for one split second, filled him with delight. But then the delight transformed like the beast in that old fairytale from royalty to a hideous creature, and the memory bittered and made him recoil.

His eyes slid over to where the ring box sat on his bedside table. How worthless the precious ring was, if he couldn't put it on Betty's finger! Yet he could never propose to her now, could he? Even if Annie agreed to his solution of retreating to the unwed mother's home – where he knew what she said was true: they would take her baby at birth, giving it to a couple whose name she would never know – even if she did that, he could never propose this Christmas. No, this Christmas would involve extricating himself from Annie's demands.

He had to talk to Betty. He knew it, and yet he dreaded it. What would she say? What would she think? *I've ruined the holidays for everyone, just like Papa used to.* Ben closed his eyes. If only shutting them would make all of his problems disappear. But they seemed to crowd more fiercely instead, squabbling for room in the darkness.

Opening his eyes, Ben sighed and heaved himself into sitting position. As he swung his legs over the side of the bed, his eyes fell on the Bible laying on this bedside table – the Bible he had read each morning and evening for months now, the Bible Betty's own dad, Reverend Cloud, had given him. He contemplated the Book for a long moment before reaching out for it. But then he withdrew his hand at the last moment, feeling dirty and alone. He had not felt this way – or at least not so intensely – since his conversion last summer. But now it seemed as though the heavens were shut to him. His nightmare of last week had come true, and he felt ashamed to knock at the door of heaven. Not until he fixed what was wrong in his life. Not until he made things right – whatever that would mean.

The telephone rang, and Betty grimaced, annoyance surfacing as the noise interrupted her playing of "It Came Upon a Midnight Clear." She had half a mind to ignore it, but she knew that the telephone's ring couldn't very well be ignored in the parsonage. Other people could ignore their telephones, but not the minister's family. Someone might need some help, someone might've gotten hurt, someone might need comfort from Mother's gentle tongue.

Though maybe it was just one of Betty's own students, canceling their piano lesson because they hadn't practiced this week, though of course they would not admit that to her.

The phone rang again, and Betty stood up with a loud sigh, ending the music abruptly with a badly-executed chord. She made her way to the entryway, where the telephone sat on the table just inside the door. "Clouds' residence. Betty speaking."

The voice that she heard made her heart quicken its tempo. "Hi, Betty. It's me, Ben."

His voice sounded strained. It was unusual for him to be calling her so early in the morning. By this time, he was usually already at a job site, fixing somebody's door, maybe making renovations on someone's kitchen, or hammering on a front stoop. Mostly, Ben's phone calls came in the evening.

But she had not gotten a phone call last night... Actually, if she wanted to be honest, Betty had felt bad about it, and now the buried irritation and uncertainty – an uncertainty that galled her – came flooding back at the sound of Ben's voice. Perhaps he had just forgotten in the busyness of his sister Grace's return to school. Regardless, though, Betty felt put out. She felt unimportant in his eyes, certainly lower down on the proverbial totem pole that she ought to have been...

So now she put a coolness in her voice as she responded. "Oh, hello, Ben." And then she let the silence drag out between them, feeling a guilty satisfaction.

Ben paused long before he spoke again. "Betty, I need to talk to you. Can... Can we get some coffee at the diner? This morning?"

Betty's heart clenched inside her chest at the tone. He was upset at something – very upset. What could it be about? She didn't want to know. She did not want to meet him at the diner, she did not want to hear what he needed to talk to her about. "I... I have a student coming for a lesson soon, Ben. Can't it wait until this evening? I'm supposed to come to your family's house for dinner, I thought."

There was another long pause. "Yeah, that's what I wanted to talk to you about. Well, at least that's some of it."

Betty couldn't think of anything to say for a moment. Her breath shallowed; her thoughts raced. "I... I suppose that I could meet you around 10 o'clock. But I can only stay for a little while. I have another student coming at 11."

"That'll be fine." He paused. "Thanks. Okay, I'll see you then."

"Fine." She paused for a moment, waiting for him to say goodbye. After all, he was the one who had called her. It was the right thing for him to be the one to end the call. But he just stayed on the line. Wanting to finish the conversation, Betty finally said, "All right. I'll meet you there."

"All right." He paused. "I... I love you Betty."

Betty couldn't speak. Though she'd sensed he felt them, Ben had never spoken those words aloud to her before. She swallowed hard, trying to find her tongue. But then she didn't need to. She heard the click of the receiver as he hung up, not waiting for a reply.

He already sat in their usual corner booth at the diner when Betty got there. He didn't see her for a moment, and Betty took that last second to touch her hair, verifying that everything was in place.

Then Ben's eyes found her, and he stood up from his place on the red-leather booth. Betty forced a smile on her lips and made her way through the nearly empty diner. "Thanks for coming," Ben said, his own mouth straight.

He really did look worried. She shrugged out of her coat, stomach clenching, and sat down. How would she drink the cup of coffee that Ben had already ordered for her? But she picked up the little cream pitcher and poured some into the black liquid and then added two teaspoons of sugar. She took her time with it. At least it gave her hands something to do while he told her... Well, whatever it was that he wanted to tell her.

"You want something to eat?" He asked, his eyes on the menu's single sheet.

"No, I'm not hungry," she replied.

"Me neither." He tossed the menu aside and clasped his hands around his own brown mug. Since she'd arrived,

Betty realized that he hadn't kept eye-contact with her. "How's your day been so far?" he asked.

She bit her lip. He'd just asked it as a way to ease into conversation, she could tell. "Fine. I had a student cancel this morning, but it worked out all right, anyway. I had some pieces of my own I wanted to practice for Christmas." She paused. "And you?"

He swallowed hard, and she saw his jaw clench. "Not so great, actually, Betty. Actually, the past two days have been... pretty bad, too." His fingers and thumbs fiddled with the handle of his coffee mug. "I've got something to say to you, but everything inside of me doesn't want to say it. But you've gotta know. You've got to be the first to know. It's not the kind of thing that you can keep quiet for long in a town the size of Chetham."

The clenching in her stomach spread throughout her body, making all of her limbs tense. She swallowed, forcing down the panic that rose into her throat. "Why don't you just tell me what it is, Ben?" If he would just spit it out, then she could face it square in the eyes and decide how to react.

"All right." His gaze stayed on the checkered tablecloth. "This is the sort of thing, Betty, that's, uh, embarrassing to have to tell just about anyone. Especially good folks. Especially somebody like you. But I guess I'll just tell it to you blunt. A girl I used to, uh, know, came to the house the night before last."

Betty bristled inside but smothered any outward display of it. With Ben's past, she was sure that his "knowing" this girl went far beyond casual acquaintanceship.

Even with that understanding, though, she wasn't ready for what Ben said next.

"She says that she's carrying a child." He paused and spoke in a near-whisper. "My child, Betty."

Betty's mind turned into bread pudding. What could she say to that? It was embarrassing enough to be speaking of such a thing as a baby born out-of-wedlock, but for that information to come straight out of Ben's lips to her ears, while they were face-to-face with one another in the diner, well, Betty felt her face blaze with the heat of embarrassment and shock.

Ben's blue-gray eyes searched her face. He must want her to say something, but what? What could she say to him after such a statement?

*Ben is a father to this girl's child.*

Her mind whirled. Her life... surrounded by a scandal over which she had no control. She could just hear the Chetham gossips now, talking about Ben's wild past, about how Betty herself had settled for a boy from the wrong side of the tracks. Illegitimate children... immorality...

And Ben himself. *He betrayed me.* That feeling rose above all the others, splitting the skin of her heart.

"She says... She says that she wants me to marry her, Betty," he murmured.

*"She wants me to marry her."*

Betty moved her lips, but no sound emerged. *This is what I get for lowering myself.* She swallowed and fingered the napkin beside her coffee cup. *This is what I get for giving into the way I felt drawn to him. Stupid me. I should have stopped myself before it was too late...*

"Say something, Betty," Ben implored. His hand crept hesitantly across the table and took hers. She let him, but her fingers rested limply in his. She felt as though she were holding the hand of a stranger, not a man whom she had been dating for the past three months.

"Are you going to?" The question finally slipped out of Betty's mouth.

"Am I going to what?"

Betty pulled her hand from his without allowing herself to feel. "Are you going to marry her? This girl?"

Ben hesitated, and she saw that he kept his hand, which hers had left, still open on the table: empty. She should feel sorrow for his sake – she knew that she should keep her hand in his, for comfort's sake, but she didn't. She couldn't. She merely felt an empty, growing ache in her chest.

"Sam says to wait – to not make any quick decisions."

She nodded, pushing away any emotion that dared to rise to the surface. "That's probably wise." She forced herself to reach for her coffee and took a sip. The creamy liquid coated her tongue, and she took her time to slowly swallow, her eyes glued to the thick rim. "It's always better to be sure. Sure that you're taking the appropriate action. That it fits correctly with your plans."

Ben stayed silent for so long that she finally let her gaze touch his. He looked at her, searchingly, a sheet of pain glazing his eyes. But why shouldn't he be in pain? Wasn't his moral failure the cause of Betty's own pain now?

"Yeah, it's always better to be sure. About everything in life, I guess."

They were quiet for a long time, or at least it seemed a long time to Betty. But when she looked up at the clock above the counter, she saw that only a couple of minutes had passed in the silence, each of them having been lost in their own thoughts.

Ben finally took his hand off the table, and Betty felt

the loss of its presence, even though she had not been willing to keep her own in its embrace. The absence of it panged her heart, though not more than his next words did.

"I... I think we need to cool things off between us, Betty, at least until I get this situation... figured out."

Betty coughed back a snort of humorless laughter. This situation? Figured out? And how was he planning to do that? The only solution, the only solution that Betty could see at least, was that she and Ben would break up, permanently, and that he would marry this girl. Her stomach twisted, and she knew that she could not drink the rest of that coffee, whether it gave her hands something to do or not.

Did he really care about her as he said that he did? The thought popped into her head. If he did, wouldn't he have fought to stay with her, however nonsensical that would be? Shouldn't it be Betty, not Ben, who said that they should cool things off? After all, wasn't it she who had been slighted by the arrival of this girl on the scene? By the arrival of Ben's unlovely past in her own present and future?

But she didn't say that to him. Not now. Instead, she merely nodded and her hands turned cold despite the warmth of the cup which they grasped.

Reverend Henry Cloud answered the knock on his office door frame with his usual cheerful, "Come in!" Ben swallowed hard, but the lump in his throat wouldn't move, and he knew that he would have to force the words past it, regardless. He poked his head through the half-open door and saw that Reverend Cloud sat behind his massive oak desk, his Bible open before him, most likely to the book of Isaiah, from which he had been preaching for some time. Around the Bible lay stacks of papers and a few other books, some of which were commentaries, Ben could tell just from the glance. A half-filled notebook sat beside the Bible, ready to receive more of the pastor's copious notes. Sunlight drifted in from the window just past the desk, shedding warm beams across the papers and over Reverend Cloud's prayer cushion, crafted by his wife and worn from decades of searching the Scriptures and seeking God on his knees throughout his sermon preparations.

Reverend Cloud's eyes lit up when he saw Ben, and his mouth, set in a rounded face, turned up into a genuine smile, the same smile that had made Ben feel at ease from his first days of acquaintanceship with the Cloud family. "Ben!" The minister rose from his desk, the chair scraping the floor behind him. "How have you been? I didn't expect to see you until this evening."

The rock in Ben's throat grew larger, and all strength left his bones. He swallowed again. "I... I have to talk to you about tonight." He had come directly from the diner and knew that Betty had not had a chance to go to her father yet. It was what Ben had wanted. Reverend Cloud had been discipling him, as he called it, taking Ben under his spiritual wing ever since Ben's conversion, even before Ben and Betty had begun dating officially. It was only right that the pastor should hear this shameful news from Ben's own lips.

At Ben's serious tone, the Reverend's face grew a little more solemn, but the kindness only deepened in the man's eyes. "Well, come on in," he said. "Come in and sit down, son."

*Would he be calling me "Son" if he knew? Knew that I just dealt such a blow to his daughter — and to his family's reputation, being associated with such as me?*

There was only one way to find out.

Ben hesitated for just a moment, and then he forced his feet fully into the room and pulled the chair out from its place before the desk. The old leather cushioning felt soft, but Ben did not allow himself to relax into it.

Allow himself? Who was he kidding? He would not have been able to relax even if he had wanted to.

He stayed silent for so long that Reverend Cloud said, probably as a way to open the conversation and spur Ben on toward speech, "Well, I certainly didn't expect to see you here this morning. I'm surprised that you're not at work."

Ben couldn't bring himself to meet the man's gaze. "I... I am going to work after this, after I leave here, but the truth is, I don't know if you will wanna see me after I tell you what's going on in... Well, after I tell ya..."

All remnants of the smile fell from Reverend Cloud's face, replaced by concern, yet his expression still retained its kindness, and Ben felt from him no hint of the drawing-back-in-anticipation that he had expected. The older man folded his hands together and leaned forward. "What is it, Ben? Why don't you just tell me?"

So Ben took a deep breath and told Betty's father everything.

Ben held the heavy door as it clanked shut behind

him. His coat slung over his arm, he shuffled down the wide church steps, happy that the cold bit at him, happy to feel uncomfortable about something, anything other than the fact that Annie had shown up in Chetham, bearing his child.

Annie... How he remembered her sweet ways. And how he remembered her temper! They had been drawn together, he knew, deep down, by each other's rebellious spirit. Despite having been together for many months, they hadn't talked much about their backgrounds, about where they'd come from, but from the little that Annie had said to him, Ben knew that her childhood had been difficult... and that it had angered her.

That had been one of the main reasons Annie had run far away from home, Ben knew. Her job at the Bousquet's, well, it was just a hideout from her strict father – a man who wasn't her biological father. Aldo, Annie's cousin, had told him as much. In fact, Aldo had told Ben more than anyone ever had about her past, though, at the time, Ben had to admit, it mattered little to him what went on in Annie's heart and mind. What mattered to him more was that they had fun together, that they satisfied each other's needs for excitement, for love, and each other's ego.

He thought that, when she'd broken up with him all those months ago – weeks before his definitive argument with Aldo, before Sam had redeemed him and taken him back to Chetham – well, Ben had thought that all ties with Annie had been cut. Their breakup was his fault; he freely admitted that. To his shame now, he remembered how she'd found him out on the town one night, after he had told her that he had to work and so couldn't take her out. She'd found him, his arm around some blond-haired chit, whose name he couldn't even remember. At the time, it hadn't registered, but now he could remember the depth of pain that had surfaced in Annie's eyes when she'd caught sight of them ... and then the coolness that had glazed over them. She'd been real hurt. But Ben had thought that she'd moved on... He'd even seen her flirting with the Bousquet's son just a week after the break-up.

And he had sure put her out of his mind. In fact, if he wanted to be honest, Ben had not thought about Annie in many months.

His mind swung back to the conversation he'd just had with Reverend Cloud, and he dropped his right hand over his empty pants-pocket. After last night, Ben had put the ring box deep into his bedside table drawer, longing for this living nightmare to end. Only then would he be able to take out the ring once more. Sickness turned his heart, knowing how unlikely such a circumstance would be.

"I think that you've been given some very wise advice from your father," Reverend Cloud had said, and, despite the fact that Ben really did think of Sam Giorgi as a father-figure to him, it still took him a moment to understand that the pastor referenced Sam and not Charlie, Ben's deceased biological father. "I wouldn't make any kind of hasty decision. God knew that this was going to happen in your life. It takes a woman nine months to carry a baby to term. So this was set in motion before you came to know Christ, and yet God knew that you were going to come to know Him. The events of your life are not an accident, Ben."

"But sometimes you've got to suffer the consequences for your sin," Ben couldn't help putting in, miserably looking down at his clasped hands.

Reverend Cloud didn't disagree, but he added, "But remember, Ben, the consequences are not God's punishment for your sin, but His loving discipline. And remember also, He will work all things together for the good of those who love Him, who are called according to His purpose. We little humans get so worried about every little iota, every circumstance of our lives, yet we know that God loves us so much that He sent His Son to the Cross for us. Won't He work out every little detail of your life – every mistake, every repentance – for your good, which is for His glory, out of His great love for you? He that spared not His own Son, but delivered Him up for us all, how shall He not with Him also freely give us all things?"

The pastor's words had not made everything better; Ben had not dared to hope for that. But his spirit did feel uplifted – well, at least he didn't feel like he should throw himself off the nearest bridge, which was how he'd felt after the way that Betty had treated him this morning.

*Cold as a clam on a winter's day.* That's what she'd been, and Ben could hardly blame her.

# Chapter Nine

After breakfast, Annie had retreated to her bedroom, still unsure of where her place was in this house. She had not expected to be treated so kindly, to be fed and offered a soothing bed, to be given so many comforts that she had never before enjoyed. It was almost as though they had been expecting her – well, Sarah, Ben's mother, acted that way.

Ben, however, was a different story.

He was changed, despite how she'd accused him otherwise early this morning. From the very little she'd seen of him, she could tell that he was, well, it was as if he was a different man. Not at all the old Ben that she knew – quick to blow up, saucy and sarcastic to his superiors, to everyone who held authority.

She'd thought that she was going to have to fight

with all the gumption she possessed to even step foot into the house. But then, that boy – well, really, young man – Paulie had welcomed her inside, with a kind of gentleness that she had not known men could possess. At least, she'd never known any who had, outside the picture-shows.

Paulie'd acted as though she was welcome in the house, as if he expected to see her and women like her, pregnant and without a wedding band on their finger. He told her to wait for his father, who was some kind of doctor. She hadn't thought about it at the time because her mind had been so focused on demanding to see Ben and confronting him, in accordance with Aldo's commands.

And when she'd found him, it had been shock, not anger, displayed across his face – coupled with intense shame and guilt. His face had actually reddened with it. She had prepared herself for anger, braced herself against it. Goodness knows she had known Ben's anger in the past - even to the point of feeling a sharp slap from his palm across her face. But shame? That was one thing that she had never seen on Ben Picoletti's face.

Now, as she sat on the bed, freshened by, who knew, probably a maid in a house like this, Annie looked around the beautifully-appointed room, the uneasiness growing inside her moment by moment. She felt as if she could not go out of her room, not because Ben's mother or anyone else for that matter would tell her to return to it, but because she did not know how to act, how to conduct herself, in the face of a seemingly genuine kindness that she'd not experienced for… perhaps forever. At least since her mother had died.

*But all their kindness won't get me to leave, won't get me to give up my rights.* Even as she thought it, though, guilt pricked Annie's heart. Pushing herself to her feet, she ignored its needling. She would go downstairs, awkward or not.

One thing was certain: She wished she'd thought through all of these things before she'd come to Chetham. It would have made her path so much clearer.

She opened the door to her room with silent fingers and stepped into the hallway, her hand resting on top of her rounded middle. Even after all these months, Annie was not used to feeling such a bulk as she walked, such a heaviness in her legs. She had always been a slim little thing; her mother had called her a little mouse, but now Annie felt more like a walrus.

The upper floor of the house was silent, so she crept down the stairs. When she had descended halfway down, she heard the rumbling of voices coming from one of the rooms towards the back of the house. She had not gone there yet, and so she did not know what the room was, but she suddenly recalled that, when she first had arrived, Sam Giorgi had come out a room from the rear of the house, a room that opened via a door to the sitting room. His home office, perhaps? Annie made her way down the rest of the stairs and into the sitting room, moving silently on bare feet until she got within hearing range. She recognized Sarah's feminine voice undergirded by Sam's low and solemn tone.

Annie turned on her heel to go towards the kitchen, perhaps to rustle up a snack, as her stomach was grumbling, but then she heard Ben's name. Without considering otherwise, Annie stopped and pressed her ear directly against the door.

"I just don't think that he should make any kind of hasty choice," Sam said. "It concerns me that Ben said immediately that he should marry her – that he thought that he *must* marry her."

Sarah was quiet for a moment. Then she said, "I agree with you; he shouldn't rush into anything." There was another long pause, and Annie held her breath, not wanting them to hear her breathing in the silence.

"But...?"

"But I'm wondering if there really is any kind of choice, you know," Sarah added.

"What do you mean?"

"Well, if the baby is Ben's – and he says that there's pretty much no doubt in his mind that it is – then does he really have a choice of whether to marry her, regardless of what he wants? Would you have him not provide for his own child and its mother? He's ruined this girl. She probably won't have many chances now, not with a baby in tow."

Swallowing hard, Annie felt the sickening truth of Sarah's words. *Not with a baby in tow...*

"She seems the type that might've already been ruined," Sam said, and Annie bristled at his dismissive comment. She imagined that Sarah must've, too, for the man's voice grew soft as he continued, "I don't mean that unkindly, Sarah. It's only that I've seen a lot of these kinds of cases in my practice over the years. When I was in upstate New York, I helped out quite a bit at the shelters they have there for unwed mothers. A lot of them were not ruined by one man, but they were in a lifestyle of ruin, sad to say. A lifestyle they'd chosen and still would like to live, if not for the child burdening them. It will take more than marriage to separate her from that kind of life."

"If she has chosen it. If she is like that. Like you say." Sarah's voice came in, not quite disagreeing with him, but adding a merciful caution, one for which Annie felt thankful.

There was another long pause, and Annie wondered if she should make her way out of the sitting room, so that they would not catch her there if they came out of the office. She was just about to take a step backwards when Sam continued, "Ben has made so much progress, Sarah. I don't know if you really realize that or not. I would hate for this to get him off-track…"

"I know my own son, Sam." Annie heard the hurt, the edge of slight anger in Sarah's voice. "I know how far he's come. But this isn't just about Ben. This is about Annie, too." There was a pause. "And about my grandchild."

*Grandchild…* Annie had not thought of it like that; she had not thought of how her story connected with everyone else's. Her own family had broken up so completely that she had not even seen her grandparents in more than a decade. She didn't know if they were still alive. She knew that Daddy's parents had passed away, but what of Mama's parents? They were somewhere out in the Midwest, though she didn't know where. The last time she had seen them was at Mama's funeral, nearly ten years ago, and she'd thought of them as ancient. She hadn't thought to write to them since then, and she knew she couldn't now, not with the shame creeping up her neck at the thought of her grandmother's angelic face. Her grandmother had probably never done anything wrong in her life. What would she say if she knew that her adopted granddaughter was carrying a child and yet wore no wedding ring?

"Have you asked her what her delivery date is?" Sam's voice interrupted Annie's thoughts.

"No, I haven't. It seemed nosy, somehow. I was hoping she'd just tell me. At any rate, it can't be far away if

ALICIA G. RUGGIERI

you add up the months. Really, I've hardly spoken with the girl. She stayed in her room yesterday, and then she went upstairs right after breakfast this morning, after she and Ben talked. She hasn't been down since."

"Do you know for a fact that she's still here? Has she left? Perhaps for that unwed mother's home that Ben suggested?"

Sam would like it if she had, wouldn't he? Annie let the bitterness swirl in her heart. For a moment, it felt good.

"Not unless she climbed out the window." This was from Sarah. "I asked the maid to let me know when she came down from her room."

A little smile tugged at Annie's lips. Obviously, the maid had not done her job.

"Besides she has no reason to leave. She came to get our son to marry her, to take responsibility for the child's welfare. Which you know as well as I that he should do."

"If it is his child, then yes, I agree. He should take responsibility, though I'm not sure that I agree with you that it means marrying this young woman."

Silence stretched out, taut as a loaded clothesline.

"Well," Sam said at last, "my advice to Ben at this point is to wait at least until after Christmas. The baby could come any day, and no good is going to come from rushing into a quick marriage, just so that the baby can be born to a married couple. It won't truly save face in the long run, if that's what you or anyone else is concerned about. All Ben and Annie's lives, people will be able to tell from the baby's birthday that the child was conceived before they wore wedding rings."

A rock settled in Annie's stomach. Aldo would not be happy about waiting so long. He had instructed her to get

124

in there, and…

Besides what would she do in the meantime? She had nowhere to stay. Sure, the Giorgis had put her up last night, but from the sound of this conversation, Ben's stepfather at least was not overly enthused about her presence. And why should he be? She had burst into the middle of a nice family – a good family – and their holidays, bringing very unwelcome news.

"Well, regardless of whether Ben marries her or not, or whether the child is Ben's to begin with, we can offer her a home here until we get all of this settled." Sarah's voice carried finality, as though she was informing her husband, not asking him. Yet her words didn't carry a rebellious tone, and relief spread through Annie as she realized that Sam Giorgi was agreeing with his wife, amazing as that thought was, considering the circumstances.

"Yes, we can offer her that," came Sam's measured reply.

"Is there any way to be sure…?" Sarah trailed off, almost as if she was embarrassed to ask.

"Sure about what? About the paternity of the child? About whether Ben is the father?"

There was a pause, and Annie imagined Sarah nodding.

"Well, I'm assuming you're talking medically. There are no ways that science has come up with yet to assure ourselves of a child's paternity. But, legally speaking, a court of law will tell us whether it believes that Ben is the father of this child…"

"I wouldn't want that," came Sarah's reply. "I wouldn't want to expose Ben or the family or this girl to the kind of publicity that comes from those court cases.

Besides, it wouldn't really make certain the only thing that matters, which is the truth."

*The truth.* Annie tried to swallow the chunk of rusted metal that suddenly clogged her throat and made it difficult to breathe.

Betty threw herself into the Christmas play with abandon, anxious to forget the whole situation with Ben, that young woman... and herself. Funny how a week ago, she'd been dreading how this play would fill up every last spare moment of her time and then some. Now, she only wished that it could keep her even more occupied.

She had busied herself in the church hall, boxes of old Christmas decorations strewn all around her, when Mother walked in and stopped short, surveying the opened packages of tinsel, the old strings of dried popcorn and cranberries, and the twisted garlands of fake greenery.

"It looks like you found a lot of things for the play," commented Mother. "I knew that Joanna Lambert kept some boxes of decorations from year-to-year, but I had no idea that it had accumulated to such a degree. I suppose she has been producing this play since 1903 and she is a self-admitted packrat, so things would pile up."

Nodding, Betty kept her hands moving and her eyes on her work. She'd successfully made it through the past day or so having avoided both of her parents' questioning gazes, telling them that she was quite all right and that she truly understood about Annie and Ben.

But Mother was no fool. And Betty knew that she could not escape Mother's probing love for long. If only she could just get through Christmas… and then just get through the wedding…

Wedding. Ben's wedding. Up until just days ago, Betty had pictured herself dressed for that day in white, clutching a bouquet of pale pink roses, with Mother's veil fluttering over her eyes. She had not decided yet whether she wanted Daddy to walk her down the aisle and then take his stand before them to perform the ceremony, or if she would rather he just be her daddy for that day, giving her away to Ben, the man to whom she had begun, ever so cautiously, to give her heart.

But the ceremony that was coming – for it would surely come, Betty felt this with a dull, aching certainty – the ceremony that would come was not her own but another girl's – a girl who didn't deserve Ben. But that was the way of God, wasn't it? Giving to those who didn't deserve. *Whereas I've toed the line all my life. And look where it's gotten me.*

She hoped, she really hoped, that Mother had not come in here to talk to her. Betty had no idea what she was going to say if pressed. *Go and sort the church's mail, Mother, or neaten Daddy's office!*

But Mother didn't move from the spot where she'd stopped when she'd entered, and Betty finally looked up to see Mother looking steadily at her, with a thoughtful expression on her rounded face.

Desperate to avoid the conversation that she felt sure brewed behind Mother's eyes, Betty spoke quickly. "I didn't realize that Mrs. Lambert kept all of this, either," Betty chattered. "Look at it: tinsel, tree trimmings, fake candles, half-used candles." Betty shook her head. "A lot of it really just needs to be thrown away. You have to start fresh with a lot of it." For emphasis, she picked up the decrepit strands of cranberries and popcorn, and a few of them fell right off the string.

Mama knelt down and took the fragile trimming from Betty's hands, her own fingers touching the red berries one at a time. "I remember when we strung these, if they are the same ones." Mother smiled. "I had no idea they could last so long. I think that you were just a tiny tot, back when Daddy and I first came to this church, and the ladies gathered together, everyone bringing supplies from home. We put together some of these decorations. We wanted to make the church a beautiful, special place to welcome the Lord Jesus Christ's nativity."

"I suppose that they were pretty while they lasted."

"Well, some things are only meant to last for a season, Betty," Mother said quietly. "God puts them in our lives for a time, for His higher purposes. His ways are higher than ours, dear daughter."

Betty picked up a piece of holly in her hands. The paint had cracked on the berries, and she used her fingernail to scrape at it viciously. She would not allow herself to voice this – and never to Mother, certainly – but sometimes she was sick and tired of the Lord's higher purposes. Sometimes, she just wanted life to be a little bit neat, predictable, and easy. To go according to her well-laid plans. Was that too much to ask?

"I just wish that life would go as planned sometimes." And that was all she allowed herself to say, all she dared to say, for she never wanted Mother's opinion of her to change – Mother's opinion of her as her good Betty: church pianist, substitute Sunday school teacher, dutiful daughter, excellent student while she had been in school, and, overall, a very sweet, obedient Christian girl – at least on the outside. No, she never wanted her carefully-curated reputation to tarnish. Wasn't that why she'd almost refused to date Ben in the first place, drawn as she was by scent of adventure that wafted off him?

And she never should have changed her mind on that score, should she have? She should have stayed with her ideal: a godly man, unencumbered by past mistakes, by a past life of lawlessness, an educated man, a man of whom everyone would approve.

Mother's hand cupped Betty's face. "Life does go as planned, my sweet Apple Betty, but the question is, do you mean God's plan or yours?"

With that Mama rose to her feet and left Betty among the dusty relics of Christmases past.

"My question is, does Ben know what he's going to do yet?" Paulie's question was voiced low, for Sarah's ears alone, but even so, Sarah glanced across the living room at Cliff whose head was bent over his drawing pad, sketch pencil gripped in his sensitive hand, colored pencils scattered here and there around him. Cliff had recently taken up sketching, and Sarah had been surprised to see that he was quite good at it. Now she saw that his concentration appeared taken with drawing an American Indian on horseback.

She turned to Paulie, who sat sectioning an orange, a book open on his lap. "I'm not really sure," she said just as quietly as he had voiced the question. Her knitting needles slowed and then stopped as she thought.

"Are the Clouds still comin' for Christmas dinner this year?" Cliff said from his spot on the carpet.

Inwardly, Sarah sighed. So his total attention had not been taken up with sketching. She sent Paulie a look of exasperation, but then she considered her younger son. At times like this, she saw that Cliff was almost a grown man, even though Sarah didn't often see him that way. She knew that he understood exactly what was going on, at least factually-speaking.

"I don't think so," Sarah replied to Cliff, who was still looking at her expectantly. Her younger son responded with a grimace. He was fond of Betty, Sarah knew, for she was the daughter of Reverend Cloud, who was always kind to Cliff, and of Bertha Cloud, who, years ago, had often sent donuts home with Grace to give to Cliff before he'd attended the church's Youth Fellowship.

Sighing, Paulie turned back to his book, and Sarah tried to return to her knitting but found that she couldn't. Her thoughts whirled. What to do with the girl upstairs? What to do with this girl who, though Ben no longer cared for her, was still carrying a child who bore his image?

And besides the child's... Something in Annie called out to something in Sarah – a part of Sarah that had died when her new life in Christ began, yet the ghost of which still rose to haunt her from time to time. Oh, she liked Betty. Who wouldn't like sweet Betty Cloud? But, despite having spent very little time with Annie, Sarah responded well to her. *Be careful, Sarah. You might be misjudging the girl. She might really be more wolfish than you think.*

Sarah set aside her knitting needles, tucking them into the basket by her feet. Even as her thoughts warned her, even as Sam had cautioned her, Sarah sensed that she was right about Annie: that the girl really was hurting in a way that none of them yet knew, that she needed love that she'd perhaps never received.

Without another word, Sarah left the room, sensing Paulie's eyes on her, though he didn't say anything. She found her way to the kitchen and, while the water came to a boil in the fat kettle, she prepared a tray with two teacups – her best – and a few slices of pumpkin bread, laid out on a beautiful, scalloped-edged plate.

Annie let the curtain fall back over the front yard. Ben's stepfather was still not home, and Annie had not seen Ben since yesterday. She let out a sigh and surveyed the empty room. It was so pretty and yet it began to feel like a prison. *A prison of my own making. I didn't have to come here; I chose it.*

Yet what choice had she really had? A single woman, obviously pregnant, without a job? Who was going to hire her?

If it had been her choice, Annie would not have chosen to go to Ben.

But it hadn't been her choice. It had been Aldo's choice.

A light knock on the door startled her out of her gloomy reverie. She surveyed the room to make sure that nothing was out that she didn't want seen. Strange thought, as she'd brought so little with her. Was it Ben at the door? Her heart fluttered in her chest at the thought. Not that she was still in love with him, if love had been what she had felt for him once upon a time. But he was the man who would decide her destiny, wasn't he?

She glanced at herself in the mirror that hung above the bureau and winced. No eight-months-pregnant woman looked very appealing by the time evening came. She licked her palm, rubbed it together with the other one, and ran her hands through her hair. Heaviness settled in her chest. Her days of being appealing were over. All she had left to do her bargaining with was the baby that she carried. Putting steel back into her eyes, Annie straightened her shoulders and turned towards the door. "Come in," she said with what she intended to be a confident voice.

But it was Sarah who stood on the opposite side of the door. Ben's mother was always clean and tidy... *But there's something about her that always seems just a tad out of place, as if she can't keep all the pieces together.* Tonight, Annie saw that in the way Sarah's stocking seam twisted toward the front of her leg, rather than perfectly down the back.

"I'm sorry if I disturbed you," Sarah said, and Annie heard a hesitation in the woman's voice. Wonder overtook Annie. *She's afraid I'm gonna reject her.*

How well Annie herself knew the feeling.

Annie allowed a little of her guard to go down. "You're... You're not disturbin' me," Annie replied. "I sure got nothin' to do here."

The slight tension left Sarah's face, and the smile grew wider. "I was wondering, then, Annie, if you would like to have tea with me in my sitting room."

Annie's back stiffened, her hackles rising. "What fer?" she asked, letting the suspicion color her words. Why was this woman being nice to her? After all, Annie was the one who had disrupted their home.

"Well, Sam isn't home yet, and I often go up to my sitting room to read and wait for him. Besides, I'd like to get to know you a little better, Annie."

Something was up; Annie could feel it. "Why?" Her voice hardened as she made the question.

Sarah bit her lip, but she didn't retreat. "I... I don't know, Annie, other than you are someone whom my son must've cared about very much."

*But doesn't anymore.*

"And, if you are the mother of his child, I would like to get to know you a little bit."

*The mother of his child...* A little of the tension drained away from Annie's shoulders. The woman couldn't be manipulating her, trying to get her to give up her child or to go into a home for unwed mothers, could she? Not if she was referring to the baby in such a way, rather than as a nuisance or a burden or an embarrassment, right?

And Annie did so want to get out of this room!

"Okay," she heard herself replying.

Ben didn't bother knocking on the front door at the Giorgi home. Funny, this had been a place of refuge for him over the past few months – a place of joy, a reminder of the new start, of the new life that he had been given in Christ at the end of the summer. But now? As he wiped his feet on the carpet just inside the front door, he let his eyes travel to the staircase. Now, every time Ben walked through the front door, every time he even thought about this house, his mind traveled to Annie and was weighed down with the sins of his past.

As Ben shut the door behind him and banged the snow off his boots, Paulie stuck his head out from the sitting room. "Hiya, Ben."

"Hey." Ben shrugged out of his work jacket and hung it on a hook inside the door. "Your dad working late tonight?" The question sat tight in his chest. Someone needed to tell him what to do. His conversation with Reverend Cloud had calmed some of his anxiousness over how the news would be received, whether or not he would be condemned by those about whom he cared most, but he was perplexed about what the right thing to do really was. Reverend Cloud had not given him an answer.

Was it wrong that Ben wanted to get this thing settled? Whether it was to accept the consequences of his actions and to marry the girl – thereby cutting himself off from a future with Betty forever – or to determine some other course of action? He wished that one of these godly men whom he admired would give him the answer he sought – an answer other than "Wait" or "You'll have to listen to the Lord."

"Yeah, Dad's working late tonight," answered Paulie. "I don't know when he'll be home. You need to talk to him?"

"Yeah." Though, while he waited, he could seek out Mama. "Did Mama head upstairs already?"

Paulie nodded "Yeah, I think she brought her tea upstairs."

"I think I'll join her. Tell your dad that I went upstairs when he comes home."

"Okay." Paulie paused for just a second before heading back into the sitting room. "Hey," he said softly, his eyes on Ben's, "I'm praying for you guys. For all of you. I know that God will show you the way."

Tears sprang to Ben's eyes, but he pushed them back, uncomfortable with showing vulnerability, especially at times like this when all his past sins seemed to be on view for everyone to see. "Thanks, Paulie." He gritted his teeth against the tears and forced a smile onto his tight lips.

Before Paulie could further the conversation, Ben turned towards the stairs and bounded up them, barely making a sound. He made his way down the hallway towards Mama's sitting room. But before he could reach the doorway of her cozy, lamplit space, he heard a shy giggle coming from within it. The sound startled him into a halt. Wasn't Mama alone in her sitting room, as she usually was, reading some good book or her Bible before turning into bed, a cup of herbal tea by her side? What in the...?

There it was: that giggle again...

*Annie.* He would know her laugh anywhere. Then came the sound of Mama's voice, low and earnest, as it always was when she was in the middle of a funny story. Ben edged closer to the door, and keeping carefully in the shadows, he peered into the crack between the door and the frame.

His heart clenched at what he saw. His mama sat in the rocking chair beside the little end table, where her tea set rested. A lamp cast its glow over both her and Annie, who had taken a seat in the other rocking chair, her round body embraced by its pillows. Each of them held a teacup – the fancy kind that Mama liked to use – in her hand. Steam rose from the cups. Annie took little sips in-between giggles, and there was a look on her face such as Ben had rarely seen there before: a look of innocence, almost, a look of sweet delight and amusement. Something clenched in Ben's chest at the sight, and he remembered the times in their relationship that had been like sunlight shining in the cold winter of his life. The confused feelings that had risen up when Annie had first walked into the door of the Giorgi house began again now, and he pushed them down. This was not love; no, it could not be that. Love – pure, undefiled – was what he felt for Betty Cloud, not for Annie.

But something struggled in Ben's chest, nonetheless, something tender, as when, in boyhood, he'd crept close to look inside a nest with hatching eggs.

He gazed at them a few seconds longer from his place in the shadows before he gritted his teeth against his feelings. Annie's coming was God's punishment – "chastisement" was what other Christians called it, when it was for God's children – His blow to Ben's back to remind Ben that all sin had a price.

He couldn't cloud this up with emotion. Ben squared his shoulders and tapped lightly on the door frame. The laughter trailed away as Ben pushed open the door. Both women looked up at him, the funny story forgotten, the laughter fainting on Annie's lips. The innocence that he'd thought that he'd spied vanished, and the old familiar defiance reappeared, hardening her eyes, causing her chin to jut out.

"Ben." Mama smiled, but Ben thought that she looked a little nervous at his appearance. Had she thought that she would have this little tête-à-tête privately with Annie? Whose side was Mama on, anyway? Ben let the anger rise up slowly in his chest and fill his heart. Wasn't anger better than the strange, uncomfortable tenderness that he'd thought he had felt a moment earlier?

"I didn't think we would see you tonight." Mama set down her saucer and cup. "I didn't bring up another cup, Ben, but there's plenty of tea left if you'd like to fetch yourself one."

Ben let his anger trickle into his words, feeling it drain like pus from a punctured blister. "Naw, you look awful cozy here, just the two of you. I wouldn't want to interrupt anything."

Eyes wide, Mama opened her mouth, but Ben wouldn't let her answer him.

"Tell Sam that I stopped by." Running on the fumes of his fury, Ben swiveled around and left the room, taking the stairs two at a time.

All of Annie's nerves tensed. She couldn't meet Sarah's eyes. The two of them sat there in silence until the sound of the front door banged shut below them.

"Well, that's the Ben I remember." The comment slipped out of her lips, without a thought. But it really wasn't, was it? The Ben that she remembered would've been even more enraged, would've been consumed by anger, would've told her long ago to get out of his house, using less-than-choice words to do it. Oh, this Ben was angry, but there was a sorrow even to his anger that Annie had never seen in him before.

Sarah's hand came to rest on top of Annie's. "I am sorry for my son's behavior, but you have to realize, this is hard for him."

Annie's eyes flashed up to meet Sarah's, but Sarah went on before Annie could say anything. "I'm not saying that this is not hard for you, too, Annie," explained Sarah, "but you've had months to get used to the idea. Ben has just learned that, well, he is tied to a past that he thought he had long since left behind."

Now Annie really felt rotten. She withdrew her hand from beneath Sarah's. "So that's what I am? A ball and chain?"

And yet she knew that the accusation was just, wasn't

it? *If they only knew...*

But they didn't know. One of Annie's hands came to rest on her stomach. They couldn't know. Not unless she told them. And that she never would. Everything depended on that.

"No!" came Sarah's soft exclamation. "Your coming here, Annie, was certainly not expected, that's certain, but that doesn't mean that it was a bad thing."

Annie looked down into her tea's amber liquid. In Ben's eyes, it *was* a bad thing – her coming here. Was it really fair to him? Was it right to take away his whole life, just so that she could have security? *It's not his whole life. He'll have a wife – and – and children. I'll... I'll do right by him. I'll make him happy.* She swallowed down the guilt that threatened to rise in her throat "I'm kind of tired," she said at last, putting down her teacup on the table between her and Sarah. "I think I'll hit the sack now."

"Alright."

Annie felt Sarah's eyes on her until she closed the door behind her.

Ben felt his feet numbing with the late autumn cold, despite the thick wool socks he had pulled over his feet. He hadn't expected to take such a long walk when he'd set out from his own house this evening, unable to sleep. Past midnight now, he headed toward Old Man Jeffries Pond – why, he didn't know. A caustic smile raised the side of his lips. *Maybe to drown myself.* At this point, why shouldn't he?

*Oh, my God, why have you forsaken me?* The cry wrenched up from his heart. He didn't know if it was wrong to say such things aloud to God, here beneath the cold starlit November sky. No one could hear him, that was true. But God could always hear him. God knew the thoughts of his heart anyway, so why not admit them? *Oh God, I am so, so sorry for the sins of my past! You know how sorry I am. But I can't go back and change anything. How I wish I could, but I can't.* His feet found the edge of the pond. The water lapped up against the worn toes of his solid boots. *And now I've hurt Betty, hurt her with actions that I took long before I even knew her.*

Must the past always haunt him? What new terror lay around the next bend of his life?

*I give you a future and a hope.*

The verse appeared like a star coming out from behind the clouds on a dark night. The tired eyes of his soul squinted at it, unsure if it was really real.

*You are mine.*

The verses that he and Reverend Cloud had worked on storing in Ben's memory over the past few months came to life now in this dark moment. No, they did not bring a sense of perfect resolution, but they gave him a raft to snatch at, as a drowning man would grab in a turbulent sea.

*You are mine.* Awe released the tension from Ben's heart almost against his will. How could he be God's when he'd done so badly? In the eye of his mind, he saw the cross; he knew that Christ had been nailed there for him.

*There is now no condemnation.*

This could be no punishment, then, but the loving discipline of the Father, a father such as Ben had never known, except perhaps a little these past few months through the guidance of Sam and Reverend Cloud. Softly and then with more confidence, Ben repeated the verses that trickled into his mind, the verses that he and Reverend

Cloud had spent so long working on. He spoke them aloud into the cold wind that blew back the rust-colored hair from his forehead; he let them run through his mind, chasing away the dark fears and leaving in their place a peace that came from outside himself.

When the sun rose on the bank of the pond, it found Ben Picoletti curled up asleep on the sand.

# Chapter Ten

"You need to forget him, Betty." She spoke the words aloud, as if saying them that way would impress them more fully on her consciousness, would inspire her to take action.

But what action could she take? *As usual, my job is to wait.* The realization pinged against her heart with a bitter twang. Taking a last sip of her coffee, Betty set her mug down on the counter. "Mother, do you want me to wash these dishes before I go?"

Mother poked her head around the side of the door. Betty could see that her arms bulged with laundry. "No, Betty. I'll take care of it."

Betty felt too weary to argue. She simply nodded.

"Where are you off to?" Mother asked, a line furrowing between her brows.

"Play practice," Betty replied and picked up her purse from where it sat on the kitchen chair. She glanced up just in time to see the line turn into a full-fledged frown.

"But you held rehearsal yesterday, Betty," her mother protested. "Surely you could have given the children one day off?"

It was not the first time Mother had questioned Betty's almost-constant preoccupation with the Christmas play.

"I just want to make sure that everything is ready," Betty interrupted. "I don't want to be caught unprepared." Slinging her purse strap over her shoulder, Betty made for the door. "I'll be back for lunch."

And wasn't that always the way it was? That she was unprepared? She had been unprepared for Ben Picoletti's arrival back in Chetham several months ago now – unprepared for the way his startling blue-gray eyes arrested her attention, for the way that his troubled soul made her want to give him answers, unprepared for the way that God might move in her life in a way so different from what she had always anticipated. Unprepared for the way she'd begun to fall in love, one piece of her heart at a time…

More recently, she had also been unprepared for the arrival of Annie. Betty made her way down the front steps of their house and crossed the short distance with determined steps between the church and the house.

*Annie.* The very name of the girl made her stomach turn. Not only because her arrival completely upset Betty's own expectation that Ben might propose to her very soon, but also because Annie's arrival reminded Betty that she was marrying someone less than her ideal. This troubled her, as it had ever since she had started dating Ben. Oh, she'd pushed it away, for it had not troubled her parents overly much, especially as Ben showed what her father called "the fruits of repentance" early on. They'd cautioned her to avoid becoming too involved with her heart too quickly, but Betty herself knew that they liked Ben a great deal – and they expected that Ben would marry Betty.

Betty's hand tightened on the doorknob of the Fellowship Hall. Something certainly had come up to throw a wrench in that plan. *Someone,* that was. How did you make a future with a man with a past like that? It was too complicated, he was too complicated, even if there had been no Annie. *What was I thinking?* She shook her head against the tears that rose to the backs of her eyes. *I must've been mad these past months to think that Ben Picoletti and I could ever have a future together.*

She stepped into the church and drew in a breath of the moist, cool basement air. Though she had rushed out of the house to escape her mother's probing eyes, she was not really late, and so she took her time putting the things she carried in her arms just so, collecting the various musical sheets she needed from the storage closet, making sure everything was arranged just right on the platform upfront. When she looked at her watch, she realized that the children would not arrive for another fifteen minutes or so. A little guilt trickled over her at the thought of her dirty coffee cup in the sink back at home. But she couldn't, she just couldn't keep facing her parents' looks of concern. Only the Lord knew what they had told her older brother, Cary, away at college. And yet, despite it all, despite how it might end up hurting Betty, her parents did not seem angry at Ben in any way. Oh, they were concerned, that was for sure, but the feeling of fear that was in Betty did not exist for them, and the knowledge that they lacked it somehow made her angry. Why, she couldn't really say, but she almost felt as if they had betrayed her by taking this so calmly, so in stride, by not getting upset about it.

Admitting that she couldn't keep her thoughts focused on the script before her, Betty jumped to her feet and headed over to the piano. Music always soothed her. She opened the hymnal directly to the center, and began to play. Just as she'd expected, the music absorbed her, and she was able to forget her troubles and enjoy herself, worry free for the first time in days.

She had just reached the second stanza of "Rock of Ages" when she heard the door slam. It always did that; it was heavy and old. Being the church pianist, Betty was used to having people hear her while she played, so, assuming that it was just one of the children arriving for play practice, she finished playing the stanza. As soon as the last note hit the air, she began to rise, but before she could turn her head to see which of the children had come in, she heard a deep voice say, "Well done. I didn't know you would become such a musician, Miss Cloud."

Betty's head whipped around, and her eyes fell on a man standing just inside the doorway, smiling broadly. He appeared to be no more than thirty, probably younger, wearing a neatly-trimmed beard. By his side, holding his hand and looking at her with an air of keen observation, a little boy stood. He looked very like the man – except, of course, he was beardless. Betty rose from the piano bench and made her way toward them.

"I'm sorry, but I don't recognize you. You seem to know me, but I'm at a loss for how we are acquainted," she began. The man smiled again, and Betty saw a mouth full of very white, straight teeth. It was a nice smile, Betty thought. *Very honest.* What you saw was what you got, it said.

"I'm sorry," the man apologized. "You see, as a young teenager, I used to pick my brothers up from grade school, and you were always there in the playground, skipping rope. I'm Jim, Jim Colbert," he offered.

Colbert... Colbert... Betty riffled through the index in her mind but could not come up with any faces of anyone belonging to the last name of Colbert. "I'm sorry," she said, frowning slightly, "but I simply don't remember you at all. Or your brothers, for that matter."

Jim smiled again. "Well, they were only there for kindergarten and first grade, I think, and they weren't even in your class, Miss Cloud. We moved out of Chetham while I was still in high school, but my parents always... well, at least my mother always wanted to come back. Now that my father's passed away and my older sister – who lives in town – is a widow, my mother decided it would be a good time to come back and reestablish her old roots."

"I see," said Betty. "I'm sorry about your father."

Jim smiled. "He passed away quite a while ago, but thank you." He looked down at the little boy by his side and then back up at Betty. "Now I hear that this Christmas play is open to children who don't attend First Baptist?"

"Yes, yes, it is. We've already gotten started with rehearsals and have cast the play, but I'm sure that your son would be wonderful for one of our nonspeaking roles, such as one of the sheep." Betty glanced down at the little boy's face and saw him smile. *His smile is just like his father's – warm as a fire in the hearth on a cold winter's night.*

"I'm sure that Aiden would love that, wouldn't you, Aiden? He's not keen on a speaking role this year. By the way, Aiden is my nephew, not my son."

Betty blushed, though she didn't really know why. It

was an honest mistake to make, wasn't it? "Oh! Your son. I mean, your nephew. Of course." *Stop babbling, Betty,* she instructed herself sternly. She tried to think of something somewhat intelligent to say. "Have you found a church home yet since you moved back?" she asked.

"No, actually, we haven't."

There was that smile again. Without her permission, Betty's heart began to pick up its pace, and her palms began to sweat. She tucked them behind her green corduroy skirt.

"We've been looking around at a few different churches in the area," explained Jim. "When we lived here before, we drove over to the Methodist church in East Providence. My mother would like to try to find a Methodist church closer to home, though."

"Oh." Betty felt a keen edge of disappointment. But why did she care what church this man attended? *I don't,* she told herself. Nonetheless, when she opened her mouth again, she heard herself say, "Well, why not try this church?" She even added an engaging smile to her words!

"Well, I'm not sure we've ever gone to a Baptist church before," Jim replied, shrugging his broad shoulders. The door opened behind him and Aiden, and several chattering youths burst in. Betty noticed that Cliff Picoletti was one of them.

"Well, there's a first time for everything," she retorted to her own surprise. *I'm being too forward.* Usually, she prided herself on being reserved, almost to the point of snobbishness. *What has come over me?* The man smiled again, and Betty couldn't help but notice the way his eyes crinkled nicely at the corners. *Look at how responsible this man is, bringing his sister's son to play practice, making sure that the boy is settled with a part.*

Betty wanted to ask him where he worked, but she knew that she had said quite enough for one day. She smiled this time at Aiden rather than at his uncle. "Well, Aiden," she said, "Let's get you set up with a playscript."

She glanced back up at Jim. "We'll be done in about an hour. We practice three times a week – Mondays, Tuesdays, and Thursdays, right after school."

Jim smiled. "Sounds fine." With a little salute to the boy, he said, "I'll pick you up very soon." Betty felt her eyes lingering after the man as he strode out, lanky legs eating up the distance quickly.

"Mama, is Ben still gonna marry Betty?" Her son's question made Sarah's hands still on her knitting needles.

"I… I'm not sure, Cliff," she said after a long moment.

"Well, I know that Betty can't come over right now, what with Annie being here and all," Cliff said, rather loudly, causing Sarah to glance over her shoulder. She was glad to see that the doorway was empty, that Annie had not heard Cliff's remark. "But I saw something today, Mama, and… I like Betty an awful lot. She's a real nice girl, you know. I'd hate to see her not marry Ben."

Sarah frowned. "What do you mean, you saw something?"

Cliff picked up his drawing pencil again and made a few quick sketch lines. "When I got to play practice today, there was a man there with a little boy. I didn't recognize him; I don't think he goes to our church, but he and Betty were real friendly with each other." Cliff pressed his lips together as though he didn't want to say anything more.

Something in Sarah's heart clenched, but she pushed it away. "Betty's friendly with everyone, Cliff."

"Yeah, but not like this. She was smiling to beat the band, like… like he was a chocolate-glazed doughnut. I just don't get it, Mama, when Ben's over here all upset and Betty just goes on as if none of it matters to her."

In all honesty, Sarah couldn't understand Betty's behavior either – just acting as if the whole situation didn't matter to her one way or the other. Why, if she had been in Betty's shoes, she would've either thrown Ben over real good or she would have hung on like a bass caught on a fishing line. She wouldn't have let her boyfriend go with a wave and a smile, so to speak.

Was that what Betty was doing then? Letting Ben go? Though Betty had often made Sarah feel uncomfortable here and there, what with her born-and-bred Christian ways, Sarah did want to see her son happy, and, at least until now, Betty had seemed like the most likely candidate to do that for Ben. *Funny, though Annie's not a Christian, I feel more akin to her than I ever did toward Betty.*

"We'll have to wait and see, Cliff," Sarah answered, as calmly as she could, feeling a little guilty at her unspoken thought. "We'll all have to wait and see."

*What am I waiting for?* He held in his hands the ring box. Nestled inside was the engagement ring with which he had intended to encircle Betty's smooth finger this coming Christmas. Now it would not embellish Betty's hand. No, this Christmas, Ben would be slipping a ring onto the finger of a girl he had all but forgotten about... or at least had tried to.

Annie wasn't the kind of girl a man forgot, though. A half-smile turned up Ben's lips, despite himself.

"I think you should wait," Sam's voice broke into Ben's thoughts once more, and he forced himself to come back to the conversation at hand, instead of paying attention to his own inner dialogue.

"Wait for what, though?" Ben's voice sounded hopeless even to his own ears, though he tried to make it matter-of-fact.

Sam's hand came to rest on Ben's shoulder.

"I'm not really sure, Ben, but this thing came so suddenly..."

"Thing? You mean Annie," rejoined Ben "and the baby." Why did he sometimes feel defensive about Annie and the child that she carried? The young woman who could both enrage him and drive him to tears, even after his conversion. *My child...*

*The two shall become one flesh...* Perhaps that was why. And yet, Annie was not the only one. There had been others, others to whom he had turned in order to distract himself, to drive away the thoughts of home that had haunted him, and, yes, most often, merely to fulfill his lusts. It tore his mind and heart when he wondered about the young women whose trust he'd won, only to spit them out of his mouth once he'd tired of them, just as he had done to Annie. How many lives had his actions destroyed? A lump grew in Ben's throat, and his hands tightened on the ring box. Could he make restitution in some way, though it might cost him everything he had hoped for?

"Yes," said Sam breaking into Ben's thoughts once more. "I mean Annie and the baby." He paced a few steps near the bookcases that lined the study wall, hands clasped behind his back.

"I just don't know why ya want me to wait to marry her," said Ben. "It seems the right thing to do. Even the Bible says as much."

"In the Old Testament," stated Sam.

"It's still in the Bible," retorted Ben.

"And what about the command not to be yoked with unbelievers? Isn't that what a union with Annie would be?"

He'd thought about that. "Ain't I already 'united' with her in all but a vow? And I'm telling you, I ain't comfortable with using my belief in Jesus as a way to skirt my responsibilities. Leavin' Annie and my kid in the dust don't seem like the best example of Christianity."

Sam turned, the exasperation plain on his face. "Ben, what you say is admirable; it's honorable of you to want to shoulder the consequences of your actions. But it may not be as simple as you think it is."

Ben almost chortled to himself. Simple? Naw, his life was anything but simple at the moment. Painful? Yup. But simple? Nope.

"You don't even know if she's telling the truth." Sam lifted an eyebrow.

"I've never known Annie to be a liar." Annie was many things, but she'd never been a deceiver. Ben had taken the cake for that one. He could still remember her betrayed face each time she'd found out about another of his impulsive flings.

Sam sighed, and Ben fought the urge to let out a sigh himself, knowing a lecture was coming. "I believe you – or at least, I believe that you believe that sincerely. I've been in medicine for a long time, and I've worked with a lot of underprivileged people. You don't know how far fear will take you from what you'd usually do, morally. Even if she isn't lying, though, Annie herself may not really know the baby's paternity. Have you considered that?"

Ben looked at Sam, frowning. "That would mean…"

"Your relationship with Annie ended in, what, March or April of last year? You were at our house after that for many months without hearing from her. You don't know if she had other boyfriends, Ben."

A strange feeling came over Ben – a strange mixture of jealousy and distrust. But why? Wasn't that what he wanted? To not be responsible?

"But there's no way to find out for sure, is there?" Ben asked.

Sam's face fell. "No, there's not."

"Then I have to accept that Annie is telling the truth, don't I?" Ben swallowed, closed his eyes, and dismissed the picture of Betty that rose in his mind. "It's the right thing in God's eyes to marry her, isn't it?"

Sam stayed silent for a long moment, his hands gripping the backrest of his chair as he stood behind it. At last, he raised his eyes to Ben. "I say this as a father to a son, Ben, because that's how I see us. And I also say it as one Christian man to another. I really believe when I pray about it, that you should wait before you commit to marry Annie."

"But wait for how long?" Something in Ben just wanted to be done with all of this, to have it all behind him, to be married to Annie and settled down in the brick house. Yet, when it came to it, how would he be able to do that? Would he be able to face Betty every week of his life attending First Baptist, knowing that he had been about to ask her to be his wife, and yet would be sitting with Annie at his side? Betty would move on. Ben was sure of it. Not being with him... Soon she would surely realize how lucky she'd been to escape him. *She'll find a guy who is more like her.*

Sam's jaw tightened "I'm not really sure," he said at last, "but unless you feel as though God is saying something very different to you, very clearly, then my advice to you is to wait at least until after Christmas."

Ben frowned. "But the baby will have been born by then. It'll be born without us being married."

"It was conceived without you being married," Sam said quietly. "Look, I think that it is admirable that you want to give up... that you want to sacrifice the future you've been dreaming of to right the wrong that you did in the past. But it's important to remember that God has already taken your sins on Himself at the cross, Ben. He took my sins upon Himself at the cross, and you know that I had many. Your marrying Annie is not going to atone for anything. Don't think of yourself as a sacrificial lamb. There is only one sacrificial lamb."

They had just finished dinner that night when Ben walked in. For the first time since her arrival, Annie had agreed to eat at the table with everyone else. She said very little, but Sarah noticed how she enjoyed everything that had been laid out on the table, from the mashed butternut squash, of which she took two helpings, to the garlicky dinner rolls.

Most of the conversation up until Ben entered had revolved around the Christmas play, though everyone was careful not to mention Betty herself. Cliff related anecdotes of shepherds who had forgotten their staffs and wisemen who did not know where their gifts were located in the props room.

When Ben walked in, Annie put her fork down, its tines clinking against the edge of the plate. It was as though she had lost her appetite. And thinking of the situation going on, who could blame her?

"Hiya, Ben!" Cliff exclaimed, jumping up from the table.

Ben appeared to be having trouble managing a smile. "Hiya, Cliff," he replied. His shadowed eyes scanned the table. "Where's Paulie?"

"Oh, he's helping down at the soup kitchen this evening," Sam said. "I didn't think we would see you again tonight," he observed, his eyebrows raised. "I thought you were going to think…"

"Yeah, well, I did think," said Ben.

Sarah heard the challenge in his voice. Her chest clenched in fear.

"How're you doing, Annie?" Ben asked. Sarah set her fork down with a startled clink. Looking around the table, she saw the same surprise written on the faces of her family.

Annie jutted out her chin in that way that she had, that way that Sarah had quickly learned was the girl's way of hardening herself against a sudden offensive. "I'm okay," she answered into the quiet that had suddenly descended over the supper table.

Ben nodded and licked his lips. His eyes left Annie for a moment, darting to Sam, but then returned to Annie. "If it's all right with you, Annie, I'd like to talk to you after supper."

Sarah's own eyes skipped between her son, her

husband, and Annie. She had not had time to talk to Sam before supper, but now she wished that she had made the time.

Annie raised an eyebrow. "All right."

At that moment, Sarah wished that she could be a fly on the wall of the room in which Ben and Annie held their conversation.

## Chapter Eleven

Betty was moving on with no regrets; Ben was sure of it. *As soon as I told her about Annie, I saw it in her eyes.*

Seeing her this afternoon… well, that had clinched his decision to talk to Annie tonight, rather than to take Sam's advice and wait a while longer. If he closed his eyes – no, even if he kept them open – he could still see Betty sitting at the same soda counter at which she'd sat with Ben just a few short weeks ago, her lovely legs twisted around the barstool, her perfectly pink mouth pursed around the red-and-white straw of her frosty coffee cabinet. And her eyes, Betty's beautiful dark brown eyes, laughing as they fixed on the man seated next to her.

Now, Ben held the door open and gestured for Annie to walk in before him into the sitting room. He gritted his teeth against the memory of that man who had leaned in across his own soda to murmur something humorous.

Ben had not waited until Betty saw him. That would have humiliated him. In the split second in which it took him to grasp what was going on with Betty and this man whom he had never seen before, Ben had already half-turned toward the door, his desire for a refreshing soda forgotten. His footsteps had taken him to the pond again. It seemed he always went there whenever he had to think about something, pray about something.

Pray?

How could he do that, when his soul nearly broke in two, when his heart and mind reeled with the drunkenness that only grief could bring?

*Man of sorrows, what a name*
*For the Son of God who came…*

The words of the hymn came to mind – and yet, with them, the sight of Betty's long fingers sweeping across the keys.

*Ruined sinners to reclaim.*

That Ben certainly was. But could he join in with the exclamation that came next?

*Hallelujah! What a Savior!*

Oh, He was a Savior spiritually. Ben had been washed, had been cleansed. He felt that. He saw it in the change of his motives, his mind, his very nature. But what of his past? There seemed no salvation from that…

He had found himself sitting numbly on the frosty grass, the moisture seeping through the seat of his pants, soaking them. How had he ever thought that he would escape the consequences of his actions? Shouldn't he just be glad that more consequences had not followed the actions that he had once taken? Something within him urged him to pray, and yet he couldn't he just… couldn't.

Couldn't exercise the spiritual muscle anymore.

Reverend Cloud's admonition weeks ago, before any of this had happened, trickled into his mind then: *"Remember, the Holy Spirit promises to pray for us when words fail us. The important thing is to come before God and wait upon Him. Someone wise once said, 'Better a heart without words than words without heart.'"*

But he was tired. Tired of waiting. Tired of sitting silently before God. Tired of lingering in grief and waiting for comfort. The easiest thing had seemed to be what he was doing now. Why should he pray about it any longer, as Sam had advised, when God's will seemed so clear?

And so he was here tonight, at the Giorgi home, moving forward.

Ben waited until Annie stepped into the living room, and then he shut the door behind them both. He took a long moment to close the door before turning to face her. She stood in the light of the lamp, a soft glow magnifying her prettiness, highlighting the child she carried in her belly. This was right then; this was the just thing to do, was it not? Every logical piece of Ben's mind, flashing with the memory of Betty sitting at the counter, with the verses in Scripture that talked about making restitution for the wrong that he had done, even with his own desire to take a strange pleasure in accepting an unpleasant fate, all combined in this moment and caused Ben to silence the warning bell that sounded in his heart.

"Annie," Ben began, "I've been thinking long and hard about the situation."

"Situation," Annie gave him a wry smile. "Ya mean the baby, of course." Her lips grew firm, and she darted a glance at Ben, her usual kind — one filled with stubborn determination. "I ain't goin' and givin' him to a stranger,

Ben, no matter what ya and your highfalutin' family say. I know ya want to marry that girl, that what's-her-name that everybody talks about here-and-there when they think I'm not listening. But you got responsibilities from your past, and–"

"I know, Annie," Ben interrupted. "And I ain't gonna leave ya in the dust."

Annie's eyes widened, shock on full display. "Ya mean… Ya mean…" Slowly, she lowered herself to sit on the couch, as if her legs couldn't support her any longer.

Ben licked his lips. "Yeah, I will marry you, Annie." The moment he said it, he expected to feel a sense of relief.

But he didn't. Instead, a numb ache swept over him, like clouds rolling in on the horizon, heralding a thunderstorm to come. Pushing aside these feelings, Ben went over to the couch, where Annie sat, forcing his feet to move, compelling his body to bend as he settled beside her. He didn't touch her; he didn't take her hand; the numbness that he felt was too great for him to make such an overture. But he did look into her eyes, sparkling with what looked like tears of relief, and he forced a smile to gentle his tight lips.

She twisted her hands, broken-nailed, in her lap. "Thanks, Ben," she choked in a mouse's whisper.

Guilt collared Ben. "Aw, Annie. I was wrong to… I just want… I just have to… to make things right. For you. For the baby."

Perhaps, in time, God would give him and Annie a new start together… a love that was good and wholesome and from God himself, rather than from their own selfish and youthful lusts.

Perhaps.

"The old Ben wouldn't have said that," Annie mumbled, half to him and half to herself.

Ben bit his lip, then released it. "The old Ben is gone, Annie. The man you're marrying ain't the same man who fathered your child. That man is dead and gone."

Annie looked at him, a small smile on her unpainted lips. "I never knew that money could do that to folks. I mean, you're so different. I guess money really does make the world go 'round, don't it?"

Ben found himself shaking his head so strongly his neck might snap. "No, no, it ain't the money, Annie. Fact is, I don't make much. I got my carpentry work, and that's going well, but the only thing I've got to my own name, free and clear, is my house and property. Sam gave it to me, from him and Mama."

Annie looked bewildered. "But I thought..." Her eyes darted around the room, and Ben knew what she saw: bookshelves loaded with the gilt-edged volumes, the piano waiting in the corner, freshly polished by the maid's hands, the exquisite rugs beneath their feet, covering the gleaming wood floors. He knew, too, what ran through her mind: the multi-coursed meals that regularly arrived on the Giorgis' table, the secure job that Sam went off to every day, the way these people used a wide vocabulary and properly-pronounced words with no slang to muddy their speech. He knew that she saw his fresh duds, always clean unless he was coming from a job, his neat haircut and shaven cheeks. He knew that, to someone like Annie, these things spoke of wealth and privilege beyond anything she could hope to attain on her own.

"It ain't no life of luxury I'll be bringing ya into, Annie, just so's ya know." Ben eyed her, wanting to make things plain. "I don't live like my mother and Sam. Can't afford to, and, to be honest, I wouldn't know what to do with the kind of money my stepfather's got. But I will promise ya this: as long as there's breath in my body, I will work to provide for ya and... and for our child." He had nearly said *children*, but something had stopped him. He still couldn't think that far ahead.

A shadow came over Annie's face, not of disappointment but of fear. Ben didn't know why. Hadn't he just assured her that they would make ends meet – more than make ends meet, in all honesty? His work paid well, and he often got referrals from associates of Sam as well, which meant customers who could pay well for Ben's work, and in cash, not favors. That sure helped.

Annie's eyebrows furrowed together. "Then what... what happened? Ya changed so much. I mean it's like you're a different man." She closed her lips, as if the words had escaped without her permission.

Despite the terrible situation in which he found himself, something good and bright sparked in Ben at the question. She had seen that there was a difference in him, not just in his circumstances, then. "It's like I told you, Annie," Ben began. "I died."

Her eyes narrowed. "You expect me to believe that?"

Ben nearly smiled despite himself. "It's hard to explain, Annie, but I'll try."

And then he told her; he told her how Sam had taken Ben in after Aldo falsely accused him. How he'd hated Sam at first, but then God... God had reached down through the undeserved kindness of his new family, and they had forgiven, forgiven him even when they'd thought that Paulie would die as a result of an injury Ben had caused. How Ben had realized that, though his family might forgive him, he was still guilty in the sight of God.

How he had repented, had come before God, seeing himself as he really was – a worm who deserved judgment and not mercy. How he had repented. He had asked for forgiveness. And God had given it so richly, making him a new creation in Christ Jesus, who had died for him. The old Ben had gone forever. He had been born into life anew.

Joy bubbled up in Ben's heart at the remembrance, filling the pool of love that he had for his Lord and Savior. He told how Jesus Christ had raised him into newness of life from the depths of despair, and when he finished, Annie sat silent for a long time. Nervousness twanged at Ben's heart. Perhaps he had not explained it well. "Does what I said makes sense?" he asked tentatively.

Annie shrugged as if she didn't care. "Yeah, but I've heard that kind of thing before."

"But did you understand it before?" Ben asked.

For it had been that way for him. Had he not heard the story of redemption all of his life, had he not seen it with his own eyes in the symbols of the Eucharist – and yet had not understood what he was hearing and seeing?

But again she shrugged. Ben felt frustration drape over him. If only she truly understood! He much preferred to enter into marriage with her as a Christian too, rather than him trying to shoulder the spiritual responsibility for their family on his own.

"So..." Annie began and Ben felt his spirit inhale and hope. Perhaps she was interested in learning more. Perhaps he had misjudged her shrug.

"So," Annie said again, and this time she dropped her eyes and twisted her hands together. "Does this mean that there's no money at all for us? Is that what you're saying?"

Ben frowned, and his spirit hardened. Money. Was

that what she was after? His mind went back over their conversation thus far. Yes, she had thought that he had come into money. And, for a guy like him, he had. He had a solid job, and he owned a house with no mortgage payment due. "Like I said, there's not much cash that I have lying around. But you'll always be provided for, Annie." He kept his voice calm but cool.

"Oh, okay." Annie's hands stiffened in her lap, as if she was forcing herself to keep them still.

Ben narrowed his eyes. "Does this change things? For us?"

Annie's eyes darted to him, alarm widening them. "No. No, of course not, Ben. All I wanted was for you to take responsibility for the baby, and for you to provide for me, too, of course. It's only fair, like I've been saying. If we have food and clothing and shelter, I'm sure that will be all right. No," she said again, as if to assure herself, "no, it doesn't change anything at all."

Despite his misgivings, Ben knew he had to let the subject drop.

Annie clenched the receiver to her ear and scanned the foyer of the Giorgi house. Good, they were all gone. At least, she thought so. In this house, she had learned that she could never tell when Cliff might pop his head around the door, or when Paulie might amble through, book in hand, or when Sarah herself might traipse down the stairs with an offer for a cup of tea.

But Annie could not afford to be interrupted now, not during this telephone call. Satisfied enough that she was alone, Annie pressed the receiver to her ear and dialed the operator. As the operator put her call through, Annie waited, her breath shallow.

Aldo didn't answer, but another groom did, one whose name Annie didn't recognize. Again, she waited impatiently, this time for that new groom to get Aldo. She listened to the faint sounds of the stable with which she was so familiar.

"Hey, Cuz," he greeted her. "Got the dough yet?"

A little anger rose to Annie's chest at the question, but she pushed it away. That was just Aldo's way; he meant to help, surely. At least, he was the only one in her family who *would* help.

"I haven't even had the kid yet," she said lightly, trying to keep the annoyance out of her voice.

Aldo tried to laugh, though it sounded curiously strained. "Look, Cuz, ya gotta hurry up things a little bit. I ain't got all the time in the world."

Although he couldn't see her, Annie still narrowed her eyes at him. "Ya ain't got all the time in the world? Whatd'ya mean?"

Aldo hesitated for just a split second. "I got some bills that need paying, you know."

A little fear tensed Annie's chest. "Aldo, this money... I just found out that there might not be that much of it to start with, anyway, but anything I get, I... I... I can't..."

"What are you saying, Annie?" Aldo's voice hardened.

Annie swallowed against the fear that now rose from her chest to her throat. "It's just that I gotta have money to get away, to live on for a good long while. I just don't know how much of it I can give ya—"

"Look," Aldo cut her off, "we made a deal. I would help ya figure out a plan. I would help ya get down there, buy your train ticket, give ya a little dough to take the bus if ya needed it, but then ya gotta pay me back, kid. *With interest.* Ya don't get somethin' for nothin' in this world. *Capisce?"*

Oh, how she understood that. You never got something for nothing in this world. Everything had its cost. She swallowed again. "I know that ya think that Ben's got alotta money, Aldo," she started, trying desperately to school her thoughts, to make him understand. "But ya didn't realize – neither one of us realized – that the big money ain't Ben's. Oh, he's got a house and all, but he don't got much else, other than a steady job."

"Other than a steady job," Aldo muttered. "Well that's more than what I'm gonna have soon, anyway."

"What do ya mean?"

"Nothin'! Forget it," Aldo barked. "Anyways, I thought ya said that ya were stayin' at some big house that belonged to Ben's family, full of rich stuff. Where's the money behind that?" Suspicion dripped from his voice.

*He thinks I'm hiding something.* Annie gripped the receiver ever more tightly in her nervousness and began to blabber. "They do. I am. I am staying, I mean, in a big house, but it don't belong to Ben. It belongs to his family – to his stepdad and his mom. They don't offer handouts, at least not in front of me, and Ben doesn't seem like he'd take 'em anyhow." The old Ben would've been different. The old Ben would've taken what he thought belonged to him, one way or the other. Again, Annie wondered at the change that had come over her former boyfriend. His explanation that seeking God had done it... Well, that just didn't hold water for Annie. Daddy was plenty religious, and he weren't half so nice as Ben was now.

"Well, there sounds like there's money somewhere. Dig for it, Annie-girl. One more thing, and then I gotta go."

Annie knew he wanted her to respond, to let him know that she was listening. "What's that?"

"Make sure he marries you before you have that baby. It's better law-wise, ya know? And another thing: Time is running out, Annie. You've been pussyfooting around too long. Ya hear me?"

Annie looked down at her rounded stomach. "Yeah, I heard ya, Aldo."

She hadn't realized that Jim would be so bold. He had seemed to be the type to know what he wanted, sure, but he also had seemed like the type who took his time.

Apparently not.

Betty leaned her head against the hallway wall, feeling dread seep through her body. Right now, in Daddy's home office, Jim was asking if he might come to call on Betty, officially. She wished that she had been able to intercept him, but she hadn't. She had only heard about Jim's arrival when Mama had given her a concerned look and told her that there was a young man – Jim by name – who was talking to Daddy in his study. Heart thudding, Betty had been bold enough to creep up towards the door to catch a few words drifting through the wood.

Words like, "your daughter" and "court".

Betty bit her lip. She hadn't expected this at all, though maybe she should have, especially when Jim had asked her to go along with him to the drugstore to get a soda after the play practice twice this week. He had clearly shown his interest. But she had brushed it off, unsure yet whether he fit into the new plans she needed to make for her life now that Ben had exited it.

However, things had taken on quite a more serious turn without her will. Lest she be caught lurking outside Daddy's study, Betty pushed herself off the wall and moved on silent feet toward the kitchen. Maybe a snack would help to ease the queasy feeling in her stomach, would help slow down the pounding of her heart, and even might stave off the terrible headache that seemed to be coming on.

What would Daddy say? He would be surprised, no doubt, and a little bewildered, too, for Betty had barely dated anyone before Ben had come along. She'd always said that she was waiting for just the right one, just the right man to fulfill her fancies. *No,* she corrected herself, *not my fancies; rather, my properly high standards.* It was good to have high standards, wasn't it? And letting them down had resulted in her getting involved with Ben.

Ben…

*I was foolish, so foolish, to let my guard down, to let him close enough to me to hurt me like this.* She stepped into the kitchen, put the teakettle on, and pulled a cup from the cupboard. After finding a box of saltines, she retrieved the jar of peanut butter from the refrigerator and busied herself by smearing the peanut butter over three of the saltine crackers. Then she fetched Mama's homemade jelly, smearing that in globs over three more crackers. Finally, she pressed those together with the peanut buttery ones.

She felt angry sometimes at her parents too, she had to admit, so angry that they had allowed her to date Ben.

Hadn't they known that he was from the wrong side of the tracks, despite being Dr. Giorgi's stepson? Why hadn't they thought that their daughter deserved better? *I do, don't I?*

Betty had just bitten into the second saltine sandwich when she heard Daddy's study door open. "Thank you for taking the time to see me this evening, sir." That was Jim's voice.

Then came Daddy's: "It was a pleasure to meet you, Jim." Her father had always been soft-spoken, even when he was in the pulpit. But soft-spoken didn't mean spineless; Betty had learned that well over the years. And now she heard – though surely Jim did not – the concern in her father's voice.

For a split second, Betty wondered if she should disappear from the kitchen, out of her father's reach, before Jim exited the house. For a reason that lurked in the shadows beyond her identification, she felt ashamed and defensive before Daddy.

But she waited too long. Before she even had heard the front door close, Daddy stood in the open frame of the kitchen doorway. He was not angry – It took a lot to get Daddy visibly angry – but was it disappointment that she saw on his face? In some ways, disappointment was much harder to bear from Daddy than anger.

Betty busied herself with putting away her saltine-sandwich fixings. "Would you like some tea, Daddy?" she asked when she couldn't stand the silence any longer.

As if he had been waiting for her to speak first, he replied, "Sure. Sure, Betty." The scrape of the chair told her that he'd taken a seat at the table.

She lifted a Lipton teabag from the jar on the counter, dropped it into a fresh cup, and poured boiling water over it. As she handed it to her dad, she forced herself to speak. "Daddy–"

But he started at the same time. "Betty–"

She waited, but, after he had looked at her quietly for another moment, he said, "You go ahead."

Betty fiddled with the handle of her teacup. She didn't lift her eyes to meet Daddy's as she spoke, as she verbally tried to make sense of Jim's visit, both to herself and to him – to make it seem like just what it was – something reasonable.

"Daddy, it's not like it seems. I had no idea that Jim was coming over here. I... I would've said something if I had. I just met him a few days ago, and we've only gone for a soda together a couple of times. He is a nice young man, though. He comes from a good family – a good Christian family – and we enjoy our time together. We're friends." She did not dare mention – actually drove it from her mind, if she wanted to be honest – the fact that Ben had seen her with Jim at the soda counter. The look of dismay on Ben's face had twisted Betty's heart, even though, at the time, she had pretended that she hadn't caught sight of him at all.

Daddy took a tiny sip of hot tea and then pulled his lips into his mouth. Betty knew the look; he was thinking hard, praying, most likely, in his mind, about what he should say to her. "Betty..." He sighed and ran his fingers through his hair, little of it though there was. At last he looked up at Betty again. "Are you done with Ben Picoletti, then? For good?"

Done with Ben? Oh, how she wanted to be done with Ben – done with every part of the painful circumstance of the last week or so. And yet, no matter how much she tried to drive the thought of him from her mind, from her heart, even Betty had to admit that Ben had nestled there in a unique way. She opened her mouth, but found that she could not reply honestly to her father's question.

After another moment, Daddy reached across the table and clasped her hands in his. "Betty," he entreated, "is this because of that young woman? I understand if you and Ben are taking a break from one another. In fact, I think that it is both necessary and wise, considering that Ben has to decide still what he plans to do about all of this. But to rush into another courtship… It just doesn't seem like you, Betty." He shook his head "It just doesn't seem like my daughter at all."

Betty felt her defenses rise at her father's words, rise to stem the flood of tears that rushed to her eyes. Daddy was right, but what could she do? God had misled her. She had trusted Him to give her something good, even though she knew she deserved better than what God seemed to be giving her in Ben Picoletti, despite her own attraction to him. And He had misled her! He had brought her to a place of broken cisterns and dry wells. She hadn't deserved that! Not after all she'd done to toe the line of His Word all her life. Not after all she'd done to plan her life properly, to set the right goals.

At any rate she was tired, she was tired of waiting for the right man to come along so that she could get on with her life. She was tired of staying home and being Daddy's little girl – of being the church pianist, of giving the mostly-untalented children of Chetham piano lessons once a week. She was tired of all the girls with whom she had gone to high school showing up at church with an engagement ring on their fingers or hearing their mothers talk about how their daughters had made the dean's list at college. She was tired of waiting for her own plans to come to life.

"I can understand how it would bother you – this situation with Annie and Ben. But God will see you through…"

"No, He won't." Betty heard herself break into her father's words of wisdom, shocking even herself.

Daddy's face mirrored her surprise. He set down his cup of tea with a quiet clink. "What do you mean?"

Tension humming through her body, Betty bit her lip, knowing that she would have to tread the ground very, very carefully to get out of this new situation she'd created with her words. Daddy would think of her as some poor soul in need of counsel, like the ones who visited his office.

But she was not like the ones who visited his office, in need of godly guidance, in need of someone spiritual to help her put her life back together. She was Betty Cloud, who always made a great effort to keep every hair in place, every note perfect on the piano, and every circumstance of her life in order. She was not someone in need of anything. Everyone else messed things up. But she couldn't say that to Daddy, could she? "I just think that maybe I made a mistake with dating Ben. So God can't be expected to get me out of the situation – a bad situation of my own making."

There. Maybe that would get past him.

Daddy frowned. "Betty, that's not how I taught you, or at least how I thought that I taught you. While we shouldn't rush into situations that we know are not God's will, when we repent, God will work all things together for the good of those who love Him. You are His child, and God will see you through this. He will see Ben through this as well."

Betty nodded, as she knew that she was supposed to. "Yes, Daddy." She forced a smile to her lips and hoped that it looked genuine.

"And I'm not convinced that your dating Ben was not God's will. In fact, I think it may have been the best thing that you've done for quite a while."

Betty blinked back the smart and trusted herself to say nothing.

Daddy looked at her for a long moment. "Well, I gave Jim my permission to see you, Betty, if that's what you want. I don't know him too well, I don't know him at all, really, but I do remember his family from when they lived here many years ago. In fact, I think I may have gone to school with his father. Though the son appears to lose no time when it comes to finding a girl, the family was a good one."

Unlike Ben's. The thought went through Betty's mind, but she didn't voice it. Ben had come from a family of drunks, abusers, and adulterers. Why had she trusted that she could have her happily-ever-after with him? He had too much in his past for her to deal with it.

## Chapter Twelve

Sarah took a deep breath, raised her hand, and knocked on Annie's bedroom door. As she did so, she silently spoke a prayer of commitment. *Help me to walk in Your strength and wisdom – Yours alone.*

"Who is it?"

"It's me, Sarah."

"Uh, come in."

As she pushed open the door, Sarah saw that Annie seemed to be tucking something beneath the cushion of her chair, but because of her pregnant belly, she couldn't manage to hide it before Sarah saw that it was the copy of the *Daily Light* devotional book that they kept in the sitting room. A little hope unfurled in Sarah's heart, but she didn't say anything. "It's a beautiful afternoon, not too cold," she started, "and I was wondering if you would like to go into Chetham with me. I have to pick up a few things at the store."

The openness that had been on Annie's face when Sarah had walked into the room turned to a split second of panic, followed by the look of a hunted deer. "Uh... Uh... I... I don't know."

The girl's eyes dropped, and Sarah guessed why Annie was hesitant to accompany her into town. People always talked, and Annie didn't want to subject herself to the stares that she would probably receive. After all, Sarah was sure that word had spread, somehow, about the arrival of a girl from Ben's past. A few days ago, Sarah would not have been so eager – or so willing – to take Annie out with her in public on the streets of Chetham. At that point Ben had not made a decision about whether or not he would be marrying the girl. But two nights ago, he'd told her and Sam that he planned to go ahead with the marriage, despite Sam's strong reservations. Sam had opened his mouth to voice them again, but Sarah had pressed a hand to his thigh beneath the table. If it had been Paulie, Sam would've protested again, despite her attempt to stop him. But when it came to Ben, though Sarah knew that Sam loved him as he loved his own son, Sam held back a little bit when it came to directing Ben's life.

"I'm not running a lot of errands," Sarah clarified. "Just down to the drugstore, and I might pop into the market quick. I also have a bread that I'd like to give to one of our neighbors. It's chilly, so we could take the car."

Annie glanced around the room. The young woman probably felt like she had been in a prison for days, hardly daring to come down the stairs. In fact, Sarah was counting on Annie feeling that way, for if she did, then she would probably go with Sarah just to escape these four walls for a while.

"Well…"

"It's a beautiful afternoon," Sarah encouraged again, "and if you're feeling the least bit tired, you can always just wait in the car while I run my errands."

At this, a small smile appeared on Annie's lips, and Sarah saw in it a hint of the lovely innocence the girl must have possessed as a child. "I guess so then," Annie acquiesced, "I just gotta get my things together."

"All right, then." Thankfulness filled Sarah's heart. "I'll be waiting for you downstairs."

Annie stayed in the car for their first stop, but at the second one, she decided to go with Sarah into the drugstore, since she needed a comb herself – She was tired of using her fingers to get through the snarls and bring some sense of order to her wavy hair. She checked her handbag once more, making sure of the generous amount of pocket money – five dollars! – that Ben had given her the other night. She had initially refused it, but he'd insisted, saying that he would provide for his own. *Ben would never've done that before.*

Now Annie drew her unwieldy bulk out of the car's interior and into the crisp afternoon. Leaves littered the streets of Chetham here-and-there, fast falling from the trees because of the sudden chill and light snowfall that had come in the last few nights. A bright sun softened the brisk temperature by gilding the edge of every leaf and tree. Adjusting her tattered hat and then arranging her clothing around her bulk, Annie became aware of the stares of two women who passed by them on the sidewalk.

But Sarah either ignored or didn't see their staring; Annie couldn't tell which it was. At any rate, Ben's mother smiled at the two women. "Good morning, Ethel, Doris," Sarah called out as the women passed by her without saying anything.

At her greeting, they both openly turned their heads to stare at the two of them, and Annie felt embarrassment rush through her body... followed by a fierce defiance. She let her coat fall open. *Give them old busybodies something to talk about.* The two women's faces twitched as if they had suddenly come under convulsions.

They settled, though, for a half-hearted smile and a timid lift of their gloved hands. Sarah's smile seemed to set more determinedly at their actions, and she turned to Annie. "Come on, then," she said, "I think you will like this drugstore. Mr. Anderson has everything you could want or need. What's on your list?"

Annie didn't have a list, but she answered anyway. "I just need to get a new comb here. And maybe some curl papers," she added. Though she hadn't really curled her hair in ages, so she wondered why that thought came into her mind.

Sarah smiled again. "Well, I'm sure you'll find exactly what you're looking for. Do you... Do you need to borrow any money?"

Annie suddenly felt awkward. "Uh, no. I've got what I need. Thanks." Should she tell Sarah that Ben had given her the money? She remained undecided until the moment was lost.

The bell clanged above the wreath-festooned door as they entered into the little drugstore. Annie remembered a drugstore like this in her hometown, though much more rundown. Across the front of the store, a line of barstools waited for customers before the long, gleaming wooden counter. Behind the counter, along with the routine soda-maker equipment, a homemade sign advertised the store's offerings, including a coffee cabinet, a drink Annie had never had before. The owner evidently had the Christmas spirit – or knew that it was good for business, at any rate – for he'd tacked a faux garland, complete with candy-canes and red berries all along the counter's edge, and festive music wafted from the large radio squatting in the corner – Annie recognized Zelma O'Neal and Jack Haley crooning, "Button Up Your Overcoat."

Away from the counter, shelves brimmed with things varying from hairbrushes to shoe polish to ipecac to dog food. No one else was visible in the store, but from the back of the store a cheerful male voice called out, "Be right with you!"

Sarah tucked her hands into her coat pockets and answered, "That's fine, Mr. Anderson. We're just looking around." She turned to Annie. "The hairbrushes and things are over there." She pointed out a rack and shelf nearby.

While Sarah went in search of the items that were on her own list, Annie found a comb – the nicest she'd ever had – before fingering a bottle of hair cream longingly. *You shouldn't spend too much. Remember you have to tuck some of it away.*

But she did pick up those curl papers. What would Ben think when he walked into the dining room for supper, as he had said he was going to, and spotted Annie with her hair all dolled-up?

She shook her head. *I shouldn't be thinking about that. Not when I know it can't last.* She gritted her teeth and went to put the curl papers back on the shelf. She needed to hold herself in check. She couldn't let her emotions run away with her, despite the fact that Ben seemed so different from the way he used to be. She had liked him before, thinking of him as the best of a bad batch, the bad batch being all men, but now... When she saw the way that he played gently with Cliff, not resorting to nasty teasing, when she observed the way he was respectful to his mother and Sam, and even his courteous way toward her in general, though she had so complicated, so disturbed his life... Well, it seemed as though a new and different man had promised to marry her than the Ben that she'd thought she was going to get.

It was almost enough to make a girl feel guilty.

Her hand hesitated over returning the curl papers to their place beside the hairpins. What would it hurt to look fine for just a little while? And why should she feel guilty? It was Ben's fault that she was here, anyway. If he'd never cheated on her, she wouldn't have broken up with him... and the both of them wouldn't have found themselves in this predicament.

With the comb and papers in her hands, Annie headed towards the register. Sarah already stood there, chatting with the bald druggist. He was wiping his hands on his body-swathing white apron when he caught sight of Annie coming up behind Sarah. The friendly smile on his face wobbled.

Annie lifted her chin, defying the heat that rose in her cheeks.

Sarah followed Mr. Anderson's line-of-sight and beckoned when she saw Annie. "Let me introduce you to..."

The doorbell jangled behind them, interrupting Sarah,

who turned to glance at whoever entered.

A young woman with shiny brown curls, clothed in the neatest-looking attire that Annie had ever seen, stepped into the store. At the sight of her, even Sarah's smile quavered. The newcomer herself halted and blinked at them, but then quickly regained her poise.

"Good morning," Sarah spoke first, her smile fixed again.

"Good morning, Mrs. Giorgi," the young woman replied in a sweet voice, but the expression on her face said that it was anything but good to see Sarah.

Sarah looked over at Annie, and Annie could see the awkwardness written all over Ben's mother's face. Up until this young woman arrived, Sarah had not showed one sign of it. So what was it about this person that made Sarah finally succumb? Anxiety rippled up Annie's spine, and she placed her hand protectively over the burden at her waist.

Annie expected Sarah to introduce her, as she had been about to do with Mr. Anderson, but Sarah didn't say anything at all. There was a moment of silence, of the young woman looking from Sarah to Annie to Annie's pregnant stomach. Then the young woman rolled her lip through her teeth and dropped her eyes down to her purse, fiddling with it as if the clasp had broken.

"Well," she said in a strained voice, "I'll let you get back to your shopping." She marched off without looking at them again.

Sarah's eyes followed the young woman as she strode down one of the nearest aisles to them, hurrying towards the back of the store. *As far away from us as possible.* When Sarah turned back to Annie, she saw that the smile on her face quivered. "We can just pay for our..."

But Mr. Anderson was disappearing into his

backroom, as quick as might be. He looked over his shoulder at them. "I'll, uh, I'll just put your items on your bill, Mrs. Giorgi."

Sarah frowned. She opened her mouth to protest. "But I can pay for them now, and Annie here…"

The man waved his hand in the air to stop her words. He tried to manage a smile, but he failed completely. "No, no, no. I've got a very important order here that I've got to fill. I'm afraid I don't have time. Not now. Have a good afternoon, Mrs. Giorgi and, uh, well… Good afternoon."

Annie looked at the items in her hands. The man did not even know what they were purchasing. *He's escaping me.* Would she always to be an object of shame to the Giorgi family? She didn't care if she brought shame to Ben, ruined his reputation… did she? *No, of course I don't!* But the Giorgis, they were nice people. She hadn't thought about how this would cost them.

*So what? So what if I hurt them?* They were rich people, used to getting their own way, used to being in the spotlight. So let them have the spotlight. They'd get over it, wouldn't they?

"I'll just write down what we have." Sarah picked up a pencil from the counter and scribbled a list on the notepad lying on the counter. Annie watched, her mind turning over the whole visit to this drugstore. She knew small-town life. The Giorgis probably wouldn't get over this. The scandal – especially if Annie did what she planned to do – would follow them for years, if not for their lifetimes. She fiddled with the bristles on the comb in her hand. *So what? What does it matter? They deserve it.*

But did they? Did they deserve to suffer for Annie's wrong? And for the wrong of their son? The words of her father came to her mind: "Each man shall bear his own sin."

A bitter smile lifted Annie's lips. But men didn't suffer for their own sins. Women suffered for them. And children. Men tended to get away with their sins.

And she wasn't about to let Ben get away with his.

Sarah's ruffled feathers seemed to settle as the trip went on. They only had one stop left to make, at the local doctor's. "I thought your husband was a doctor," said Annie as the car stopped. She had not spoken much on the drive, but now she could not resist. Why would a doctor need to pay another doctor?

Sarah smiled as she opened the handle of the door. "Dr. Philips is a family doctor. Sam's a specialist. We like to go to family physicians for our general medical care. Sam doesn't like to mix the two together unless there is an emergency."

Annie nodded as if she understood, but she really didn't. Wasn't one doctor the same as another? Imagine, having more than one doctor!

An unsmiling older woman answered the door to Sarah's knock, and Annie watched Sarah hand an envelope to her. The severe look on the woman's face lifted into a hint of, well, not exactly a smile, but at least less of a frown. Then the woman caught sight of Annie in the car, looking at her through the glass. The woman's face hardened, and she stared, squint-eyed, until Sarah turned to see what was the object of her gaze.

Then Sarah said something to her, gesturing towards the car with a friendly expression. Annie guessed that

Sarah was explaining who Annie was. The warmth crept up Annie's neck once again. Well, what had she expected, coming to Chetham, demanding that a prestigious citizen's stepson take responsibility for the child she carried? She had come publicly; it was no wonder that people felt that they could respond to her in kind.

Despite Sarah's open smiling and gesturing, the woman's frown did not lessen. She held Sarah's white envelope against her crisp printed apron and kept her eyebrows raised just a bit. When Sarah finished speaking, she saw that the woman spoke nothing in response. Even Sarah seemed to wilt slightly at her hard demeanor.

Annie rolled down her window just a little bit, not caring if the persnickety woman at the door saw. She heard Sarah say in a strained voice, "Have a good afternoon, Mrs. Philips."

The woman merely nodded, and Sarah turned and made her way down the steps. Without turning again, she opened the door of the car and joined Annie inside.

"Where to next, Mrs. Giorgi?" the driver inquired.

Annie looked at Sarah. Sarah sat there silently for a moment and then reached up and unpinned her hat with a sigh. She laid the hat on her lap, and then answered, "To Emmaline Kinner's, please, Taylor. I think we both could use a cup of her tea."

Receiving the relieved smile that Sarah sent her way, Annie hoped that Emmaline Kinner would not be like the other people she had met – or at least whom she had seen, since they seemed unwilling to actually meet her – since coming into town this afternoon.

The sun was nearing the horizon when Taylor brought the car to park beneath the canopy of a sturdy maple tree. "You'll come in with me?" Sarah asked.

Annie noticed how Sarah had not said, "Do you *want* to come in with me?" For some reason, Sarah wanted her to meet this Emmeline Kinner. Annie's curiosity rose, in spite of herself. Carefully tamping it down, however, she shrugged. "If you want," she said in a carefully careless voice.

Sarah smiled, a genuine smile with none of the forcefulness that had undergirded it throughout the day thus far. "Good. I think that you'll like Emmaline. I know that she'll be glad to meet you."

Annie couldn't help the surprised expression that spread across her face, though she did her best to mask it quickly. Glad to meet her? Was this another one of Sarah's delusions? What kind of woman would be glad to meet a girl like Annie?

Taylor came around to open the door, and Sarah stepped out of the car. Joining her on the sidewalk, Annie looked up at the modest but well-kept white house before them. On each of the ground-floor windows, a small piney wreath hung by means of a scarlet ribbon. Annie darted a glance around the yard, taking in the sleeping flower gardens and rose bushes whose colors must sing when the warm weather came. The brick paths invited her feet to stroll down them and the gentle willow trees coaxed her to rest beneath their soft boughs, were the temperature warmer.

"Emmaline has been my dear friend for the past few

years. She has… helped me so much." Sarah said to Annie before starting up the walkway leading to the front door.

From inside the house, Annie could hear a woman singing. Her voice was not exquisite, but she held the tune well, and joy sparkled in her voice, making it seem more lovely.

"What can wash away my sin? Nothing but the blood of Jesus. What can make me whole again? Nothing but the blood of Jesus. Oh, precious is the flow that makes me white as snow! No other fount I know; nothing but the blood of Jesus."

Sarah stood waiting outside the door, without knocking, until the woman finished singing the verse. Then she rapped on the door and called out, "Emmaline. It's me, Sarah, and I brought a special guest."

Annie could think of multiple ways to describe herself. An unwanted guest. A disruptive guest. An intruder. But a special guest? Annie wondered if that was Sarah's nice way of saying all those things without saying them.

The door whisked open, revealing a woman who wiped her wet hands on a dishtowel. Her face lit up as she looked from Sarah to Annie, and she pushed the door open more widely, encouraging them to enter. "Hello, Sarah. And you must be Annie." The woman smiled and offered Annie her hand.

Put off-balance by the woman's open and immediate kindness, Annie hesitated for just a moment before taking the woman's hand and shaking it a little gingerly. She nodded, then swallowed and forced out, "Yeah, I'm Annie."

Annie caught sight of a blonde head peeping out from behind the woman's printed skirt. "Say hello to your

Auntie Sarah," Emmaline said to the little boy, who appeared to be no more than three years old, Annie thought.

Auntie Sarah? Annie stole a glance at Sarah and saw a strange look pass over the woman's face – a look of resignation, of longing, of intense love. Was this Sarah's nephew, then? Were Sarah and Emmeline sisters? Or were they just such very good friends that Sarah was called by a family title? Annie didn't know for sure.

Sarah knelt down, despite her bad knees, and opened her arms. The little boy let go of his mother's skirt and gave her an unrestrained hug, squeezing her tightly around the neck. Sarah's hat, pinned back on quickly in the car, came loose and fell to the floor. Sarah laughed, picked it up, and rose to her feet again. "You're growing every time I see you, Davey," she said. "Soon you'll be as big as your daddy."

Emmaline smiled down at the toddler again and said, "Will you ladies have some tea with me? I just put dinner on the stove. It's only some soup, so it can cook itself."

At the mention of soup, Annie sniffed the air. "It smells good," she heard herself say aloud, and then her face warmed. She didn't know this woman, she was a stranger in her house, and here she was, commenting on her soup! *You're just a tag-a-long, Annie. Keep quiet.*

But Emmaline smiled at her, and Annie's embarrassment faded. "Oh, that's an old chicken soup recipe of my mother's. Easy to throw together, you know?" Beside her, the little boy tugged at her skirt, and Emmaline reached down and picked him up, settling him on her hip. Annie wondered at the woman's seeming sense of joy. She didn't have about her the air of drudgery that so many women did who stayed at home cleaning, cooking, and caring for sticky children.

Sarah didn't have that manner either, Annie mused, as she followed the others over to the square kitchen table. But she always discounted Sarah, anyway. Who wouldn't be happy, who wouldn't be carefree, if they had the kind of money that the Giorgis did? Yet here was joyful Emmeline Kinner, not wanting for a simple meal to put on her table, but also wearing a patched, though neat, apron.

Emmaline sat down with them. "I had just put on the water to boil before you came. I was looking forward to the break before Geoff came home." She smiled, and Annie decided it was a very nice expression, one that didn't seem to hide away a different motive. However, Annie kept herself on guard. No one was really without guile. She had learned that the hard way.

"Emmaline's husband, Geoffrey, works at the high school," Sarah explained to Annie.

Annie gave a nod. So the woman's husband did have a secure job. That was what brought peace, that was what brought security to this home, then.

*But what about Bousquet's home? Plenty of money there, but there weren't no peace or security.* She pushed away the thought of that place as quickly as it came.

And of him...

"When are you due, Annie?"

Her mind elsewhere, Emmeline's question took Annie by surprise. "In January," she replied without thinking. As soon as the words came out of her mouth, panic tightened her chest. "I mean, December. I get 'em mixed up a lot. What with Christmas in there and all." Now what kind of sense did that make? Fear fused together every bone and muscle in her body.

A shadow of question passed over Sarah's face, but

she said nothing. Annie could've kicked herself.

Oblivious, Emmaline smiled. "What a gift children are, aren't they?" On the old model stove, the teakettle whistled, and Emmaline jumped up to get it, still talking. "It's so good that you could come to Chetham and—"

The screen door opened again, interrupting Emmaline's words and ushering in a gust of cold air. Annie peered over her shoulder and saw a tall brown-haired man stride into the house, carrying a worn leather briefcase in one hand and a stack of books and papers under one of his gangly arms. He stopped short when he saw the women gathered around the kitchen table, and a smile broke out on his face, making his plain features attractive, Annie decided. "We've got company," he observed, his tired eyes sparkling behind his wire-rimmed spectacles.

Emmaline had already scooted over to his side, and Annie watched as she went on tiptoe to give him a kiss on the cheek. "Yes, Sarah's brought…" Emmaline paused for just a second, and Annie knew that she was probably figuring out how to introduce her.

"Annie," she settled on at last. For one split second, Annie wondered why she had not been introduced as Ben's fiancée; then she realized that Emmaline probably didn't know.

For some reason, Annie was glad that the smiling man must not know that her pregnancy was an illegitimate one. She tucked her unadorned left-hand beneath the table.

"Welcome, Annie," Emmeline's husband said, setting down his books on the table. "I'm glad to meet you. I'm Geoff Kinner." The little boy had run up to him in the meantime and was tugging on his pants leg. Geoff reached down and lifted his son up in the air, planting a kiss on the pudgy cheek. "Hey, Davey."

"You're home early," Emmaline stated, giving Geoff a smile. "Supper won't be ready for a while yet."

"Yes, well, I didn't end up needing to go to the board meeting after school as I thought I would. For which I am mightily relieved." He gave an exaggerated sigh.

"That's good," Emmeline smiled. "Well, we'll eat in about an hour."

Geoff nodded and let David down from his place on the man's hip. "I think I'll use that time to get some papers graded, then."

"Sounds good," Emmaline replied. "Do you want a cup of tea to take with you upstairs?"

Geoff shook his head. "No, thanks. But Davey can come up with me and read some books on the floor if you'd like."

Emmeline looked down at the little boy. "Do you want to work with Daddy upstairs for a few minutes?"

The little boy gave a grin that could leave his mother in no doubt. He gave a heavy nod.

"Okay, then."

With another smile and a-glad-to-meet-you, the man exited the room, his son's hand in his. Annie found her eyes wandering after him. She had never seen a father be so kind and gentle with his little son. She remembered the way that her father had been stern with her as a child, demanding obedience, rarely rewarding good behavior, not letting her know of his love – if he possessed any for her – the kind of love at least that Geoff evidently had for his child.

"Do you got any other kids?" she asked Emmaline.

Emmaline smiled, but there was a hint of sadness

there. "No," she said, taking her seat at the table once again. "David is our only living son. The son of our hearts, but not of our bodies, you know."

Annie stared at her. What did the woman mean by that?

"David is adopted," Emmaline went on.

Annie could not help but stare as the waves of memory passed over her mind. *Adopted...* "You mean, he ain't yours?" For was that not what adoption meant? At least, it had in her family – she had been one of them in name only, and Daddy had made sure she knew it. *"One of Dorothy's charity projects,"* she'd heard him mumble more than once.

"David is ours, Annie, in a very special way. He is ours by choice: both the choice of his loving mother and my choice to take him into our home and to receive all of the love that he can give and to give it back to him."

The patter of feet came from the other room, and David reappeared.

"I thought you were going to read upstairs while Daddy worked?" Emmeline asked.

"Need my train-train." The little boy looked around the room until his eyes lit upon the wooden toy, hiding near the hutch.

As he fetched it and hurried from the room, Annie could not help now but watch him and see how very different his appearance was from that of Emmaline and Geoff. Anyone who knew that he was adopted would see it. In her own family, she could remember all the times that she had wished that her appearance had matched that of her brothers and sisters. If it had, if she had fit in better, would Daddy have taken to her better? Though could she even call him Daddy now, seeing that he had disowned her? She remembered so well his words before she left: "You're no daughter of mine," he had said loudly, making sure that she knew – that everyone around knew – that she was ill-begotten, not of his flesh, not of his bone. "I rue the day I took you in."

"Annie?" Emmaline's voice interrupted her thoughts. She shook her head free of the memories crowding in and opened her mouth to ask something about David. But what came out instead was, "I was adopted." The surprise on their faces surely was mirrored on her own, though, of course, for different reasons.

"I didn't know that." Sarah set her cup down on its saucer and looked at Annie with curiosity in her eyes.

Well, she had to go on now. "Yup."

She looked down at her still-full teacup, staring into the liquid as if it were a pool of remembrance. "But it weren't into the kinda family that David's got here." She let the words tumble out of her mouth. "My adopted dad made it pretty clear from when I was young that I wasn't the same to him as his other kids, that I was different but in a bad way." The emotion lowered her voice. "He said that there was something bad about my real parents that made me do the bad things I did as a kid. If any of his kids did anything wrong, I mean, the kids from him and his wife, I usually got blamed for it because I was a bad seed – that's what he called me. He used to say that even if you put a bad seed in good ground, it could only grow more bad seeds."

Annie glanced up to see how Emmaline and Sarah had taken her words. Would they judge her, as he had, as the spawn of an immoral woman, as her father had always said? She could recall how, when he felt particularly strong about her misbehavior, he would sometimes even quote the Scripture, saying that an Ammonite should not enter the assembly of the Lord until the tenth generation had passed. And to him, she was that Ammonite.

Yet there was only grief in Emmaline's eyes, grief and... something else. Something Annie recognized but had not seen in anyone's eyes toward her since the woman she had thought of as her mother died years ago. *Love.* Love that Annie had not earned. But why would this woman love her, a stranger, and one from whom she couldn't profit in any way?

She drew yet another bucket of memories from deep within. "My adopted mama was not like Daddy. She... She loved me, maybe not the same as all her other kids... I don't know... She certainly never took my side against Daddy. But I think she cared about me still. She used to say that she loved me when she talked to me at night, when I was little."

She fought against the tears that were welling up at the remembrance.

"Then, a few years after Mama died, Daddy told me I got to go." A blush heated her cheeks.

"How cruel," Emmaline murmured. "He just told you to leave for no reason at all?"

She glanced down at her hands clasped around her teacup. "He...He caught me kissing a boy out in our toolshed." She looked up just in time to see Emmaline exchanging a glance with Sarah. "He told me that I must be just like... was just like my real mother." He didn't really say mother, but Annie felt awkward to use the phrase that Daddy had used when describing the woman who had borne her. "Said he wouldn't have no part of harlotry."

"And where did you go?" This came from Sarah.

Annie shrugged. "I had a cousin… Well he ain't my blood cousin. He's a cousin of Daddy's family. He said they could use me as a maid in Bousquet's house if I wanted to come on up. And so I did. There weren't nowhere else to go."

"And that's where you met Ben." This came from Sarah, who had sat quietly throughout the conversation.

Annie looked up, a little afraid of what she would see on the older woman's face, now that she had confessed her roughshod past.

But there was only thoughtful compassion there – the same compassion that still shone at Annie from Emmaline's face as well.

Sarah's hand came across the table hesitantly, and covered Annie's, still warm from clasping the cup of tea. "Well," she said, "I'm certainly glad that you have come to our family now. That you have become a part of our family now, dear Annie. You are a blessing from God to us, I'm sure of it."

Annie tried to return her smile but found she couldn't manage it. *If they only knew…*

Ben came for supper that night. He sat beside Annie by choice and offered her each dish as it was passed. Annie could never have said that he was romantic toward her at all, but there was a strength to his kindness toward her. He had not been unkind to her before – Well, except for those first couple of days when, no doubt, he had still been completely shocked by the turn of events that had upended the Picoletti-Giorgi world, but now… Now, living in the Giorgi household felt like a little piece of heaven. She had been afraid that, after she'd spilled the beans about her upbringing, the family would be harsh towards her. But they were not. In fact, even Sam, who always struck her as being a little suspicious of her, was much more openhearted.

They must think her a pathetic case of charity. A little of Annie's pride wrestled with that idea, but the family's benevolence was such that she soon surrendered to it wholly. In a small corner of her heart, she began to wonder: Could she truly have a life like this? Could this go on forever?

# Chapter Thirteen

Reverend Cloud had not been angry.

Instead as Ben had choked out the confession that he really was going to marry the pregnant girlfriend of his past, that he really was going to give up Betty in favor of Annie, Reverend Cloud looked at him calmly from across the desk. The only sign that Ben's words affected the man in any way came from the flickering of emotion in the man's eyes – the spark of compassion and, perhaps, of grief as well. But he did know that the man was not angry, and this was both a relief to Ben and a source of confusion.

"Do you think that I'm doing the wrong thing?" he asked, desperate to hear some word of advice. Desperate for the man to tell him that he was doing right.

But Reverend Cloud had shook his head. "Ben, I

ALICIA G. RUGGIERI

can't tell you what is right or what is wrong for *you* to do in this circumstance. You've mentioned to me the discussion you had with Sam about how the Scriptures mention both an admonition to beware of uniting with unbelievers… and yet also a responsibility to make right offenses others have against us, especially in such things as this."

Ben felt a little impatience rise within him. "Well," he said, "can't ya tell me what ya would do in my situation, at least?"

The pastor's face softened as he leaned forward to look Ben in the eyes. "You've been getting a lot of advice: from Sam, from your mother, from your own heart, I'd guess. But the only thing that I can tell you, Ben, is this: I would pray and I would seek to hear God's voice amid all the advice you've been getting. Listen to Him, rather than to the whisper of your feelings or thoughts, rather than to the logic of worldly common sense."

Frustration joined the impatience in Ben's chest. "But you yourself have said that God speaks sometimes through wise counsel. Isn't that what I'm after?"

"All the wise counsel in the world is not good enough as a substitute for hearing God's voice on something that burdens you, Ben. As I pray about this matter, I can't sense God telling me to say anything to you, any word of counsel other than what I have already said – that is, to seek to hear His voice. You may get something different from someone else. I don't know. I do know this – that God has not directed me to tell you anything specifically other than to seek Him. And I know through the Scriptures that if you seek Him, He will make your way plain. He will direct your path."

Ben picked a little dirt from underneath one of his thumbnails. "But… ain't ya upset, even just a little, about how all this affects Betty?"

"Of course, I'm saddened that this saddens her. But upset?" Reverend Cloud smiled. "No, Ben I'm not. God is not wringing His hands over this. He has his own purpose for Betty's life, and He will make her path plain just as He will make yours clear. I would've loved to have you as a son-in-law. You know that. But if God has something else for you both, who am I to argue with Him? God will take care of Betty. Don't worry about that."

A sense of relief came over Ben at the man's words, and he was suddenly glad that the man had not given him a fresh flood of advice as to what he should to. The lack of human guidance coming from him, the sense that Reverend Cloud had directed Ben towards God's guidance for him instead, refocused Ben and refreshed his soul. "I haven't been seeking God's guidance as much as I ought," he admitted. "I've been so worried about getting the situation settled… Well, I knew the situation couldn't keep going on forever like this, and it seems the smartest course of action. Then I saw Betty…" Uh-oh. He had not meant to say that. He clamped his lips shut as Reverend Cloud narrowed his eyes in question.

"What do you mean, you saw Betty?"

"Aw, nothing. It's just… I felt like I couldn't go on any longer with things unsettled. I knew she felt the same. And I wish her well… no matter what."

And Ben did wish her well, despite how his heart might be aching, despite when he thought of her sitting on that little stool next to a handsome, tidy man. His heart ached, yes but he also wanted the best for Betty. *And I sure ain't that.* "I want what's good for Betty, Pastor, and I know that I'm probably not what's good for her." When Reverend Cloud opened his mouth, Ben hastened to go on. "I mean, I know that I'm probably not the one God has for her." There. That would settle better in the man's ears, rather than Ben's earlier words that had rung with a slight sense of self-pity.

"And you've given your word to the young lady?"

"To Annie? Yeah." Deep within, Ben knew he should have prayed longer about it. Should've listened more. But what was done, was done.

Reverend Cloud stayed quiet for a long moment, looking down at his hands, folded across his desk. Then at last, he glanced up at Ben. "You and Annie will be in my prayers, Ben."

A lump formed in Ben's throat. He didn't deserve such kindness. "Thanks," he managed.

"Are we still meeting tomorrow?"

Ben looked up, stunned. "What... What do you mean?"

"Our Bible study together. I know you have a lot on your mind right now, but I'd like to continue it if that's all right with you. I think it's good for both of us. I know I've learned so much from it."

Now tears really did sting Ben's eyes. He blinked them away. This man, Betty's father, still wanted to continue their friendship together, a friendship so precious to Ben.

Weakened by the mercy he had been given, Ben nodded. "Yeah," he said, "I'll be here tomorrow."

"The usual time?"

"The usual time."

Betty twisted the tube of Tangee and applied just enough to her lips to enhance the color but not enough that she would look like a painted woman. Mother had reluctantly allowed her to start wearing the tinted lipstick last year, and Betty didn't want to make her mother regret her permission. Gently rubbing her lips together, she had begun to run her fingers through her curls, letting them mesh together naturally, when a knock came on her door. "Who is it?"

"Me, dear," came Mother's voice through the white-painted wood.

Betty closed her eyes and sighed. She had hoped that Mother would still be out visiting at this time, that she would fly in just before dinner and then be occupied with getting their meal on the table.

That she would be too busy to interfere in Betty's life again.

Interfere? When had Betty ever thought of Mother as someone who interfered?

Only when she had started to go against Betty's own plans. Only when she had started to object to the way that Betty reacted to the situation with Ben.

"Come in," Betty called back and put on her brightest smile as she swiveled on the chair before her petite vanity table so that she could face the door when Mother entered.

The door swung open. Mother peered around it and then inched forward into the room. "Are you going out tonight?" What was not spoken, but Betty still heard: *And you didn't tell me?*

"Uh, yes. I'm going out with Jim." She hoped that Mother would not object, would not voice her concern with Betty going.

Yet why should Mother object? After all, Jim was

from a good family, unlike… Betty pursed her lips. She didn't even want to think about… about *him* any longer. Not that she was miffed or anything. She had simply moved on.

But Mother didn't say anything more about Jim as she quietly entered Betty's room. Glancing in the vanity mirror, Betty could see that Mother was eyeing the blue-plaid wool dress lying on Betty's bed. Mother fingered it gently.

"Betty, your father told me about Ben's decision," Mother said at last.

"Oh." She made certain that her voice held exactly the amount of nonchalance she wished it to carry: one-hundred percent.

Mama approached from behind as Betty watched in the mirror. Mother laid her plump hands on Betty's shoulders, letting them rest there gently, though Betty felt as irritated by the gesture as though they restrained her. "Is that all you want to say about it?" Mother asked.

Betty shrugged. "What more is there to be said, Mother? Ben made his decision. Besides, I'm not sure if we really were well-suited to one another."

A slight hint of a frown came upon Mother's face. "Not well-suited? You could have fooled me, Betty. Why, certainly you're different, but the two of you get along like peanut-butter-and-jelly."

Betty stifled an urge to sigh aloud and stared into the mirror. The curl to the left of her face would not lie correctly. She took a smidgen of pomade, brushed it through her hands, and smoothed it onto the hair, hoping that would tame the waywardness. It didn't. "Well, Mother, life is a little more complicated than just making a sandwich. There are other things to consider you know.

Ben never really measured up to my ideal. You know that."

Now Mother really frowned. "Your ideal? I know Ben still had a lot of growing to do in his walk with the Lord, but your father said that he saw signs of maturity – tremendous growth in Ben. Personally, I would have advised you both to wait a while before marrying, but…"

"I'm not marrying Ben, Mother!" The words exploded out of Betty's mouth, harsh even to her own ears.

Mother looked at her, stunned at the outburst. "I know that."

"He's marrying Annie," Betty stated. "Not me." She couldn't help the crack in her armor, nor the tears that sprang to her eyes, despite how much she gritted her teeth against them.

Mother's arms came around her then. "Oh, my dear Betty. This is certainly a time for trust."

Trust? She *had* trusted. She had trusted Ben not to hurt her. But he had. She had trusted God to lead her in a straight path, but this was a crooked one. She should have gone with her gut instinct and not allowed herself to get carried away by her feelings and by notions of redemption. "I was a fool with Ben," she stated, "but I will be wiser with Jim, Mother."

Mother dropped a kiss to her head, but it did not melt the coldness from Betty's heart. "Betty, none of us could have known that this was going to happen, that a girl would show up out-of-the-blue like this. But God knew. And in His wisdom and in His love, He will work all things together for the good – for your good, for Ben's good. And even for Annie's good." Mother was quiet for just a moment. "Maybe… just maybe, this circumstance will be what leads Annie to know Christ. And wouldn't that make it all worthwhile?"

Betty nodded as she knew that she was supposed to, but inside, she shook her head violently. *No. No. No!* Losing Ben, being hurt like this, everything inside of her said that it was *not* worth Annie's salvation to her, even though Betty knew that it should be. If this was the way that God worked when she submitted to His will, as she had done when she decided to go out with Ben against the calculated judgment of her brain, well, then Betty would try to get along on her own for a while. Who knew if she really had ever heard Him right in the first place?

She stood up. "I've got to get dressed," she said. "Jim will be here any minute."

He was treating her with more kindness than she had thought possible from Ben. Really, from any man. He'd even sat down beside her at the table tonight, rather than across from her.

"Would you like more potatoes?"

Annie realized with a jolt that Ben was addressing her, not in a cool, detached tone, but with kindness in his voice.

"Yes, I'll have some." She reached for the platter. He was just handing it to her when she gasped. A sharp pain drove up her abdomen, and Ben had to rescue the platter to keep the potatoes from tumbling to the tabletop.

Annie knew that she must look wild, but she could not keep from gripping the edge of the table with white-knuckled hands. The pain drove straight into her lungs.

Sarah and Ben both rose to their feet with a swiftness

that nearly upended their chairs. Annie looked at them wide-eyed, and she felt Sarah's hands on her shoulders. "What is it? What's wrong?" came Sarah's question, but panic numbed Annie's tongue.

Was she going into labor? It was too soon, far too soon, sooner than anyone but herself recognized. Annie clutched at her stomach and stared up at Ben, who actually looked genuinely concerned. The sight of his face – caring, kind – at that moment almost took Annie's mind off of the pain.

Almost.

He voiced aloud Annie's own thoughts. "Is she gonna have the baby now, Mama?"

From behind her she heard Sarah say, "I don't know, Ben. Are you in pain, Annie?"

Why did people ask dumb questions like that? Still, Sarah meant well, and Annie managed to nod.

"I wish Sam were here," Ben mumbled.

"He's working late at the hospital tonight," Sarah replied. "Besides, this is probably nothing to worry about. A lot of women have false labor pains in their last weeks."

The pain lessened. Annie began to take deeper breaths.

"Come on," Ben urged. "We should get ya to the hospital."

Terror raced afresh through Annie's body. If they brought her to the hospital, would they know? Would they find out the truth? She could not afford to let that happen. Thus far, she had swatted away all attempts to get her to see a doctor in Chetham. She forced a smile onto her face, as if the pain had left. "No, I don't wanna do that. I... I think I must've ate too much supper," she lied. She pushed out a hopefully realistic-sounding laugh. "Guess I won't be having more potatoes after all."

Sarah looked unsure though not overly-concerned. But Ben's mouth was set in a straight line of worry. Something inside Annie softened at the look of concern on Ben's face. Was he anxious for the welfare of his child? Or for her welfare? Ben had never expressed any kind of concern about her while they had been a couple. It had always all been about his own desires, his own needs, just as Annie's had been. But now...

She decided to take a cue from Sarah's suggestion. "Might be false labor pains. I... I been getting them on-and-off for a month. I saw a doctor about them," she continued to lie, anxious to get the notion of her traveling to the hospital off the table. "He said that there wasn't nothin' to worry about."

The concern on Sarah's face dissolved, and Annie looked over at Ben and saw him shrug his shoulders, face relaxing. "Well, if you've been having them off-and-on, and the doctor said there wasn't anything to worry about..."

Annie nodded vigorously. "Yeah, that's what he said."

"And you're feeling better now? The pain is gone?" Sarah slowly removed her hands from Annie's shoulders and began to return to her own seat.

Annie nodded. Though the pain had not completely abated, it *had* gone down a little bit.

"I still think that we should ask Sam about it when he gets home." This came from Ben, who had picked up his fork again and was twirling it in his potatoes restlessly. "And get ya in to see a doctor here in Chetham as soon as possible."

Why did he care? Her coming had only troubled his

life. Unless he really had begun to care for her... A small blade of hope sprang up in the dark soil of Annie's heart.

His eyes caught hers, and there was something in them that she could not understand: a new honesty perhaps.

It made her feel ashamed.

"Mama, I'm gonna stay here tonight."

Mama looked up from folding laundry, the surprise evident on her face. And no wonder. Ben had not stayed overnight for months, ever since he had gotten the old Picoletti house livable again. "Why?" Mama asked, never one to beat around the bush.

He hesitated. How could he explain it, this new feeling of anxiety about Annie? This sense of caring and desire for no ill to fall upon her or upon their child? "For Annie's sake," he replied at last. "I wanna be here just in case... I know that she said that everything was okay with the doctor and all that but..." He trailed off and picked up a pair of Cliff's socks, tucking them into a ball, just for something to keep his hands busy.

"Sam should be home soon," replied Mama. "If anything happens, we can telephone you." Ben had installed a line in his own house this past fall.

Ben picked up another pair of socks. "Yeah, but sometimes Sam gets held up at the hospital. If anything were to happen, I wanna be here."

"All right, son," Mama replied as she placed another folded T-shirt on top of the pile of laundry. She didn't meet Ben's eyes – that was Mama – but Ben heard her say in her quiet, low voice, "I'm real proud of you, Ben."

A wave of embarrassment, rich and warm spread through Ben's body. "Proud of me? Why should ya be proud of me, Mama? I would think that, this past week alone, I've given ya enough to be ashamed of to make ya hang your head forever. It sure does make me wanna hang my head forever," he added.

"It's what you are doing now that I'm proud of, Ben. The way that you are taking responsibility for this. Sometimes people feel that since God's grace covers all of their sin, they don't need to make any reparation for the harm that they may have done to others in the past. Some folks think that once it's forgiven by God, they can forget all about it. And I guess that's true in the sense that, yes, they are forgiven. Their sin will never be held against them. But a really repentant heart – I think that kind of heart'll want to make reparations if it can."

A lump rose in Ben's throat at Mama's words. "I didn't wanna at first, Mama" he said softly. "Ya know that. I was scared, scared to face the past, scared of what it might do to my present."

"You were afraid of losing Betty," Mama stated.

"Yeah." He blinked hard. "And I did lose her." The words could barely make it past the boulder wedged in his throat. *I lost Betty.* Even now, he could hardly believe it.

"You didn't lose her. You gave her up. There's a difference." There was a long silence, and Ben heard the *swish-swish* of Mama's skin as she folded the socks, her palms passing each other. "Nobody who gives up houses or lands, or wives or children, or anything for the kingdom of heaven's sake will not be repaid in this life and in the life hereafter." Mama glanced up at him. "And that's the truth, son."

Annie heard the drain slurp the last of the water from the bathtub behind her. How wonderful it felt to be able to have a long soak in a hot tub of water. And bubbles! Sarah had told her that she was welcome to use anything at all in the bathroom cupboard, and so Annie had taken full advantage of that on this, her third soak since she had come to live (however temporarily) in the Giorgi home.

She looked in the oval mirror above the bathroom sink and frowned at her face. The past few days had put a couple of pounds on her, it seemed, though she had always been too skinny, anyway. Taking down her pigtail, she fluffed her hair, then unlocked the bathroom door.

She stepped out into the hall and made her way down the corridor towards her room. As she turned the corner that would bring her right to her door, she saw that Ben stood in front of it, his hand raised as if about to knock.

Why did her heart leap into her throat at the sight of him? She couldn't be falling in love with him.

Could she?

*You're a fool if ya are, Annie.* She would just end up having to do what she planned, anyway, she reminded herself. Better to rid herself of silly notions like love. Love always brings a risk. Her mama's face flashed before her eyes – Mama, the one person that she had truly loved in all the world, loved without reservation, had died. There were many days when Annie wished that she had never known such love – only to lose it.

"Ben?"

At her voice, Ben turned with a start.

"I was just coming to see if you were okay," Ben said after a moment. He shifted uncomfortably, pushed his hands into his pockets, looked down at the carpeted hallway, and finally allowed his eyes to meet hers again.

Annie shoved away the sharp desire to be held, to be nestled safe and close in this man's arms. "Yeah, I'm okay," she said, unable to maintain eye-contact with him. There was such kindness in his eyes – kindness that she had never seen there before. It attracted her... and it frightened her. Who was this Ben Picoletti? He was so different from the man that she'd known last year. It was as if that Ben had died, and a new one had been born and become a full-grown man in less than the space of twelve months.

"I just took a bath," Annie said to fill the long shadow of silence that stretched between them.

She glanced up in time to see Ben nod toward her robe, a smile making its way onto his face. "I figured that." He shifted again, his hands moving in and out of his pants-pockets. "Look, Annie, I'm stayin' over here tonight. Just in case... something happens, ya know. I wouldn't want ya to be alone. I would wanna be here."

Annie's heart softened at his words. He was being so kind to her when she was all but using him for her own ends. *But he doesn't know I'm using him,* she reminded herself. *He used me, too, all those months before he cheated on me.* Though in the back of her mind, she had begun to hear her conscience whisper, *And didn't ya use him as well?* Aloud, she said, "Ya don't gotta stay, Ben. I'm sure it'll be fine. I don't got no more pain."

And it was true. The pain had completely subsided while she had been in the bath.

"Well, I'm stayin' anyway," replied Ben. "I'll be

downstairs on the couch if ya need me. Ya know I'm not a light sleeper, so don't be afraid to give a good yell to wake me up."

He started to turn away from her then, and Annie could not resist letting her hand reach out and grasp his forearm. It was the first time that she had touched him on purpose since her arrival, and he turned to her with surprise, looking down first at her hand on his arm and then up to her face.

"Why are ya bein' so kind to me, Ben?" She asked it bluntly; she needed to know. Was there a trick up his sleeve? "I know ya ain't happy about the fact that I turned up here."

He was silent for a long moment, and Annie defied her panting fear of what he would say to her. Why should she be afraid? Harsh things had often come out of his mouth when they had been together, and harsh things had come out of hers as well.

"We love because He first loved us." His response to Annie's question didn't make much sense. It sounded as if Ben was quoting, like he always had with the poetry she remembered him reading on occasion in the past.

"What's that supposed to mean?" She let her old sassiness pop out of her mouth.

Ben looked at her for a long moment, so long that Annie began to feel uncomfortable. But then he spoke. "It's like I told ya before, Annie. Everything that's happened to me since I come back to Chetham – It's like – It's like I've been reborn. That's what the Bible calls it – being born-again. I'm a new man. I ain't – I'm not the same Ben that dated ya."

Annie looked at him skeptically. "Whadaya mean?" Sounded like Ben was talking crazy. "Course you're the same man. Unless you're a ghost."

Ben smiled at her, and Annie noticed a kind of joy in that smile that made her own heart tense with craving. "No, I ain't no ghost, Annie. But the old Ben did die, and Christ came in and took me over. It's the new Ben ya see, the Ben that Jesus has created anew."

"Sounds like you're talking gibberish again," Annie replied. Something inside her pushed against understanding at the same time that something else within her lunged toward it. The tension made her more uncomfortable, and she let the irritation show in her tone. "I don't understand a word of what you're saying. Didja decide to become a better person or somethin'?"

Ben shook his head. "Nope. I couldn't become a better person on my own, that's for sure. Ya know that better'n anyone." He paused for a minute, his eyes on the floor, then he lifted his gaze to meet hers again. "Look, Annie, are ya tired?"

Well, that came out of nowhere. *Guess he's trying to get rid of me and my pesky questions.* With spite, she lifted her chin. "No, I ain't tired, Ben Picoletti," she snapped back.

He looked surprised at the way she answered, as if she had completely misunderstood him. "Well," he said, "if ya ain't tired, do ya wanna come downstairs and have a cup of coffee or something, and I'll tell ya the whole story of how everything changed in my life these past few months?"

"I don't really like coffee, Ben," she reminded him. What else had he forgotten about her? Or never cared to remember in the first place? "And ya already tol' me all about all this."

"Okay, how about a glass of warm milk?" he asked. "And I know I told ya before. But I figger some things are worth hearin' more'n once."

She found herself nodding, drawn and not wanting to resist. And for the first time since she had come to the Giorgi house, Ben reached out to her with his hand. She hesitated for just a moment before grasping it in her own. It felt warm. Secure. She clung to it like a small child as he led her down the lamplit hallway toward the staircase.

Many hours after he should have been asleep, Ben stared up at the living room ceiling. As his head rested against the sofa pillow, he replayed the evening's conversation in his mind, praying, thinking, waiting for insight. He prayed for clarity. He prayed to understand what God was doing, what God would do in his life, in Annie's life.

When he could stand the tumble of his thoughts no longer, Ben threw back the blankets and knelt to pray beside the sofa. The room became a sanctuary that night as he poured out his heart to God, sometimes with words that could be spoken, sometimes only with tears.

Had he been too hasty in giving up the dream of Betty to accept the reality of Annie? He knew he should be thinking more about Annie's salvation than about any time-bound happiness for himself. Yet memories of Betty continually flickered in his mind – remembrance of how her small hand fit in his, the way their voices blended in song, the purity of her heart, the way she always dressed so neatly, so prettily, like a picture in a magazine…

He remembered, too, the way that Annie had clung to him this night like a small child, as he led her down the staircase. He'd only meant to guide her. She had sat here at this couch that had now become his altar, just across from him, a mug of steaming milk clutched in her white hands. Every so often she'd taken a sip, but her expression had not changed much throughout the whole telling of the story. The big green eyes had stared over the rim of the cup. She looked so alone, so lost, even if she didn't realize it…

If it wasn't for Betty… He remembered how he had been attracted to Annie once, how her feistiness and rebelliousness had called out to him.

*Father!* Ben's heart cried out, and he buried his face into the cushion. *Is this how it is meant to be? Is this how my life is meant to go? I feel so confused, so torn in two. I've got a tenderness in my heart toward Annie, and I long to correct the wrongs of the past, but the love that is in my heart for Betty's real, too, and I want a future, a fresh start with her.* He sucked in a breath and smelled the clean, slightly dusty fabric of the couch. *Father, ya know the longings of my heart better even than I do. Help Annie to see Your salvation. Help me to…* His mouth stayed open for a moment as his heart tried to form the words.

*Help.*

## Chapter
## Fourteen

"Ben says he was born two times." Annie's remark broke the silence that had settled between her and Sarah. The two of them were in the kitchen; Sarah had invited Annie to help her roll out sugar cookie dough and to make some cutouts in preparation for Grace's arrival this coming Friday. Grace would be home for the holidays and her semester break; she wouldn't need to return to the Conservatory until two weeks after New Year's Day.

Now at Annie's words, Sarah's heart skipped. "Yes, that's right," Sarah replied with a smile.

Silence lingered for a moment, and then Sarah ventured again, "Did he explain what that meant?"

Annie looked uncomfortable, and her hands mushed into the dough more forcefully than necessary. "Yeah, he did."

Sarah studied her out of the corner of her eye. She couldn't help the hope that rose within her. Why would the girl bring this up unless she had a desire to understand more, to know this God who had delivered so many from Sarah's family from living a life of bondage to sin and fear and death, and had brought them into His unable-to-be-extinguished light? She fought to keep her voice steady and nonchalant as she asked, "And what did you think of it? Did you understand what he said?" She literally bit her tongue to stop herself from saying any more, from mumbling on as was her tendency when she got nervous or excited.

Annie's face raveled into a grimace. "Yeah, I understood it. The words at least, I guess. He was speakin' English. But… I dunno, it just all seems so far-fetched to me. Why would a God who had everything Himself, who didn't need us at all, why would He give up His only Son to save people who are of no account? Who didn't do nothin' to earn His forgiveness, who didn't earn His mercy? Why should He care about them? What does He get out of it?"

Sarah's heart swelled as she thought about the redemption that God had given in His Son, a perfect gift so often rejected. How to explain it to this one, this girl who had perhaps never known selfless love? How to make her understand? She could try, Sarah knew, but she also knew that it might not be just with words that Annie came to understand the love of God but with actions as well. "He did it because He loves us." The words were so simple, yet brimful of meaning: *He loves us.* "He loves you, Annie. He made you, and His love for you comes through that Cross that Jesus died on. He gave up his best because He loves you."

Annie stared at her, expression blank for a long moment, then she shook her head. "It just don't make no sense," Sarah heard her mumble.

"What doesn't make sense?" Sarah asked, hoping that she was not pushing too hard, yet also wanting to push hard enough.

Annie raised her eyes to look at Sarah. "Why should God love me?" And Sarah heard in the question once again the words Annie had spoken before: *What's in it for Him?*

There was no answer to this but the simplest one. *Lord, make her understand.* "God is love, Annie. That's who He is, so He acts in a way that makes sense with who He is."

Annie stared at her for a moment, then went back to rolling out the dough. In her nervousness Sarah broke off a piece of raw dough, popping it into her mouth to give her tongue and teeth something to do so that she wouldn't be tempted to rattle on.

"Well, I'll say one thing."

Sarah darted a glance at Annie. "What's that?"

"Ben's a whole different person here than the Ben that I knowed at Bousquet's."

Sarah felt a smile stretch up her lips. "I sure hope so, Annie. I sure hope so."

Annie squeezed the receiver tightly against her ear and lowered her voice to a whisper. "I told ya, I would call ya when I got the chance, Aldo." She ran the fingers of her free hand through her hair, tucking it behind her ear.

"Don'tcha pretend to be my brother when ya call next time, either. What if I'd told 'em my brother's name? My *real* brother's name, I mean."

Aldo just laughed. "Ya don't got no real brother, kid. They all threw ya over the side of the boat."

She clenched her teeth. She had nothing to answer him with, no sharp retort. The lump rose and grew in her throat. *Because he's right,* she thought. *I don't got nobody.*

"I'm the only person ya got left. Remember that next time ya decide not to give me a ring like ya told me ya would." A threat tinged Aldo's voice, but the only thing that went through Annie's mind was: *I've still got Ben and Sarah.* And Paulie. And Dr. Giorgi, even if he was a little aloof and still acted suspicious toward her.

Her silence spurred Aldo on. "Look, kid. I know how people like that act. They either give ya the boot from the get-go, or they put on an act and get ya to trust them. Then they really give it to ya. So don't fall for it. Okay?"

She was quiet. For the first time in a while, the lie he wanted to hear stuck in her throat.

"Okay?" The threat in his voice cut into her clearly.

She swallowed down the clot. "Okay."

"Good, glad to hear ya still got brains in your skull. Now, I've been thinking. At first, I thought it was better if ya stayed until after ya had the kid, but now I've been turning it over in my mind, and the place you're staying at – that's the rich place, right?"

Annie nodded but then realized he couldn't hear that, so she forced herself to answer aloud. "Yeah. It's Ben's stepfather's house. I'm staying here until after we get married."

"Oh, good. Keepin' things nice and proper." He snorted. "And is there any word on when the wedding's gonna be?"

Annie glanced around the foyer and darted a look up the stairs, but no one appeared to be coming. "No, we haven't got a date yet."

For some reason her words tickled Aldo's funny bone. He laughed. "Ya haven't *got a date yet?* Just listen to ya, talkin' all fancy, as if everythin' was right and proper, as if ya were the beloved bride. Not the one wreckin' Ben Picoletti's life and stealin' all his dough!"

Annie swallowed again, desperate to get rid of the lump that kept rising. "Not all his dough."

There was a long pause. "What're ya getting at, Annie?" Aldo growled.

She forced herself to answer. She had to, now. "I... I just feel kind of bad, ya know, Aldo? I mean, it's not the guy's fault, after all. Ben – well, he turned out kinda nice." What was she saying?

Aldo's voice jerked with a laugh. "Turned out kinda nice, did he? What, has he gotcha fooled again, Annie-girl?" His tone turned serious. "Listen to me. He's just wrappin' ya around his finger. Him and his hoity-toity new family. They wantcha to trust them so they can get outta ya whatever it is they want."

"What in the world would they want from me, Aldo?" She had nothing, nothing whatsoever that any of the Giorgis or Picolettis could ever want. She looked down at her stomach. *Except... I think that Sarah kind of wants this baby.* She didn't know yet about Ben. It still seemed that he was just accepting his responsibility for creating the new life.

"What have ya got that they want? You've got the key to their happiness. If you walk out right now, no dough squirreled away in your pockets, well, then their lives go back to their happy normal. They want to get ya on their side, Annie. They want ya to believe them – that they mean everything they do for your good, when they really don't. Rich people always got something up their sleeve. Mark my words, they've got some way in mind to get rid of ya before they lose this game."

Aldo blew out a big breath. "I remember Ben Picoletti all too well. He always had some new trick to play."

Annie didn't say it aloud, but she thought it all the same: *And so did ya, Aldo. Ya always have had another trick up your sleeve.*

"Anyway, when I didn't hear from ya for too long, I figured I'd better see what was up. See if ya had any tricks up your own sleeve. Any I didn't know about, if ya catch my drift."

She swallowed back the fear that noosed her neck. "No," she forced the word out of her strangled throat. "No tricks, Aldo."

"So we're going right along with my plan?"

In her moment of hesitation, Annie thought that she could feel his silent threat breathe over the line. She hurried to answer. "Yeah, just like ya planned."

They hung up quickly after that, as Annie thought that she heard a car pulling up the driveway: Sarah coming home from running her errands. Annie had pleaded off this morning from accompanying her, saying that she still felt kind of tired. She realized that she was so used to lying at this point that the lie barely stung as it passed over her lips.

She hurried up the stairs to her guest room and sat down on the bed. Below her, she heard the front door open and close and she thought that Sarah might be asking the maid a question. Probably about her, whether she'd been downstairs or not. Annie jumped up from the bed and ruffled it a little bit again to make it look like she had been lying down for a nap. Then she went over to the little vanity mirror and mussed her hair so that it would look like she had risen from slumber. She suddenly looked at her reflection in that mirror, the big eyes staring out of the freckled white face. *What if I was to stay? What if I never left? What if I stayed here as Ben's wife – for keeps?*

Stay as his wife? Her own eyes opened wide at the thought. It seemed unbelievable – for her to be considering something she would've so thoroughly rejected just weeks ago! But the Ben she had known then was a very different Ben from the one to whom she was now… engaged.

But was it fair to Ben? She frowned at the question and raised her chin. Why wouldn't it be fair to him? She could tell that he wanted a wife and children – a family of his own. And she'd be a good wife to him, couldn't she, if she tried hard enough?

With a shake of her entire body, Annie glared at her reflection. What was she thinking? How could she even consider this? But then another part of her thought, *What do ya mean, Annie, how can ya consider this?* Why was going through with it, marrying him and then staying with him, worse than marrying him and running off, leaving him with the baby and the only option of divorcing her for desertion? Running off with his money to who-knew-where Aldo would direct?

She clenched her teeth, ran her tongue over them. There was no easy way out of this for anyone. *What did I get myself into?* Any way that she cut the cake now, someone would get hurt: herself, Ben and his family, and… She looked down at her protruding stomach, thinking of the baby she had grown to love, despite all the trouble its existence had caused…

The trouble that *it* had caused? Guilt settled heavily over her shoulders and she heard her father saying the wages of sin is death. Well, she was reaping what she'd sown, wasn't she? It had nothing to do with this innocent little baby.

Looking in the mirror, she set her jaw. She'd done wrong, that's for sure, in a lot of ways. But this little life inside of her had not – this little person had done nothing wrong. *I won't let anyone hurt ya,* she mouthed the words silently. Could the baby within her hear the thoughts of her heart?

And then and there, she made up her mind for good.

She would make the best choice for her baby, not necessarily the best choice for Ben, surely not the best choice for Aldo. And herself? Well, she would have to live with her decision. With her guilt.

*It'll be my punishment.*

Betty looked down at the paper in her hands, sighed, and picked up a pen. Holding the paper against the wall, she scratched off yet one more of the shepherds. *Good thing that the Bible doesn't specify how many there were.* How many more children could possibly get sick before the performance or find some other activity to which they realized they'd already committed?

"At this rate, I'm going to have to fill in for one of the shepherds myself," she said aloud, leaning back in her desk chair. She actually wouldn't mind doing that, though she hated to admit it to herself – It seemed a little beneath her dignity – but she was already playing the piano and in charge of telling the children when their time to go onto the platform was. Could she really don a shepherd's headdress, pick up a crook, and join them on stage as well?

*At least it would distract me from thinking about Ben and… and… that girl.* No matter how many times she tried, Betty couldn't erase the memory of coming face-to-face with… with *her* in the drugstore. Nor could she erase the pain each fresh remembrance brought. Thinking of that girl – really, any girl – replacing her in Ben's heart brought the pain of an internal papercut to Betty's chest – invisible (she hoped) to all around her, but nevertheless real as any wound.

She shook her head again. "Really, Betty," she scolded herself aloud in a murmur, forcing her eyes to run down the cast list once more. She – Betty Cloud – mourning the loss of run-around Ben Picoletti? Was it even possible?

Yet she knew that it was. She knew it as surely as she knew that she was using Jim to bandage, and to attempt to heal, her wounded spirit, thus far in vain. She knew it as surely as she knew – though she was unable to admit it – that she felt betrayed – not just by Ben – but by God for her loss. Deep inside, she pushed down the protest that she couldn't and didn't want to dislodge: *You had no right, Lord; no right to do this to me, to ruin my plans.*

"Grace is coming on the train this afternoon?" Ben

drained the last of his coffee and set the brown mug down with a clunk.

Across from him, Paulie eyed the dessert menu and grinned. "Yeah, on the four o'clock, before the church play starts. I'm picking her up, you know."

Ben quirked his eyebrow and smiled. "Well, I figured that, pal."

Paulie just laughed and called the waitress over. After he ordered a piece of cold grape-nut pudding, extra whipped cream, Sally turned to Ben. "You want anything?"

Ben shook his head. "Naw, thanks." With everything on his mind lately, sweets were the last thing he cared about. In fact, he'd wolfed down his meatloaf, green beans, and mashed potatoes with barely a thought to their taste, though he knew they were good.

With only a nod, she turned away, not even offering him a refill of his coffee. Ben tried to not let her coolness bother him. Some folks in town still held Ben a little low in their esteem, and no wonder: He'd been a liar, a playboy, a gambler, and the son of the same kind of man. Who knew what ran through Sally's mind every time she saw him?

*But you were washed…*

The verse trickled into his mind, and he forced himself to accept it, to let it sink in once more.

*Washed by the blood of Jesus. No merit of my own. 'Tis mine but to receive…*

The waitress brought Paulie's dessert. As she put down the plate, Ben's eyes caught on Sally's ring – a plain gold band. His mind went to the ring he'd kept, unable to give it to Annie when he'd meant it for Betty, yet also unable to return it to the jeweler's. It wasn't that he held out hope that he would ever be able to give it to Betty; but he'd attached the love he'd had for Betty to it. He couldn't think of another woman wearing it.

*Had?*

Who was he kidding? As if his love for Betty had died with the arrival of Annie!

He gritted his teeth. *God, help me. I can't go through life like this – committed to one woman, yet keeping feelings for another.* "Have you and Grace set a date yet?" he asked, more to distract himself from his own thoughts than in a true quest for information.

Paulie swallowed the bite in his mouth and smiled. "This is really good," he said, pointing to the remainder of his pudding with his whipped-cream-smeared fork. "You sure you don't want a piece?"

"I'm sure."

Paulie shook his head, as if he couldn't comprehend Ben's lack of desire for grape-nut pudding, but then answered Ben's question. "No date yet. Grace has two-and-a-half years still to go at school, and I've got even more, so..." He shrugged. "Have to say, I'm looking forward to going back to Brown for spring semester."

"Ya ever thought about movin' out to New York? Getting married before ya finish school and moving out there to be with Grace? You could go to school out there – transfer, or whatever it's called."

Surprise bloomed on Paulie's face. "Huh? Why would I do that? Chetham's home for me."

Ben nodded. "Yeah, I guess."

Paulie was quiet for a moment as he forked his last bites of pudding into his mouth. "Why would you ask me that?"

Ben felt so tired of keeping everything tucked away inside, like too many clothes stuffed into a dresser drawer. "I didn't mean anything by it. Sometimes, though, I wonder if I'd be better off moving away myself, I guess. With Annie, I mean. After the baby..." He couldn't continue. The circumstance was still so embarrassing to him, despite the weeks that had passed since her coming, despite the head-knowledge that he had been forgiven for his sins – all of them – despite even the fact that he had engaged himself to Annie, had done the right thing for her, for the baby to come.

"You'd move away from Chetham?" Paulie stared at Ben, the empty fork still held in his hand. "Why? You've got your house here... your family. You're doing good with getting work; I can tell that by how you've been begging me to help you out here-and-there, even though we both know that I'm not too great with a hammer. Why would you go away? You've never mentioned this before."

Ben picked up the napkin that lay crumpled beside his plate. He fingered its edge, trying to figure out how to explain all this to Paulie – one who had known so few repercussions in life as a result of his own little sins. He had to try. "I...I'm committed to Annie and to ... this baby." He stopped, unable to go on, unsure if Paulie would condemn him for being so weak.

"I know that." Paulie stared at him. "So...?"

Ben glanced at the waitress, who hovered a few feet from their booth, very busy with arranging the salt-and-pepper shakers on the next table over. "She probably wants us out of this booth so she can wipe down the table."

Paulie glanced over his shoulder. "Sally, we'll take our checks, please."

A smile brought relief to the older woman's face, and she hurried over with her notepad. After she'd placed the two checks on the table, both men dug into their pockets.

Ben's meal had come to twenty-nine cents, Paulie's to forty-three, due to his dessert.

Ben saw that Paulie added an extra dime to his total for the tip – generous of him, especially since crusty old Sally was trying to push them out. He thought for a second and then added a nickel to his own total.

"That's all set. We'll be sitting here for a few minutes longer, just so you know," Paulie informed her, his pleasant manner softening the unspoken demand that she leave them be.

With a nod, she picked up their payments. "All right, boys."

Paulie returned his focus to Ben once the waitress had left their area of the diner. "So you were saying that you're committed to Annie and the baby, but what?" he asked in a low voice, which Ben appreciated.

Ben tightened his jaw, trying to figure out how to say this. "I just don't know how I can stand by and watch it all, you know?"

Paulie shook his head. "Watch what, exactly?"

Ben sucked in a breath. He wished he didn't have to spell it all out, but... "As the years go by, I'll be watchin' as Betty dates and marries – maybe this new fellow in town, Jim. I keep seein' her with him. She'll have her own children, build a new life for herself... A life without any place for me in it."

Paulie's eyebrows came together in sympathy. "But you'll have your own life, too, Ben. With Annie."

A hollow spot opened up inside Ben at those words. He swallowed hard. "There's that, too, though, Paulie. How's it fair to Annie for us to stay here in Chetham?"

"What do you mean?" Paulie squinted, as if confused. "How would staying be unfair to her?"

Ben closed his eyes for a moment, trying to piece together all of his swirling, broken thoughts in a way that would be at least intelligible. Finally he just said it plainly: "How would *you* like to be married to Grace, knowing she'd once loved another man, a man who lived in the same town as you?"

Paulie's eyes darkened. "Even the thought of Grace loving another man shreds me inside, Ben." He shook his head. "Last year, when I found out that man at the conservatory was asking Dad for his permission to ask Grace to marry him... I nearly lost it."

Ben nodded in agreement. He couldn't do that to a woman to whom he'd sworn to be faithful, in heart as well as mind, in thought as well as body: He couldn't tempt himself to sin, nor could he tease Annie toward rightful jealousy. Betty, though... It probably wouldn't matter one iota to Betty.

Even so.

He leaned forward, his gaze meeting Paulie's. "So you understand why I'm sayin' that maybe it's for the best if Annie and I go someplace else?"

Distress rippled across Paulie's face, even as he slowly nodded. "In a way, yeah, I guess that I do. But what about everyone else, Ben? What about your mother? This is her grandchild Annie's having. And Cliff. He looks up to you so much. I hate to think about what your leaving will do to him. I sure can't take your place there." He paused and then went on, picking his way through words as if across a rocky beach. "Don't you think that, as time goes on, you'll learn to care for Annie and, well...?" He trailed off.

Ben heard what was left unspoken: *And forget your love for Betty?* Even the thought sliced his heart, left it bleeding and raw.

Yet he also knew that Paulie was saying only what needed to be said. And some small part of him hoped that there was truth in it.

For if God was not merciful, if his love for Betty did not slowly fade from his heart in the presence of Annie, how could he go on in his life? God's taking away Betty's love from his heart, in that case, would be a mercy, though he might not see it now.

Even so, a move away from Chetham might be for the best for everyone.

# Chapter Fifteen

Ben's little brother, Cliff, had begun to eye her with just a smidgen less suspicion, Annie thought. For that matter, even Sam seemed to have warmed up a little to her once Ben had made up his mind.

*He can never know the truth. None of them can ever know.* She swallowed down the guilt that rose in her throat. Guilt? No, it must just be indigestion; yeah, that was it. A lot of pregnant women got indigestion. Though she couldn't say that she'd been eating much to cause it. Ever since she had decided to go against Aldo – Yes, she really finally had – she had been unable to eat. *What'll he do when he finds out?*

He really couldn't do anything, could he? It wasn't *his* child, after all, nor did Annie belong to him! He was only incidentally involved as her cousin – well, sort of cousin:

cousin of the adoptive family that had disowned her. Aldo wasn't truly involved at all! He should have no say in any of this. She raised her chin and stared at herself in the mirror. She really should eat up, because, for the length of pregnancy she was supposed to be, her belly didn't look very large. She bit her lip as she looked down at the new dress that Ben had given her.

That Ben had given her...

In all their months of dating, Annie couldn't remember him ever giving her a gift just because he wanted to. Oh, of course he had given her the obligatory gifts: when she was mad at him, he'd given her a cheap bottle of perfume to try to soothe her; or, when she'd hinted so strongly that it was her birthday that a blind owl couldn't miss it in broad daylight, he'd found some trinket at the five-and-dime and handed it to her, hastily wrapped by a store employee. Gifts like that he had given.

But a gift that came with no strings attached? A gift for which she'd given no hint? A gift that seemed to come from... could she dare hope... his heart?

That kind of a gift she had never received from Ben.

Until now.

Last night, he had found her, brushing her fingers over the spines of the books on the shelves. She'd been wondering how many the Giorgis had really read. Were they just here for show? Or were they beloved volumes, the stories dear to the reader's heart? She guessed the latter, unbelievable though that might be, for the spines were cracked a little in places, and when she'd slid out one of the books, she'd found a few pages that had been dogeared or upon which notations had been made in pencil.

Tentatively her fingers had found one volume with

worn edges that looked like it may have been read more often than some of the others around it. The title on the spine read, *The Way to God* by D.L Moody. What did that mean? Was there a way to Him, truly? Had Ben found it? Sarah had told her that she might take out any volume from the library that she wanted to.

And then Ben had cleared his throat behind her. She'd whirled around, hiding the book under her arm, though she didn't know why. She'd been given permission, so why did she feel guilty? But she hid it nonetheless. Her eyes came to meet Ben's.

If she could call this man Ben. She knew that was still his name, but, oh, how changed he had become. This new softness to his face, a softness Annie had never seen there before, as he looked down at her. What had happened? He and Sarah had said that he had been born-again. Despite their explanation, though, Annie just could not understand what they meant. And a man like Ben didn't just become a better person. Annie knew Ben. He wasn't the type to change so thoroughly, so deeply, not on his own. No, something – someone – had changed him.

He stood before her, a little awkwardness playing on his face.

"Hi," Annie said, to break the silence.

"Hi," Ben answered, smiling, and Annie noticed that he carried a shopping bag in his hand, the kind a fancy department store gave.

"What's that?" Annie had asked, never one to beat around the bush.

"Oh." Ben glanced down at the bag and then lifted it up. "I… I got you something."

"What is it?" Annie couldn't keep the surprise out of her voice.

Ben took a couple of steps forward and held out the bag to her. He kept his expression vague, carefully guarded. "Look and see."

She stepped forward across the carpet and took the bag from his hands, her fingers brushing his. With one more glance up at his face, Annie pushed aside the tissue paper that veiled the contents of the bag and dug her hand down deep to pull out a mass of material. *A dress. For me.*

She let the bag fall to the floor with a quiet thud as she stretched out the garment before her eyes. She had never owned something so beautiful. It was the darkest burgundy velvet – perfect for Christmas-time. The design was very simple, without the fussiness Annie despised. A few pearl buttons danced down the front, coming to rest just above an empire waist. A maternity dress. She could hardly believe it.

She looked up at him, nearly speechless. But not quite. "How didja…? How could ya…?"

A small smile played about his lips. And in the moment Annie felt something stir surely inside her own heart for Ben that she had never felt before. "My mother helped me pick it out. I hope you like it."

He seemed unable to find any more words, but Annie didn't care. She held the dress up to her shoulders. The color glinted in the lamplight, warm and rich and red, like a hot Christmas cinnamon punch, as the length fell to mid-calf. She knew that, even so heavily pregnant, she would feel beautiful in this dress.

"I thought that you could wear it to the Christmas play at church."

The gentleness in his voice so attracted her that she willingly tore her eyes away from the masterpiece in her hands to look him in the face. "To the Christmas play?"

She had gathered that Ben's old girlfriend was the one putting all of that together. Annie had assumed that, regardless of whether Ben went or not, she would not be welcome. In fact, she would not have begrudged Ben the chance, one last time, to sit by himself at that play and watch the girl he loved. Sure, Annie would have felt bad, but she would've expected that of any man, even a so-called good one.

But this? This dress, and, with it, the invitation, no, the assumption, that she would be going with him to the play caused her throat to tighten. Tears, the first to rise in her eyes for so long, prickled at the edges of her lids. She blinked them away. She would not cry! She would not cry over a fancy dress, nor over the way that this young man – this man who had cheated on her, who had backhanded her, who had left her alone at the mercy of other like-minded men – she would not cry over his kindness, his generosity, nor even over the love that she still could not admit that she longed to receive from his hand.

"It's tonight, you know," Ben said into the quiet.

Annie clenched her teeth together and willed the tears away, but she could not will away the new softness that she felt towards him, try as she might. "And ya want me to go?"

He gave a nod. "Yeah, if you'd like to, I'd like ya to go... with me."

She couldn't say anything. The lump closed off her throat.

Then he reached inside his jacket.

And pulled out a tiny box. Annie's heart nearly stopped.

"I also gotcha this, Annie." He swallowed hard and opened the box on its noiseless hinge. "I hope ya like it," he said, his voice quiet, controlled.

She looked at the ring that he offered to her across the small space between them and reached out a hand to take it. Was it really hers? This band of gold, topped with a small brilliant, clear stone – a real diamond, surely. "Thank you," she said. "It's beautiful." How insufficient the words seemed!

When she raised her eyes, she found Ben looking intently at her. He stepped forward, taking her aback, and reached for her hands. She felt the roughness of his carpenter fingers, the skin calloused by the hammer and nail, by lifting boards, by hard work diligently done. Yet, despite their roughness, she felt a new gentleness, a touch without the selfish passion that had once filled them.

"Annie, I have somethin' to say to ya. Somethin' that needs saying." He glanced over his shoulder at the couch. "Could we sit down for a second?"

She managed to nod. "Sure."

As they both took a seat on the sofa's edge, she wondered why her heart thudded in her chest as it did. It was just Ben, she told herself. Ben – the one who'd betrayed her. Ben – the one whom she was betraying…

She shook her head ever so slightly in order to stop her thoughts from muddling together. She wasn't betraying him! She was just getting what was owed to her. It wasn't her fault that the senator's son wouldn't…

But was it Ben's fault? Much as she had struggled, much as she tried to justify using Ben in the way that she was doing, she knew that one thing was true: that she was responsible for her own actions, for her own choices, just as Ben was, just as the senator's son was. But knowing something and doing what you knew you should do were so often different things.

He kept hold of her hand, and she felt small and delicate, and, unbelievable as it was, sincerely cared-for. Cherished.

She watched as he swallowed hard. "I don't know why I haven't said this before. I should've. I should've set it right when ya came, but this whole situation… this whole thing, well, I, I got scared. I was thinking more of me than I was of you. I was thinkin' more of me than of… of our child."

*Our child.* Annie's heart stilled, as if unable to decide between warming at Ben's words and cowering with guilt.

"I'm sorry, Annie," he said, and Annie met his eyes, seeing in them once more an honesty that she had never known in the past from him. She felt ashamed in the face of it, for she knew that she was anything but sincere. Anything but honest.

He went on, scattering her thoughts. "I'm sorry for leaving ya like I did, for being such a jerk while we were together. I'm sorry for cheating on ya. If I could do it over, I would do it so different, but I can't do it over. So all that I can say is, I'm real sorry. I'm real sorry for everything."

He swallowed. His thumb moved restlessly over her knuckles. Annie stumbled deeper and deeper into the valley of guilt as he continued. "When ya came to Chetham at first, I've gotta be honest, I was mad."

She nodded. She could understand that. "I know ya were mad at me," she offered. "I get it. You found a new life here and…"

"No, it wasn't really that, Annie," he said shaking his head. "I was mad at myself – the old me, the one that had made all them mistakes." He shook his head. "No, let's call 'em what they was. The one who'd committed all them sins. And, yeah, like ya said, I was already in a new life, but what made me mad the most was seeing how the sins of my past would hurt the people that I cared about."

"Like Betty?" She asked the question but thought that she already knew the answer.

Ben hesitated and then nodded. "Yeah, Betty for one. But Cliff and Paulie and my mama and Sam, too. And you, too, Annie, strange as that sounds, given how I acted. And this baby."

He blew out his cheeks and hung his head. "When I come back here, I had already messed up my own life. I had no idea where I was going. Everything behind me – it was as though it was a road strewn with broken bits of glass. And everything before me – well, that was all darkness. I was angry, Annie. I've been angry all my life, as far back as I can remember, and I didn't care how I treated people, how I used them, 'cause I was so hurt and so angry inside. I couldn't see past the end of my own nose. And as I hurt other people, I also hurt myself. Even the ones I claimed to love, well, I hurt them, too."

His head hanging down, his eyes didn't meet hers anymore. Annie wondered about this confession. She knew that Ben had been raised Catholic; maybe she was kind of like his priest right now? He was making a confession?

She was about to say something, anything, just to break the silence, the uncomfortable openness that Ben's confession had brought.

But then he spoke again. "I'm real sorry, Annie. And I wanna truly make things right between us. All this, it didn't happen the way I wanted."

Could she feel any rottener? She tried not to let the inward wince that she felt show on her face, but it was tough. She couldn't cover it up with a smile; that certainly wouldn't be appropriate. So she covered it up with words instead. Words that she had been longing to speak to Ben for some time now, though she could not trace back to the day when she had first felt the longing. "Ben, what *really* changed ya?"

His head rose, and he frowned, confusion apparent in his eyes. He licked his lips. "I've told ya, Annie: It wasn't a what; it was a *who*. Jesus changed me. Jesus Christ."

A little disappointment seeped into Annie. This was the same old thing again that Ben and Sarah had both spoken of before. Annie's own adoptive father had talked about Jesus Christ, but he was not a changed man, or what he had changed into was not like what she saw in Ben. "Oh. Never mind."

"Ya don't believe me," the words came softly from Ben's lips. He must've seen the disbelief on her face.

She quickly tried to get it off her face, to hide it from him. "No, no, it's not that." But her expression had already spoken, and her lips could not wipe away what had been wordlessly said.

"Well, you may not believe me, Annie, and I don't blame ya, though I don't know how else ya think I could've changed, at least I hope I've changed enough so that you'd notice." He smiled ruefully. "I certainly couldn't have changed myself. I didn't even know that I needed changin'."

"Ya did have life hard," Annie said and then stopped, barely able to believe that she was defending him. "I mean," she amended, adding crustiness she didn't feel to her tone, "we both had life hard. It ain't a wonder we're the type of people we are."

She shocked herself at the words that had come out of her mouth. Had she really just equated herself with Ben

Picoletti's former badness? She, who had blamed him for her deceitfulness, for her bitterness, for the child even that she carried outside of wedlock? Even so, they both had excuses... didn't they?

But Ben was shaking his head with the gentleness that softened the judgment. "Naw, Annie. I ain't got no excuses for the way I was. Sin, the sin that was in me, not the circumstances of life that surrounded me, made me the way that I was. I was in bondage to sin, and I couldn't do nothing else, no matter how much I tried. I was a slave to myself, a slave to my own desires, a slave to sin."

Sin... How many times had she heard her adoptive father talk about sin and its wages? How many times had Daddy told her that she was a product of sin? And now Ben was here telling her that the way to become a whole different person was by not doing this thing called sin? Was that it? It made no sense to her at all. "So, you just stopped sinning, and it made you a different person?" This time, she couldn't keep the disbelief from tainting her voice.

Now his head shook more violently. He leaned towards her earnestly, so much so that she actually found herself drawing back a little. "No, Annie! I couldn't stop sinning in and of myself. I didn't have the power to be a good person, as some people call it. There's only one good person."

Only one good person? What in the world? But she couldn't stop the question that came out of her mouth, "And who's that?"

"Jesus Christ."

There was that name again.

She felt a tinge of longing when she heard it; she felt a tinge of dread, too.

"Jesus Christ is the only One who's good enough, Annie, to take bad men and women and to make 'em good."

"And how's He do that?"

"Through the cross. Jesus Christ came to earth to save sinners, sinners like me and you. He was perfect, and so He didn't deserve death. He didn't deserve the judgment of a God who's perfect. He was God Himself and human flesh. That's what Christmas is all about, Annie: God sending His Son as a baby, in human flesh."

She shook her head in bewilderment, but she didn't pull her hand from his. It felt so warm and comforting. "I don't understand. How could a baby, no matter how good He was, how could a baby make anybody good?" Her mind struggled to connect the pieces of the puzzle that Ben handed to her.

"God sent His Son into the world, Annie, not to condemn the world, but so that the people in the world might have eternal life. The only way that He could do this – the only way that He could give people real life was by takin' away death for them. And not just death itself, but the thing that caused the death, the incurable disease that they had. That disease is sin. He took away the sin of the world by dyin' for us. Jesus died in the place of everyone, so that everybody who trusts in Him can live."

She had seen a cross before, many times. But she had never given much thought to what it meant. She had never heard all this before. "Why'd He do that? Why'd He give up His own life to come die for people who had done wrong against Him? Who'd sinned?"

"He did it outta love. He did it outta love, Annie. He loves you, and He loves me. God wants us to be right with Him. That's why He got rid of the sin that was blocking us from Him. He is the only way to goodness, the only One who is good. And He wants to make us good, too. Not that we would have a righteousness of our own, but that our righteousness would come through Jesus Christ. He will make us clean, if we ask Him. He'll give us a fresh start. He did it for me. He can do it for you, too."

A fresh start…

He loved her…

Could it be true? This God? This God, who her father had always told her was angry with her, was waiting for her to make a mistake, reluctantly forgiving her, perhaps if she was *really* sorry, could this God be the One whom Ben was talking about? Could her father have been wrong, all this time? And maybe, maybe if what Ben said was true… *Maybe Daddy is the way he is because he don't understand this!* If only this were true!

If it were true… Oh, why did she struggle to know whether it was true or not? "How do I know if what you're saying is true?" she voiced aloud.

"Know?" he echoed. "Well, to know, ya got to first believe. Believe God's Word – that what He says about Jesus is true. That's what the Bible calls obeying the Gospel."

A leap into the dark? She recoiled and stiffened. That was not her way. Not her way at all. She had to be careful, always, lest somebody took advantage of her. She narrowed her eyes at Ben, whose own gray-blue eyes met hers earnestly. *Maybe that's what he's doing now.* Maybe he was trying to trick her, manipulate, take advantage of her for some reason. Maybe this was all part of an elaborate plan to get rid of her! How, she didn't know, but she knew she had to be careful. Believe? Before you could know for sure? Everything within her shivered at the thought.

"I better start getting' ready," she said.

Ben blinked at the startling change in subject. Slowly, he sat back, withdrawing his hand from hers, the confusion dancing across his face. "What?"

The intimacy that had developed around them dissolved, and Annie felt the chill of its loss around her shoulders. Yet her accustomed aloneness returned in its place, more comfortable to her than the warm intimacy with Ben. "I better get goin' if I'm gonna be on-time."

Ben's eyes met hers. "Yeah, all right." His voice came quiet... and kinda sad.

What had he done wrong? Ben wondered as he looped his tie around his neck, staring into the mirror hanging above his dresser. All the while that he'd scraped his chin of its five o'clock shadow, as he changed into clean duds, ironed by Mama, like always, while he had a quick supper of a bologna sandwich and some leftover mashed potatoes – all the while, he thought about that conversation with Annie. What had he said wrong? She had seemed so open, so interested in what he was saying, almost on the verge of accepting Christ as her Savior, when something had happened. He had actually seen the moment when the shutters closed over her eyes.

*Lord, I tried.* His hands fell to the sides, having completed knotting the tie. It was one that Betty liked, he realized. While Mama had chosen his shirt and pants, Ben had selected his tie. He hadn't even thought about the fact that it was Betty's favorite, had he? It had been a subconscious decision, almost second nature now to him, to want to please Betty.

*But no more.* He hardened his jaw against the thought and raised his chin. He couldn't do that anymore. His hands reached up to unknot the burgundy tie. He laid the tie down on the bureau top, next to the ring that he could not bring himself to return.

*Oh, God, why's it so difficult?* For all of his brave words to Paulie about moving out of Chetham, he wondered if he could ever move Betty out of his heart. He knew that God could put a love for Annie inside his heart; yes, Ben knew that for sure, for had it not been God who had put love inside of his heart, and real love, not the selfish kind that he had always carried about with him, for every person that was in his life now? Yes, he could certainly love Annie, but could he ever put out of his heart the love he had for Betty – the special love that he carried for her?

*I've got to.* In order to be faithful to Annie in every way, he must put out of his heart this love for Betty, this love that he had thought came from God.

But now God had asked for it back. And he must give it back to the One who had given it to him in the first place. Ben let his hands travel over the ring box and decided then: He would return the ring tomorrow, first thing. He could no longer tease himself. Even tonight, when in his flesh his heart had leapt at the thought of seeing Betty once more at church; he'd seen so little of her in the past week or so, ever since he had broken things off with her. He knew the craving was not right. He rebuked himself.

*Help me to do right by Annie. Help me to do right. I am so weak in my flesh. But You are strong. Be my strong tower. Be my rock. Strengthen my heart.*

"Whadaya mean, you're stayin'?" The threat in Aldo's voice cut Annie's ears.

She held her ground, though she knew her voice trembled. "I mean just that. I'm not comin' back to ya, Aldo. I'm not runnin' away from Chetham. I'm gonna stay here. With Ben."

The silence hung between them.

"You mean you're goin' to stay – *married* to him?"

Annie swallowed down the boulder in her throat. "Yeah," she croaked.

Her heart thundered so loudly she wondered if Aldo could hear it on the other end of the line. "Okay," he said at last, drawing the word out. "Well, I guess you've made your choice, then, Annie. Just remember, if ya ain't loyal to me, then I ain't got no reason to be loyal to ya. You're on your own, kid. I mean that. You're really on your own."

After Aldo voiced a few more threats, Annie heard the phone click down quietly. She shivered. Quiet anger was so often the worst.

*You're on your own, kid.* She looked down at her protruding stomach. But she wasn't on her own, was she? She had Ben now to take care of her. She didn't need Aldo, right?

*Unless Ben ever finds out…*

## Chapter
## Sixteen

Betty looked out over the darkened sanctuary. Mama had come in just a few minutes ago, and she had lit the candles in the windows. On the raised platform in front, the nativity set rose up, a stable made out of cardboard painted to look as though it was crafted from wood. Adjoining it, a stable door stood, firmly shut. From there, Betty knew that the innkeeper would tell Mary and Joseph that there was no room for them inside, but they were welcome to stay in his stable. Inside the stable set, the feeding trough – the manger – waited, full of hay, the swaddling cloths hidden behind for Mary's use. All waited for the Christ Child. Gazing around, Betty saw that the place looked holy, calm, a fit place for the Christmas play to occur.

And yet inside Betty, chaos boiled. She felt anything but calm.

Ben would be here tonight. And with him, that girl – his fiancée – Annie.

Even the girl's name kindled a flame of anger to lick at the edges of Betty's heart.

But she suppressed it, knowing that she had no right to feel such. It was not the girl's fault that she had become pregnant, was it?

Though, of course in a way it was. Just as it was Ben's fault.

Betty tried to reframe her thoughts. It was not the girl's fault that Betty had fallen in love with Ben. That she had been so foolish as to believe that God could mean for her to join her life with that of a man whose past was filled with shadows.

Jim. She should think about Jim. He would be here tonight, too.

But try as she might, no matter how many times Betty recalled Jim's charming smile, his twinkling eyes, even the strength of his hand – for the first time, he had reached for hers when they had walked home together the other night – she could not drum up the enthusiasm that she wanted to have for their relationship. No matter how much she tried to stretch her inner vision so that she could see the plan for her life from this moment forward: smooth, unruffled, with four children, a house in town, and a husband who was perfect for her in every way. *He fits my plans, surely.*

*And God can't mess this up.* It was too neat and tidy. There was nothing in it that would allow Him to.

She startled at her own thoughts. She didn't really believe that... did she? Was she really trying to find a way around God's meddling in her life?

She shook herself. "Enough of this nonsense, Betty,"

she sternly told herself in a whisper. The children would be arriving soon; some probably had already, entering through the basement door and getting ready there with their mothers. What kind of director was she, to not be down there with her students?

Someone who didn't want to be a director, that's who. Someone who was doing the job because she was expected to do it. Someone glad to do it only so that her heart did not feel.

With her heartbeat thundering in her throat, Annie made her way down the wide staircase to the entryway. She could hear the quiet chitchat of Sarah and Sam as they waited below for others to join them. She was wearing soft-soled shoes, also Ben's purchase, and so they did not hear her descent until she was almost upon them. When they turned, Annie saw their eyes light with surprise.

Sarah spoke first. "Annie, what a beautiful dress! You look lovely."

Her heart lifting up at the words of approval, Annie allowed her eyes to drift just for a moment to Sam. What would he think – this man whose eyes had held suspicion every time they looked at her for the first few days, though nowadays, they held only resignation and concern?

His face had softened, though, and the look on it surprised her. His face... Well, she'd always wished to see such an expression on Daddy's face. "You look lovely, Annie," he said in his quiet, confident way. Then, shock of all shocks, he stepped forward, took her hands in his, and bent to give her a quick peck on her cheek.

This was something new altogether. In the past, Annie had only known two reactions from men. One, that they had been allured by her, looking at her with lust. Or they had looked at her with disgust or pity, knowing themselves to be better than her.

But what was this? As she allowed her eyes to linger on Sam's face – really, as she was unable to pull her gaze away – she saw neither lust nor disdain, but only undeserved… love.

"Ben should be here soon," Sam said, releasing her hands. "I am looking forward to accompanying all of my children to the play tonight." He smiled at Sarah.

Awkward with the intense emotion, Annie tried to think of something to say. "Where's Cliff?" She tried to keep her voice light as if she was unaffected by the warmth of the Giorgis.

"He'll meet us there. He ended up being recruited as a shepherd, even though he protested that he was too old for the part." Sarah shook her head, smiling.

The door burst open behind them just at that moment, and Paulie strode in, drawing with him a petite golden-haired young woman. Immediately, Sarah gave a cry of welcome and Sam's face broke into another large smile. "Grace!" Sarah wrapped her daughter in her arms. "I thought you weren't going to make it in time."

Paulie grinned so hard he looked as though he might burst. "Her train was running a little late. We thought we were going to have to meet you at the church."

Annie looked on awkwardly as the greetings continued among all with obvious affection. She was just an outsider; she didn't belong…

But then, the young woman turned to Annie, her eyes alive with interest. "I'm Grace," she said a little shyly.

"You're Annie, right?"

Annie nodded and smiled with a little less strain than she felt. "Yeah," she managed.

Grace extended her small hand and took Annie's in her own. "It's very nice to meet you," she said. "Paulie has told me a lot about you."

Annie's eyes darted towards Paulie where he stood, grinning like a fool at Grace. Exactly what Paulie had told Ben's sister about her, Annie wondered. There wasn't much good to tell. But for all that, Grace looked actually pleased to meet her.

"I'm so glad to be getting a sister," Grace went on, "and a new little niece or nephew."

Annie could only nod numbly. For all their strangeness, Grace's words actually seemed genuine.

Sam broke into the exchange. "Well, shall we be getting on to the church?"

Annie looked toward the door, a little worried. Was Ben not coming for her after all?

Sarah must've seen her look. "Don't worry, Annie. Ben sometimes gets delayed with his work. He'll meet us there if it gets too late."

Annie nodded, more nervous than ever. To enter this church, she had been counting on Ben's presence by her side to calm her, to provide a measure of protection from... *From what?* She put her worn coat over the beautiful velvet dress, her ears deaf to the happy murmur of Paulie, Grace, Sarah, and Sam.

It must just be that telephone call earlier that had shaken her up; yes, that was what it was, Annie decided. But what could Aldo do? All he had said was that she was on her own, right? Despite her own reassurance, she still hugged herself to stop the shiver that ran down her arms.

"After you." Sam held the door for her so that he would be the last to exit and lock it behind them.

*"I'm invested in this. And I'm going to get back what's coming to me."* Aldo's threat, midway through the call, came back to her. What did he mean? She assumed that he meant the bus ticket and the train ticket for which he had paid so that she could get to Chetham. He certainly didn't mean any of the clothing that she wore or any of the few things that she had carried with her; no, those were all her own, poor though they were.

"I'll work to pay you back, Aldo," she'd assured him. "You'll see."

"I'll see?" He'd laughed then, but without mirth -a harsh sound that pierced her ears. "Like heck ya will. I ain't dependin' on ya anymore," he'd said just before hanging up.

She trembled as she tucked herself into the back seat of Sam's car. Grace and Paulie would follow them in Paulie's secondhand Ford; Annie was sure that they would be glad to have some time alone. *The lovebirds.*

She clutched her coat tighter to herself. Sarah glanced back just then. "Are you too cold, Annie? There is a blanket on the back seat if you want to put it over your lap."

"Uh, sure, thanks," Annie said and reached for the blanket, as if her sudden chill had to do with the December temperature and not with the memory of her cousin Aldo and his threatening words.

Ben pulled into his stepfather's driveway, glad that he

wasn't late for once.

But something was wrong. Only the porch light shone. Had they already left? He had been sure he was early. His heart started to beat a little fast. He looked down at his watch. It was six-twenty-five; he had arrived with plenty of time to get to the church for seven o'clock.

The play was at seven, wasn't it?

His heart in his throat, Ben scrambled to see if he had possibly left the Sunday bulletin in the backseat of his car.

Sure enough, there it was. He opened it, his eyes dreading to see the time of the play in the announcement section.

Six-thirty. Ben groaned and put the car into reverse.

*Where is he?* Her eyes should not be looking for Ben, should they? But they were.

From the front row, Jim sat and smiled at her, looking very smart in his well-brushed suit. She smiled back at him, as she knew she should, but her eyes continued to rove until they fell on the pew in which the Picoletti-Giorgi family typically sat.

Her heart landed in her stomach. There the young woman sat, dressed regally as the Virgin Mary in medieval paintings: her face pale and pure.

A bitterness tanged on Betty's tongue as she looked at the girl. Though she didn't deserve it, God was giving Annie exactly what she wanted, wasn't He? While on the other hand, Betty was getting exactly what she didn't want from Him.

And where was Ben? The question came back to her

as she looked down the pew and saw Dr. and Mrs. Giorgi, Paulie and Grace, and… that girl. But no Ben.

Betty was about to turn away to join the two dozen children who waited for her final instructions when she saw Ben in the foyer that adjoined the sanctuary: tearing off his coat, unwinding his scarf from around his neck, pulling off his mittens. Then, quick as a wink, he came into the sanctuary with that eager stride of his. Her eyes met his over the congregation.

He smiled.

He smiled. How could he smile, though the expression was tinged with a little sadness?

But still!

Betty turned, unable to repay the smile with one of her own, unable to believe that he could possibly be happy at the turn of events. She walked backstage and nearly tripped over a child dressed as a lamb. She bit back the sharp words that leapt to her tongue and smiled down at the child instead. "We're almost ready to begin," she said, ignoring the angry pull at her heart.

The lights dimmed. Reverend Cloud offered the opening prayer. All of the congregation hushed, the darkness blanketing them softly. A light gleamed from each of the doorways that led to the backstage area. Then Annie saw it: a teenager – Cliff, she thought – stood on top of the wooden covering of the baptismal, holding a scroll in his hands and reading from it.

Annie had never been to a play before. She didn't know quite what to expect. She hadn't known that the churches performed plays! When she'd said that to Sarah, earlier this week, Sarah had replied that at Christmastime, things sometimes could be a little different.

*Well, this sure is different from any church service I've ever attended.* Though, to be honest, in recent years, her church attendance had been scanty – really, non-existent. She settled more comfortably on the hard pew.

Silence settled over the congregation, and Annie wondered what was going on. When she looked intently at Cliff, she saw that his face – obscured by a beard affixed by two loops over his ears -seemed a little nervous. Had he forgotten his lines?

But then she heard beautiful piano music, a stirring tune. When she glanced toward the source, she saw Betty, her fingers moving deftly over the keys. Standing beside Betty, a child sang sweetly:

*"Come, Thou long expected Jesus*
*Born to set Thy people free;*
*From our fears and sins release us,*
*Let us find our rest in Thee.*
*Israel's strength and consolation,*
*Hope of all the earth Thou art;*
*Dear desire of every nation,*
*Joy of every longing heart.*
*Born Thy people to deliver,*
*Born a child and yet a King,*
*Born to reign in us forever,*
*Now Thy gracious kingdom bring.*
*By Thine own eternal Spirit*
*Rule in all our hearts alone;*
*By Thine all sufficient merit,*
*Raise us to Thy glorious throne."*

As the soft words of the child faded, Cliff began to

speak. Despite the fact that Annie could tell that his beard was composed of a paper plate pasted with painted cotton balls and that he wore an old bathrobe, the words that he spoke caused wonder to rise in Annie's heart:

*"And there shall come forth a rod out of the stem of Jesse, and a Branch shall grow out of his roots:*

*"And the spirit of the Lord shall rest upon him, the spirit of wisdom and understanding, the spirit of counsel and might, the spirit of knowledge and of the fear of the Lord;*

*"And shall make him of quick understanding in the fear of the Lord: and he shall not judge after the sight of his eyes, neither reprove after the hearing of his ears:*

*"But with righteousness shall he judge the poor, and reprove with equity for the meek of the earth: and he shall smite the earth: with the rod of his mouth, and with the breath of his lips shall he slay the wicked.*

*"And righteousness shall be the girdle of his loins, and faithfulness the girdle of his reins.*

*"The wolf also shall dwell with the lamb, and the leopard shall lie down with the kid; and the calf and the young lion and the fatling together; and a little child shall lead them."*

Re-rolling his scroll, Cliff stepped off the baptismal through the curtain that covered it from side-to-side. Annie could hear the clunk of his feet as he descended.

The lights went off, followed by a shuffle of darkened activity onstage. When the lights returned, Annie saw that on the left side of the stage, a girl, probably Cliff's age, stood before a small table. She wore some kind of blue material as a long-sleeved tunic, and a solid-colored cloth covered her head, sweeping down onto her shoulders, like a humble bride's veil. When Annie peered at it closely, though, she could see that it was a pillowcase! The girl acted as though she stirred something in the bowl before her.

A new actor entered from the righthand side of the stage. A tall teenager, he was dressed completely in white – Annie wondered if they had used a bedsheet for that. His feet were bare, and it looked as though they had put something glittery on his face. Raising his hand, he pretended to knock. A *tap-tap* accompanied the motion, and Annie realized with wonder that they must have contrived some way of making the sound effects.

The young lady dressed in blue put down her spoon and went to open the door. She let in the newcomer, who said to her, "Blessed are you, chosen of the Lord!"

The young woman appeared a little afraid, Annie thought. "What do you mean?" she asked, clasping her hands in front of her tunic.

The young man went on to explain. Annie soon came to understand that he was an angel and that the unmarried girl was Mary, the one chosen to have a baby – Jesus, who as the angel said, "would save His people from their sins."

*How? How can a baby save people from sin?* The words spoken by Ben and Sarah over the past two weeks trickled through Annie's mind. Her heart lurched, suddenly desperate to make sense of them.

After Mary had said, "Let it be to me according to thy word," Annie sat in the darkness, oblivious to the sound of scurrying feet as the stagehands worked to change the scene. In her mind, pictures played as she reviewed the scene. Why did it touch her so? This story that she had heard before, though she had forgotten it?

She was not like the young woman on stage, Mary – not at all. She was unmarried, that was true, and she, too, carried a child in her womb, but she was not chaste like that young woman was. But then Annie continued to think, even as the lights went on, musing over the way the angel had said that the baby Mary bore would save His people from their sins. This baby – Jesus – would save His people from their sins. And wasn't even Mary one of His people? Maybe... Maybe the issue was not with the outside, but with the heart – what only God could see.

As she sat and watched the old Nativity story play out before her eyes, with bedsheets and pillowcases worn as homemade costumes, with cardboard cutouts standing in for the town of Bethlehem, she wondered. Her mind, her heart opened up as attic boxes, long closed to the sunlight. She had heard this story before. Why had she not seen the things in it that she was seeing now? Why was her understanding opened to understand things that were not even spoken aloud on the stage? She felt like she had been in a dark tunnel and that suddenly she had turned a corner and had come out into the light. She still stood in that tunnel, but she felt that she could now step into the light, if she chose.

*He will save His people from their sins...*
*He will save His people from their sins...*
*He will save...*

She could barely blink as she watched the story play out. Now, Joseph and Mary, who was now heavily pregnant, stood at the door of an inn. Joseph reached out his hand to knock on the door, and the cardboard cutout nearly fell, but he steadied it with his hand. Whoever was supposed to come to the door did not respond right away, anyway, so Joseph knocked again. Then he called out, "Innkeeper, Innkeeper! Are you there?"

There was the sound of running from out of the room off the stage. A little boy, clad in a tunic drawn up around his knees to aid him in running, ran past Betty at the piano. As he passed her, he called out, "Sorry, Miss Cloud! I had to use the lavatory real bad!"

Laughter rippled through the congregation, as the boy took his place behind the cardboard cutout. Joseph knocked again, and this time the cardboard door opened. "Yes, what do you want?" said the newly-arrived innkeeper in a grumpy voice.

Joseph gestured towards Mary. "Please, sir, we are looking for a room. Do you have any available? My wife is ready to have her baby."

The innkeeper crossed his arms. "Rooms? What do you mean, rooms? I have no rooms. Bethlehem is flooded with people coming in from that census. Be gone with you. I have nothing to offer you."

Annie's heart stitched together tightly. No room? No room for Jesus? How could the man turn away this pregnant woman, this woman who did not deserve the innkeeper's scorn and this gentle Joseph, who was trying to take care of her?

Joseph sighed heavily and turned away. "Come, Mary."

But then the innkeeper stuck his head out the door one more time as he saw them turning to go. "Wait."

They turned.

"I… I have a place in my stable. At least it will be dry. There's some hay down there for bedding if you didn't bring any blankets."

And so Annie watched as Mary and Joseph went to the stable room. They shared that space with small children dressed up as lambs, cows, and even a donkey, who gave out the occasional bray. The lights dimmed, and when they rose again, the same scene stood before Annie's eyes, yet now, Mary held her Baby, wrapped tightly in cloths.

A small group of children, dressed as angels, came to the righthand side of the stage. They opened their lips and sang together, clearly:

*"See the eternal Son of God*
*A mortal Son of Man,*
*Now dwelling in an earthly clod*
*Whom Heaven cannot contain!*
*Stand amazed, ye heavens, look at this!*
*See the Lord of earth and skies*
*Low humbled to the dust He is,*
*And in a manger lies!"*

Tears prickled at Annie's eyes. Why was she crying? It was just a story, wasn't it? And yet something in her wanted to… respond. Longed to step into that light at the end of her dark tunnel.

Longed to run into the light that this Christ-Child offered.

*Come, daughter.*

*Come.*

Her heart heard the words.

The angels' song ended. And then one angel stepped forward, a little boy, his hair shaggy over his ears, and in a clear voice, his candle held stiffly in front of him, he sang,

*"What can I give Him, poor as I am?*
*If I were a shepherd, I would bring a lamb.*
*If I were a wise man, I would do my part.*
*But what can I give Him?*
*I can give Him my heart."*

She stared at the scene onstage – Child cradled in His mother's arms, amidst the humble coziness of the stable – and couldn't stop the tears from running down her cheeks.

He came… to enter their hearts.

To enter Annie's heart.

*But what can I give Him?*

*I can give Him my heart.*

She sat quietly, for the first time that she could remember, completely still in her soul. *Yes, Lord Jesus. I give you my heart.*

The play engrossed Ben. He had never seen a performance of the nativity story before; they had not done them at the Catholic church in which he'd grown up. Christmas had been held in high honor there, but they had not had a play, and so this was a new experience for him.

Something in the way that Joseph acted towards Mary especially drew Ben into the narrative. He thought about how he would have felt if he had been Joseph: If he had found Mary had betrayed him, he would have been angry, so angry that he was not sure that he would have dealt justly with her as Joseph did. *Maybe I would've wanted to stone her.* But Joseph was merciful, though at the time he had not believed Mary deserving of mercy.

At that point in the play, Ben got a little lost in his own thoughts. The Bible called Joseph a just man – a man who acted with righteousness. And the one mark of acting with justice, the very action that qualified Joseph to be called just, was giving mercy to a person who did not seem to deserve it.

*To be just is to be merciful.* Not only to give what someone deserved, no more and no less, but in God's eyes to be righteous was to be *merciful,* strange though it was. It didn't seem to make sense to Ben's human mind, but there it was, right in the Bible.

And because he was just, because he was merciful, Joseph became the laughing-stock of the town... and yet he had not deserved it. He bore Mary's seeming shame.

*As Christ Jesus bears our shame.*

Beside him, Ben heard sniffling, ever so slight. He turned his head a fraction of an inch and peered from the corner of his eye. Tears ran down Annie's cheeks, her gaze fastened on the stage before her. He had never known her to cry before, not even when they had broken up. Rather, sparks had flown from her eyes as she'd spat out her anger on him. Anger, not grief, was usually Annie's response to emotional pain.

But here she sat beside him, with tears trickling down her cheeks, her eyes fixed on the simple story being played out before them by children and teenagers, while his Betty played the piano.

*My Betty.*

Despite his recent acceptance of his situation, the phrase that had so naturally sprung to his mind still stung his heart. He pushed it away and rephrased it to himself: *Just Betty.* Not belonging to him, but just her, by herself. Instead, this one who sat beside him, whom he had never thought to see again, who now carried his child in her womb – this woman was his. Would he, like Joseph, accept this?

How else could he possibly respond but in obedience to the One who had called him out of darkness? In his heart, Ben bowed himself in painful yet glad submission.

But actions would speak louder than words. Ben slid his hand over Annie's where it rested on her lap. He took her hand in his and laid their joined hands on the pew between them.

He had startled her; that was certain, for she turned wide, tear-blurred eyes to his for one quick second. He squeezed her hand, and peace settled in his heart as he refocused his attention to the stage, and saw from the corner of his eye that Annie did the same.

She kept her countenance placid, composed, like always, as if nothing had ruffled the interior sea of her heart. Yet, inside, waves crashed. Even as her fingers moved with practiced grace across the ivory keys, Betty's mind tumbled.

Why did they strike her so now, those words of Mary to the angel? She had heard them often enough. The play went on from that point, but Betty's attention halted there, the words swirling round and round with hurricane force.

*Let it be to me according to Thy word.*

*According to Thy word…*

And yet in her own heart, Betty knew that this was not what she wanted. *I want my own will, not Yours.* A cold grief settled over her heart as the outright realization stared her soul in its face, stripped of its blindfold. When had it come to this? When had she come to wanting her own will, not the will of her Heavenly Father, in her life? Oh, she wanted His will, alright, as long as it coincided with her own plans.

But that didn't count for anything, did it?

Over and over again in her mind, Betty saw Mary kneeling in submission as the words came from her lips: *Let it be to me according to Thy word.* Her wants, her desires had been swallowed up in God's. Mary must've had many dreams, many desires for herself, and being shamed in her hometown could not have been one of them. And yet she had accepted it, for it was God's will for her, and she knew it was good.

And so all women had called her blessed for the past two thousand years.

Mary's example shone a search-light on her soul, and Betty cringed away. Tears prickled at the edges of her eyelids as her fingers played the hymns she had long-ago memorized. How long had she thought that she was like Mary? Pure, undefiled – though even Mary needed a Savior, despite her willingness to be the vessel for Him.

At last, the play reached a point during which Betty need not play. Her fingers stilled on her lap. *I'm not like Mary. I am not like her at all, Lord. I am so sorry. So sorry.*

From some corner of her mind, Betty recalled a sermon her father had once given. Like a shadow, the memory came back to her now, filled with new meaning. Mary, he had said, meant *bitter* or *rebellious*. Yet out of that bitterness, out of that rebellion, God had brought salvation in Him. Mary, a woman named *bitter*, a woman named *rebellious*, had accepted God's difficult will for her as sweet, had accepted God's hard and yet marvelous plan for her with a bowed head and a glad heart.

*Oh Lord,* Betty cried silently, *let me do likewise. Let me welcome Your interference in my life in the way that Mary did – with joyful gladness, with heartfelt obedience. I repent. Change my heart, O Lord.*

There was a difference in Betty at the end of the play.

Ben could see it, though he didn't know if anyone else, save maybe her parents, would notice. But despite the fact that he and Betty had only been dating for a few months, he had studied her well enough in that short time to know when something was wrong... Or different, in this case.

As she thanked everyone for coming to the Christmas play and as she accepted the flowers that one of the mothers of the children in the cast had brought for her, her face shone clear, clearer than he had ever seen it, in fact – free of the aloofness that often coated it like a candy shell, covering her heart. In its place, she wore a look of peace worthy of Mary herself. Ben wondered what had transpired. Had the play touched her heart as it had touched his? As it seemed to have touched Annie's as well?

Before dismissing the congregation, Reverend Cloud encouraged everyone to be sure that they got some Christmas cookies and hot chocolate on their way out. Ben turned to Annie, who still wiped away tears. Her face wore a blurry smile, and there her eyes glowed with childlike wonder. She licked her lips as she looked up at him. "Thanks, Ben. Thanks for bringin' me here."

Ben longed for her to tell him what her tears meant, but this was not the right time. Instead, he placed a hand on her shoulder, feeling its slender femininity tremble beneath his hand as the last shudder of tears coursed through her body. "Would ya like to stay for cookies and hot chocolate?"

She nodded hesitantly, almost shyly. So strange, for one such as Annie. "Sure, if ya want," she replied and turned to pick up her raggedy purse.

Ben dropped his hand from her shoulder and picked up her small hand in his. He led her from the sanctuary to the fellowship hall, where the smell of cinnamon and chocolate welcomed them with open arms.

# Chapter Seventeen

Annie selected a chocolate-dipped snickerdoodle, while Ben had his hand on a large, heavily-frosted-and-sprinkled egg biscuit. Annie must feel nervous, and Ben couldn't blame her. He remembered how he had felt when he had first moved back to Chetham and had been around "church people." Made him feel funny, like he couldn't fit in. He didn't want that to be the case for Annie, though he knew it would take a lot of gumption for these small-town church folks, well-intentioned though they might be, to accept completely Annie as one of them, with all of her known and unknown history.

"Merry Christmas," the voice came from just behind them – a familiar voice that still lifted Ben's soul when he heard it.

He turned, never more conscious of Annie at his side.

Betty stood there, the same quietness on her face that he had seen settled there at the close of the nativity play just a few minutes earlier. Ben wondered at it, for it became her well, enhancing her natural beauty, making her brown curls glisten even more under the soft church lighting, her skin appear soft and warm…

But he tore his mind away from those thoughts and instead considered the woman who was to be his wife, the woman who stood just beside him. With some effort, Ben resisted his desire to reach out to Betty and instead placed his hand at the small of Annie's back. He felt her tense in surprise, but he ignored it. "Merry Christmas, Betty," he replied at last, speaking past the marbles clogging his throat. He ought to say something about the play. "Uh… The play was great. Really, ya did a wonderful job with it."

She smiled, the irritatingly-confident expression that she often wore somehow having slipped away. "Thank you," she said, "I had a lot of help, and, in the end, God brought it all together. I was thankful for your brother Cliff. He filled in at the last-minute for me. Who knew he'd make such a great shepherd *and* prophet?"

Ben could tell that she was making an attempt at humor to lessen the tension between them.

"So…" He tried to think of something to say, for Betty lingered. "So, uh, will your family be spending Christmas at your house this year? Or are you spending it with Jim's family?" Darn it. Why'd he let that last bit slip from his mouth? He'd put that behind him, hadn't he? He thought that he had been at peace with it all. Maybe he was. Maybe that was why he was bringing it up now: to show himself, to show Betty and Annie, both of them, that he was truly at peace with the situation before them all.

Sure, that was it. *I need Thee every hour, Lord.*

Betty looked startled for a moment, but then she shook her head. "No, Jim and I are only going to be friends right now. Our families don't know each other very well yet, either. Besides, my own brother's coming back with his family. We'll be spending the holidays with them."

*Jim and I are just friends.* That was what she had said, but Ben could not allow himself to dwell on the words. Not with Annie by his side. Not with their baby inside her body. *Lord, I accept Your will. Create in me a love for this gift You have given me. Let me see it as a gift. Not as a burden. Let me be like Joseph.*

Something was different inside of her; Annie knew that. She was the same Annie; yet she was not the same Annie. *What happened?* she wondered as she ran her brush through her hair later that night. She stared at her rounded form in the mirror, clad in the new white nightgown that had appeared recently in her room. "Who am I?" she asked her reflection. She believed – oh, how she believed – that Jesus was the One who God said He was – His only Son, the Savior of the world. In her heart and in her mind, everything had turned a full circle. She felt as though she had been living under the water all her life, and now, now she stood on dry land and heard and saw afresh, with clear ears and eyes. *I feel like I've been born-again.*

She had kept so silent on the way home that Ben had asked her whether anything was wrong. She had only been able to shake her head and say, "No, nothing." It was so hard to put into words what had occurred. She had just sat there, saying over again in her heart and mind, "He saved

His people from their sins."

*He saved me from my sins.*

A love such as she had never known descended on her. She was His. The belonging to Him freed her.

She could not understand it all, but she knew it all in the depths of her soul – She knew that something eternally shattering and healing had occurred for the first time in her life.

God was near, not far. He was purest love, not anger.

A giggle raced up her throat and out of her mouth before she could stop it. She slapped her hand over her lips and stared back at her reflection with her bright shining eyes. "Was this what happened to Ben?" she said aloud. No wonder he was so different! Everything was different now.

She gave a little jig in place with her feet, only to nearly stumble beneath the sudden thought that sobered her.

Everything was different...

For the first time since the play, Annie's heart plummeted.

*Everything is different...*

"I have to tell the truth," she said to herself in the mirror. The twinkle in her eyes was replaced with a solemn fear.

*How can I do that?*

Yet at the same time she knew that there was no other way. *I have to tell the truth.* Oh, but how? She had estranged Aldo; her cousin would not help her now in any way. And what would Ben say? The thought of that made her insides clench.

And Sarah and Sam... All of them trusted her, all of them believed her words! Would they call the police?

Would they throw her out into the cold? Would they demand repayment for her stay at their home, for the food that she had eaten, for the inconvenience and embarrassment she had cost them?

*It doesn't matter. I still gotta tell them the truth.* Her heart dreaded it. Yet she had thrown herself upon Jesus Christ for her salvation. Was she willing to throw herself upon Him, was she willing to trust Him, in this as well?

The test to her new faith had come suddenly, much sooner than she had ever expected, if she had expected one at all.

She bit her lip, staring at her reflection. Should she go to Sarah first? Or was it better, more fair, to go straight to Ben? A thought darted into her mind then: Perhaps, perhaps she could just leave them a letter, a note, explaining everything. Then she would be out of their lives – on the street, that was true, with nowhere to go – but at the very least she would not need to face them. And, as soon as she told them, that's where she'd be anyway.

But then she looked down at her child, nestled within her. "Oh, little one," she sighed quietly. "I can't do that to ya, can I?" She knew that her only real, safe option, if she left the Giorgi household, would be to go to a home for unwed mothers; Ben had mentioned that there was one in Providence. There, they would take care of Annie – feed her, clothe her, even find her some training or employment – but they would also take away her baby as soon as it was born. In exchange for their care for her, the child would be given to some stranger, someone that she did not know, given away in a closed adoption. Lost to her forever and without any assurance that it was loved or safe. She couldn't do that. She knew that the home tried to find good families for the children, but she also knew what it was like to grow up unwanted and unloved. "I can't do that," she murmured again, and her heart swelled with a greater love than she had ever felt before for the small life growing inside of her.

But what, then? She also could not continue in deceit. "Oh, Lord, what do I do?"

*Tell the truth.*

The knowing came to her heart, as surely as if a voice had spoken aloud.

*Tell the truth.*

She stared wide-eyed at herself once more before nodding in resignation. She would do it tomorrow, come what might.

# Chapter Eighteen

Ben had a job near River Avenue the next morning, so he decided to stop by Mama's house for breakfast. It was a hard thing for a man to resist French-toast casserole and sausage, along with fresh grapefruit, freely provided on his stepfather and mother's table. This morning, though, another thing also helped to propel Ben up the brick walkway into the Giorgi home: His curiosity had only grown regarding the change that he had seen come over Annie last night. Why had tears written both joy and sorrow on her face? He was curious about the silence that had enveloped her, too, except for her quiet, "Good night, Ben."

Giving just a gentle tap on the door before he strode

into the entryway, Ben plucked off his hat and unwound his scarf, then tossed down his mittens on the side table. As he hung up his coat, he pondered what last night could've meant to Annie. Had Annie...? Could it be possible...? *What if Annie believes?* If that were the case, a small spark of hope might ignite in his heart for their marriage to be a blessing to them both... eventually. How good it would be to be united with her in spirit as well as by law! And maybe then their hearts might eventually unite as well.

He followed his nose into the dining room, where he found their cook placing a large platter of sausage on the table, just as he'd hoped.

Tabitha tried to look sternly at him, but Ben could see that she was secretly delighted that he'd come for breakfast. "Now, Mr. Ben, you don't go eating all of my sausage," she commanded him, turning on her heel to go back to the kitchen.

"How about just a few of them?" he asked, chuckling as he sat down and tucked a white napkin into the front of his shirt. It might not be proper by high-society standards, but it'd keep the grease off his checked shirt.

"Have Dr. Giorgi and my mother come down yet?" he called toward the kitchen.

Tabitha poked her head through the doorway. "Oh, the doctor left for the office already. That man works himself to the bone. The bone, I tell ya! Your mother will be down shortly, as will Miss Annie." The cook added that last bit with a small frown attached to her words, but Ben chose to ignore it. The staff would learn in time through his actions how Annie was to be treated and respected in this home.

Tabitha vanished again into the kitchen, and Ben

bowed his head and thanked God for the food that was set before him. He had just poked his fork into a juicy sausage when Annie rounded the corner. She stopped short at the sight of him.

Hoping to set her at ease, he smiled around the bite and swallowed quickly. "Morning, Annie."

Her eyes dropped down and then flickered up to meet his. "Good morning, Ben," she replied softly. The old arrogance that had often tainted her voice had disappeared.

He gestured towards the table when she didn't move. "Come on and help yourself to some breakfast, Annie," he encouraged her. "Tabitha's French-toast casserole is the best I've ever tasted." As if to demonstrate how much he loved it, Ben forked another piece onto his plate.

Annie hesitated for a moment, then shuffled forward and sat at the table across from Ben. She took her time unfolding her napkin and laying it across her lap before pouring herself a cup of tea, adding two square lumps of sugar to it. Beyond the happy cloud of pleasure that enveloped Ben as he ingested his breakfast, he noticed that Annie took an extremely long time to make her tea. "Are ya not hungry this morning?" he asked, suddenly a little worried. Was the baby making her sick or giving her pain again? But he wasn't really sure how to ask her that. Uneasily, he forked another piece of sausage in his mouth and chewed, all the while keeping an eye on Annie's facial expression, which wore a look of perplexity and seriousness that he had never seen before there.

And determination – so much so that Ben finally stopped chewing, put down his fork, and stared openly at her. "What is it, Annie?" he asked, his appetite lost.

The bright winter sun made its way through the panes

of glass to Annie's left, haloing her reddish-gold hair. As Ben watched, she seemed to force herself to speak. "I need to talk to you about something. Soon." She said the words without emotion, steadily.

"Is this about last night, Annie?" Had she been bothered by Betty coming up to them? Or did she want to tell him the reason for her tears during the performance? He'd take either explanation. He sure did want some clarification with regards to all that had occurred with the two women in his life last night.

"No, it's not about last night," she answered him hurriedly, but then amended, "Well, maybe it is a little bit. A lot. Sort of."

Perplexity swallowed him whole. Ben surveyed what was left on his plate and knew that he wasn't going to get down any more of it until he heard more. "What is it, Annie? Whatever it is, ya can tell me."

Her eyes darted up to look at him and he saw fear there. "I promise, I won't get mad," he assured her. He'd given her plenty of reason in the past to think of him as a man who reacted in anger. *Lord, help me, whatever it is. Help me to deal with it through Jesus Christ, not my own strength.*

Her eyebrows raised just a little bit. "I think ya will. How could ya help but get mad?"

Her words hurt a little bit. Aside from the first day or so that she had been in Chetham, Ben had not lost his temper with Annie. Not at all like the months in which they'd dated, when he had lost his temper frequently. He knew that the Holy Spirit was working in him, by God's grace alone.

"Well," he said a little subdued, "wouldja like to tell me? I've got some time now. Do you want to talk now?"

She glanced at his half-full breakfast plate, keeping

her own pale fingers wrapped around her teacup. "What about your breakfast? Won't it get cold?"

He shook his head and rose to his feet. "I couldn't eat if I tried. Not when you've got somethin' important to talk to me about."

He could tell that he'd surprised her, but she did not protest as he led her towards the door, then stood to the side to let her precede him to the hallway. "Why don't we talk in the library?" he suggested. "Nobody'll bother us there so early in the morning."

She nodded, and he ushered her into the room. Around them, the shelves of books rose up to the ceiling, silent as if listening to the tick of the clock and waiting for the two humans in their midst to speak. Annie didn't sit down right away, and Ben certainly didn't want to sit, either. His heart jumped up around his throat, why, he couldn't tell. What more shocking news could Annie give him? She had already turned his life inside out with her arrival a few weeks ago. In truth, he hoped against hope that her revelation now would be that she had come to know Christ.

But if that was the case – if that was what she was about to reveal to him – why did she seem so afraid? So nervous? It didn't fit.

Trying to set her at ease, he took a seat on the sofa but found that his knee jabbed up and down as soon as he sat. *Oh, God, what's going on here?*

Slowly, she, too, took a seat. When she still remained silent for a few long moments, Ben prodded, "Ya said that this was not about last night – not completely – but is it? Did something happen to ya last night, Annie, that ya wanna talk to me about?"

She nodded fiercely, her eyes on her clenched fists

lying across her knees. "Yes," she whispered. "I... I believe what they were talkin' in the play is true. I've heard things like that all my life, growing up in church, Ben. Somehow, I'd heard it all, but it never was clear to me, never sank in until last night. I... I asked God to forgive me for my sins through Jesus."

Joy flooded Ben's heart, and all fear that he had felt over what might come out of Annie's mouth drained away instantly. "Oh, wow! Annie, that's just... that's just swell!" He fell to his knees before her and grasped her hands, raising his face to look into hers, expecting to see joy blooming there.

Peace did light her face, yes, but a troubled expression shadowed it, too. Her hands wrapped around Ben's, as if she was a drowning person grasping for a piece of driftwood on a turbulent sea. "Yeah, it is wonderful, Ben. I can't even say what kinda joy that I felt when I knew that I'd been forgiven my sins, that I'd been given a new start, that I was born-again in Jesus Christ."

The words that came from Annie's mouth amazed Ben. He knew that he was looking at his beloved sister in the Lord now, not just an old girlfriend from his past. The joy bubbled up so in his heart that he could not help himself from reaching over and embracing her. For a split second she clung to him, but then drew away.

When Ben looked at her, he saw that tears had risen in her eyes – tears of sadness and not of joy.

"What is it, Annie?" His heart panged.

She shook her head. "I hate sayin' it, but I've gotta, Ben. I wish I didn't have to, that we could just go on in the way that we've been going, but I know in my heart that it ain't right." She looked at him intently, as if she thought that he should understand exactly what she meant.

But he didn't. "What are you talking about, Annie? What's not right?" Wasn't that what they were trying to do – do the right thing by getting married, giving their child a home together, and now, by God's grace, being united in Christlike love for one another?

Annie struggled to speak through her tears, and frustration rose within Ben alongside the tenderness. He pushed back at it, determined not to let his feelings have their way, resolved to be gentle with her despite her inability to control her tears, to let him know exactly what was so deeply troubling her. "It ain't right, Ben," she repeated, sniffling. "It ain't right for ya to have to give up Betty and to marry me. As much as I want ya to." She broke down into weeping again.

He sat back on his heels and spoke the truth. "It *is* right, Annie. I wanna give our baby a home. I wanna give this child a mother and a father who are united together. I want it to know it's wanted. I didn't see it that way at first, and I'm real sorry for that, but I know now that this child is a gift from God - a perfect gift from His hand. I'm startin' to see that clearly.

"I'll be honest with ya, Annie," he went on earnestly, her cold hands inside his warm ones. She kept her head lowered, and he felt the spatter of her tears on his knuckles. "I was having a hard time with givin' up Betty, but God is givin' me peace about it. I know that He'll work out His plan for her life, just as He's working out His plan for yours and mine. I know that God'll give me a deep love for you, and it'll be even better because it comes from Him, not just from my own desires. I know I weren't the best boyfriend to ya when we were together before, but I promise, by God's grace, I'll try to be a good husband. I'll…"

But she was really weeping now, great gulping sobs that wrenched from her, and the rush of Ben's words slowed. He rose from his knees and sat down on the sofa beside her, awkwardly placing his arm across her back. She did not lean into him, which surprised him, but sat rigidly, with his arm around her, weeping and weeping into her hands. He wondered if he should go to his mother. Surely Mama would know what to do. He was just about to rise and tell her that he would be right back with Mama when Annie seemed to gain back a measure of control. "Ben... Ben, there's something I gotta tell you. I..."

Her words were interrupted by the sound of knocking on the outside door. "Someone'll get that," Ben assured Annie, continuing to give her his full attention. Whoever it was out there, they were banging away like there was no tomorrow.

Still, Annie could not control her heaving sobs. She wiped her nose on her sleeve, leaving a long wet smear on the cheap, raggedy fabric. Ben reminded himself that he needed to get her a new dress to replace this one, too. *Next time I get paid from a job, I'll get her a fine-looking dress, straight out of Shephard's Department Store.* Something proud – in a good way – settled into Ben's chest at the thought, even as he tenderly reached out a hand to steady Annie. Unlike his father, by God's grace, he would provide fully for his family – for his wife, for his children.

*Children.* At that moment, Ben realized that he was not just thinking of this child that Annie carried as his, but also of their future little ones. *He will give you a future and a hope...*

Brooking no thought of what he had lost by Annie's coming, but only of what he had gained, he enfolded her against his chest. He knew that he had startled her; he could tell by the way she stiffened against him. But then, as if unable to fight against the gentleness any longer, she gave herself up to it, to him, melting into his strong embrace.

Truly, in that moment, Ben felt like Joseph, tenderly encircling Mary with his love, his protection.

"Annie, ya can tell me anything. I promise," he tried again to assure her, but his words were cut short by the repeated loud banging on the door.

Grimacing, he gently released her. "Lemme go see who that is." *Whoever it is, they'd better have a good reason for bothering the Giorgi household like this so early in the morning.* Ben checked his anger a little when he reminded himself that Sam was a doctor; occasionally, patients dropped by the house, rather than going to the office he shared in town with another physician.

*Keep a lid on it, Ben,* he sternly reminded himself as he rose from the sofa and strode across the carpeted library toward the door that led out to the entryway.

But he never made it to the door.

Instead, the knocking stopped suddenly as he heard the muffled sound of the entryway door unlatching and swinging open, followed by Grace's quiet greeting and another person brashly answering her.

Ben frowned and quickened his steps.

The library door burst open. "Please! Just wait a moment while I get—" Grace's petite form attempted to block the man from entering, but he pushed her aside – making Ben's blood go from a simmer to a boil.

*Aldo.* The breath completely left Ben's lungs as he stared at the young man whom he had cheated more than once, with whom he had worked, who had stabbed him in the back at the end of their friendship. Mouth hanging open, Ben couldn't force out any words. All he could hear was the pounding rush of blood in his head. Why was Aldo here, in Chetham?

Grace, her face flushed, looked from Aldo to Ben. "I tried to get him to wait in the entryway, but as you can see, he wouldn't," she said, folding her arms across her chest with all the huff of a disgruntled prizefighter.

Ben shook his head, numb at the sight of Aldo, who was not only present but who looked strangely triumphant. Then, something snapped. "Get out." The words left his lips without Ben bothering to think them through. For if he'd thought them through, perhaps he would've had to think of what the Christian thing to do might be – to offer his enemy a drink, perhaps, or a place to sit down?

A smile curled Aldo's lip up at the corner. His hair was long now, almost hanging in his eyes, and shadowed his face. "Nope."

The anger rose in Ben, a mighty tide crashing on the shore. He took a step forward and pushed Aldo in the shoulders. Memories of his own treatment at Aldo's hands less than a year ago – deceit, trickery, betrayal – overpowered him. "I said, get out!" He had felt relief at that first push at Aldo's wiry body and now couldn't resist leaning forward to give another shove.

But Aldo caught Ben's wrists. For one so skinny, Aldo possessed a steel-like strength. His fingers wrapped around Ben's wrists, squeezing them. "Don't lay your hands on me again, buddy," Aldo said smoothly, softly, calmly. That was always his way: unruffled while he prepared to drive a knife between his opponent's ribs.

Ben struggled against Aldo's hold, but Aldo didn't let go. The two stood there frozen in a stand-off while Ben stared into Aldo's concrete eyes. "What are ya doin' here?"

Ben finally bit out between clenched teeth.

Aldo raised one eyebrow. "Didn't ya know? I come to visit my cousin Annie. Got some business to do with her. And with ya, Benji-boy."

Ben's heart thundered in his ears. Why had he not thought of it before? Annie was Aldo's cousin – adopted cousin, anyway, though they never made much of the fact when they were both working at Bousquet's.

"You ain't welcome here, Aldo." The little voice came from behind Ben. He heard fear in it. But why was Annie afraid of Aldo? She had never seemed so before.

With a jerk, Aldo let Ben's arms down. From the corner of his eye, Ben saw Grace slip out of the room. *She's probably going to get Mama.*

"Not welcome? Well, Cuz, I sure do feel hurt by that." Aldo smirked. "Especially when we've got so much unfinished business to do together, don't we?"

Ben turned in time to see Annie lift her chin. She folded her arms across her chest, above her rounded belly. "We got no business together, Aldo."

Aldo pretended shock. *He really should've been on the stage.* "No business together? Since when?"

Ben watched as Annie swallowed hard. "I told ya the other day on the telephone. I... I ain't got no more business with ya, Aldo."

Any words he had left died on Ben's tongue. *The other night on the telephone?* What in the world did that mean? Well, the answer was obvious; she had been keeping in touch with Aldo, his enemy, right here, under Ben's own nose. The tenderness that he had felt towards Annie in those few moments before Aldo had burst through the door morphed into something cooler, sharper, altogether different. What kind of game was she playing?

He watched as Aldo took a few strides across the room, the smirk on his face saying, *See, I told ya so.* He moved towards Annie. Her face whitened as her cousin approached, but Ben could not force himself from his own spot. "Well, maybe ya ain't got business with me no more, Annie-girl, but I sure as heck got business with ya."

Annie looked him straight in the eye, though her voice trembled. "No, ya don't. Our business together is done." Shaking, she clutched the edge of the couch for support.

"Our business," Aldo stated, his voice stepping light-footed as a cat through the dim twilight, "ain't over until I get my money back. With interest. Like we said at the beginning."

*His money back…*

It dawned on Ben then – he was a little slow on the uptake, sometimes, he could admit this – that Annie owed Aldo money! Money almost always drove Aldo's machinations. Ben wondered how great Annie's debt was for Aldo to travel all the way to Chetham to collect it. *It's gotta be a lot.*

Annie's eyes darted to Ben. The initial sharpness that had settled into Ben's heart wore away again, replaced by softness. Had she turned to Aldo in desperation, borrowing money? Had she done it because she was pregnant and out-of-work? Because Ben had abandoned her, though he had not known at the time she was going to have a child? Protectiveness rose inside of his heart for Annie, and he stepped toward her, as if to show Aldo that he would stand with Annie against her cousin, if need be.

For some reason, Aldo found this funny, so much so that a rat-like grin spread across his lips as he looked at the two of them. Ben felt his face redden at the mockery he saw in Aldo's dark eyes. He moved directly to Annie's side, placing his arm around her shoulders, drawing her towards himself. "Anything that Annie got owin' to ya, Aldo, I'll pay."

At this, Aldo snickered. "Looks like ya *will* pay all Annie's debts. Looks like it." He switched his eyes from Ben to Annie. "Well, Annie-girl, looks like ya got yourself a real champion here. And never did a girl deserve one more, did she?"

Ben gritted his teeth, more than ready for this show to be over. "How much does she owe ya?"

Aldo raised his eyebrows. "You're really going to pay for her, ain't you? You're really going to get her outta this?"

Ben didn't deign to nod. He just stared straight at Aldo, wishing that his gaze could slice the man in two. *But such were some of you...* The verse trickled into his mind, while internally he shook his head. Had he really been like Aldo just a few months ago? Yet he knew that he had.

*While we were still sinners...*

Ben gritted his teeth against the verse, but he couldn't shut it out completely. *Oh God, help me to forgive him.*

But try as he might, he couldn't force the feeling of forgiveness to come. No matter. Reverend Cloud's counsel came to him in that moment: *"When you don't feel like it, admit your feelings to God, but act upon the facts, Ben."* That's what the middle-aged minister had said to him across his office desk, the sunlight of the warm autumn afternoons spilling over his balding head. *"Your feelings will follow the facts when you act on them."*

Ben forced his face to relax. He knew that forgiveness did not mean to treat the sin as though it didn't matter. Rather, it meant to treat the sinner with love, with mercy, not giving them what you knew they deserved. What Aldo deserved was rudeness. What Aldo deserved was a shove to the door.

Though Aldo wasn't asking for forgiveness...

And yet, Ben was required to forgive, though, at the same time, to refuse to countenance Aldo's abuse of Annie.

"How much do ya owe him, Annie?" Ben asked, keeping his eyes on Aldo. He wouldn't trust that snake for a second.

"Ain't ya even going to ask me what it's for? Why she borrowed it?" Aldo sneered.

"That's between me and Annie, Aldo," Ben replied, keeping his voice taut and, with great effort, civil. "Annie," he asked again, "what do ya owe him?"

But beside him now, he only heard the sound of weeping. A glance at Annie told him that, sure enough, her face was buried in her hands as sobs wracked her body.

Ben looked back at Aldo, and saw that his face wore another smirk, more pleased than before if that were possible. "Ya want me to tell him, Annie-girl?"

Annie did not reply, except for a fresh onslaught of tears.

Ferocious anger overtook Ben, and he turned on Aldo. "How much?" he ground out. May God forgive him if his anger was unrighteous.

Aldo raised his eyebrow, as if to tease him.

"How much? If I hafta ask ya again, Aldo, I'll be callin' the police."

A look of fright skidded across Aldo's face for a split second, but then he laughed. "That's rich. You, callin' the police?"

Ben kept his stare locked on him.

Finally, Aldo sighed, with all the drama that Ben had always associated with him. "All right, all right, I guess nobody's up for a joke today. Annie-girl, how much ya figure ya owe me?"

But only sniffling answered him.

"Well, whether she knows or not, I do. Let's just round it out to an even four-hundred smackers, to make up for my inconvenience – having to come here to collect it and all."

Ben swallowed. It was a lot, far more than he had expected. "Is that true, Annie? Do ya owe him that much?"

But before Annie could answer, Aldo said, "It's whatcha promised me, ain't it, Annie-girl? For all my work on your behalf?"

Ben gritted his teeth. "A lot of good your work on her behalf did her, whatever it was, Aldo."

"Oh, it sure as heck did a lot of good." Aldo grinned. "Looking around here, I can see that. Here she is, sittin' pretty."

Ben wondered at that remark. "Four hundred, Annie?" he asked, trying not to let the panic settle in his voice. Four hundred dollars – nearly a third of what he would make in a year. He didn't have that kind of money, not in cold cash, just lying around to give to Aldo.

Annie wiped her eyes on her sleeve. "Yeah," she blubbered. "But it's not the way that ya –"

Aldo cut her off. "See, Ben? I told ya so. Aldo's never wrong, is he?"

Annie tugged on Ben's arm. "Ben – "

Ben swallowed hard. "Hush, Annie. I-I-I'll get it for Aldo. It's no problem. I'm glad to do it."

She wouldn't relent. "But, Ben –"

He wished that she would stop. He was taking care of it. "Be quiet, Annie," he said, a little sternly, and she dissolved again into a crying mess by his side, so unlike her. What kind of a hold did Aldo have? Ben's anger increased.

He knew what he had to do. "Come with me to the bank, Aldo. I'll get you the money there." He hoped the bank would give it to him, at least. The Picoletti house had been paid off now for almost two years; Sam had done that when he'd married Mama. Surely, based on the fact that he was connected to the Giorgi family now and made a steady living, the bank would give him a small loan. If four-hundred dollars was a small loan!

But Aldo slunk over to the sofa and sank into its cushions, putting his dirty boots up on the other end. "Oh, I think I'll just wait here. Take myself a little nap. I've had a long trip." He closed his eyes and rested his head against one of the plump pillows.

"Get your feet off my furniture, please." Mama's commanding voice cut across the room, and Ben's head whipped around to see her standing like a military general in the doorway, Grace by her side.

At the new voice, even Aldo shot up in surprise. In fact, he was so startled that he removed his feet as she asked and sat up.

Mama strode forward to stand before him. With him sitting down, her short form towered over him. She still wore rags in her hair, and she appeared to have dressed in haste. "I don't believe that we have met," Mama stated. "I am Mrs. Giorgi. And you are?"

Aldo actually rose to his feet, nervousness making him clench and unclench his hands. Ben looked on in wonder. He had never seen Aldo like this. "Aldo." Aldo cleared his throat. "The name's Aldo."

"And why are you here, Aldo?" Mama asked.

Apparently recovering enough from his surprise, Aldo raised his chin in defiance. "Pardon my French, but it ain't none of your beeswax, madam. I got business with Ben and Annie. And I ain't gonna leave until I got what I come for."

Mama looked from Annie to Ben. Ben gave a slight nod. Her jaw set, Mama turned back to Aldo. "All right, Aldo. Would you like some coffee? Or tea?"

Startled, Aldo looked to Ben. Ben couldn't help the smile that inched onto his lips. Mama was acting like a queen. "Uh, I guess I'll have some coffee."

Mama nodded shortly and took a seat on the sofa. "Very well. Grace, will you get Mr. Aldo some coffee, please?"

Annie watched as Ben handed over the envelope to Aldo. It was thin, so thin that Annie couldn't believe that four-hundred dollars were tucked inside. So much money! And yet she couldn't tell Ben. Not until after Aldo left.

For, in the little space of time when Sarah had gone to answer the telephone and Grace had left to fetch coffee, Aldo had taken Annie aside. Gripping her elbow, Aldo had hissed into her ear, "Don'tcha dare say anything until I'm out of this house, ya hear? Ya ain't gonna ruin this windfall for me."

She had wrenched her elbow out of his hand, feeling his nails grate against the fabric of her dress. "Ya don't own me, Aldo. And I hafta tell them the truth. As soon as

Ben gets back."

He laughed, keeping it soft just in case, she assumed, somebody was coming into the room at that moment. "You, tell the truth? That'll be the day, Annie-girl. Besides, you've got nothing to gain from doin' that, do ya?"

*The truth will set you free…*

When had she heard that? She didn't know, but the very words acted like a key on her heart, making it long to fly into the freedom that God had offered her through His Son. She didn't understand it all, how could she after just being one of God's children for one night? But she knew – *she knew* – that she would have to obey.

"I am going to tell the truth, Aldo, and so should ya. I… I was wrong before. I was a sinner."

Before she could go on, Aldo interrupted her, laughing. "And what are ya now? A saint?"

"I… I'm born-again." Wasn't that what Jesus had said to Nicodemus last night in the reading that she had done in the book of John? Born, not of blood, not of flesh, not of the will of man, but of the Spirit? Again, she didn't know what it all meant, but she knew it was true. And she knew that she could not have anything to do anymore with the works of darkness. "Aldo, ya don't have to do the things that ya do either, ya know. Jesus came to save sinners, like you and me, and He –"

"Shut your lips." His harsh words cut her off. "I don't want to hear none of that stuff. Don't try this church nonsense on me. You got whatcha wanted, Annie, and now I've gotta get what I need. What ya promised me. You can do all the tale-tellin' ya want after I'm gone – see if I care. But lemme get my dough and get out of this house. Then do whatcha want. Ruin your life for all I care."

She felt as though he'd slapped her. "I… I don't

wanna ruin my life, Aldo. I just want to tell the truth."

A smile had brushed his lips. "Well, I think ya can get more than ya bargained for when you tell the truth, Cuz."

Now, as she watched Ben hand over the slim envelope, Annie shuddered. As soon as Aldo walked out the door, she would take Ben into the library; she would tell him…

"I got a feelin' this is a permanent goodbye, Benji-boy," grinned Aldo.

Ben just looked at him.

Annie's heart hurt as she thought of all Ben – and all the Giorgis – had done for her. What was more, she had pain deep in her side, physical pain that had not been there before. Maybe all the stress wasn't that great for her, carrying this baby and all. She remembered Aldo's words to her – that she would get more than she bargained for when she told the truth. Much as she wanted to see Aldo walk out that door, she also dreaded the words that she would have to speak in the moments that followed.

"Goodbye, cousin," Aldo smirked, pocketing the envelope. He slipped out the door. Ben closed it quietly behind him and leaned against it with eyes shut.

There was no time like the present. Annie let her eyes rest on Ben one last time, looking at him – this man whom she had come here despising, this man whom she had begun to love. *I'm gonna lose him forever.*

"Ben," she started, holding her hand to her side. The pain nagged. Yet she knew that after she'd told him, she would need to gather all her things and walk straight out that door. Where would she spend the night?

But Ben's eyes fluttered open at her voice. "Don't worry about Aldo, Annie. You're part of our family now." A smile struggled to his lips.

How Annie's heart groaned! Part of their family... Oh how she wished for it! She had never known that such a longing could be in her heart. Funny, she had come here looking to grab some money from them and leave, like Aldo had done, and here Ben was, having just paid the way for her to stay.

Tenderness toward her shone in Ben's eyes, and Annie allowed herself to bask in it for one moment longer before she opened her mouth. "Ben," she began again, but she couldn't stop from clenching her teeth a little in pain.

His eyes fell to the hand that she held on her side. "Annie, do ya need to lie down?"

She did, but she couldn't admit it to him right now. She shook her head. "No, I just need to talk to ya about something. Something important."

"Can it wait, Annie? I'm real late to work. I told Mr. Dickerson that I'd get to his house by 8:30, and it's already quarter-to-ten."

She wanted to shake her head no, but she knew that the truth was, it could wait for a few more hours. It would do no harm, except to her own heart, which would wait in agony, like an animal with its paw caught in a trap.

"Yeah, I guess so," Annie murmured. Maybe it was for the best anyway; surely, she would feel better by this evening. And maybe they would let her stay for one more night. That would give her a little more time to make plans.

Ben pushed another smile onto his lips. He looked so weary, and the day had hardly begun. "I promise we'll talk tonight," he said.

## Chapter Nineteen

Sarah heard the groaning as she passed Annie's door. Her heart skipped a beat. She didn't hesitate to put a hand to the door, knock, and call out, "Annie? Annie, are you all right?"

No answer came, so Sarah pushed open the door and entered into the room lighted by the weak winter sunshine passing through the white curtains. "Annie, I heard you..." Sarah trailed off as she took in the sight of the young woman curled up beside the bed, her eyes closed, limbs trembling.

Sarah rushed to her side and knelt down as quickly as her bad knees would allow her to. She brushed back the silky hair near Annie's ear. "Annie, what happened? Did you fall?"

But Annie shook her head. "It... It hurts," she

mumbled, opening her eyes for only a moment.

"Where does it hurt?" Sarah asked urgently.

Slowly, Annie's hand moved down to where her child nestled within her.

"Why didn't you get me sooner?" In dismay, Sarah shook her head but didn't wait for Annie's answer. After all, the girl hadn't, so they must deal with the situation as it now existed.

"I'll be right back," promised Sarah, rising to her feet. She glanced behind her just once as she went to the door, knowing that she didn't need to tell Annie not to move.

Downstairs, Sarah rang up Sam first at his office. The nurse put her through immediately to her husband. "Get her to the hospital," was Sam's immediate response to Sarah's inquiry about Annie. "Don't waste any time. There's no way of knowing whether it's serious or not. I knew we should have insisted that she see a doctor. Well, it's no good saying that now. Bring her, and I'll meet you there, Sarah."

She banged the receiver back into place and dashed back up the stairs. When she reached Annie's room, she found that Grace had come in her absence. Relief came over Sarah at the sight of her daughter kneeling beside Annie. It was good to have help. She reined in her own emotions, not wanting to scare either of the girls. "I talked to Sam. He said that we should go to the hospital. Grace, will you get her other side? Come on, Annie. We're going to get you some help." She slung one of Annie's thin arms around her neck, and Grace did likewise.

"Where's Paulie?" Sarah asked Grace, hoping against hope that her stepson was around to drive them, as their usual driver had gone to town on some errands. If Paulie wasn't home, they'd have to wait for a taxi to come.

"He's home," Grace said, and Sarah felt profound relief. *Thank You, Lord.*

She stood still when they emerged into the hallway. "You go get him, Grace. I'll wait here with Annie."

Grace made sure that all of Annie's weight rested on Sarah, and then she flew down the hallway. Her feet clattered down the stairs as she called out for Paulie.

It seemed a long time, but Sarah knew that it was probably only a minute or two before she heard her stepson bounding up the stairs, accompanying Grace's lighter steps. When Paulie assessed the situation, a look of concern quickly entered his eyes, but he acted quickly. With the gentleness that Sarah recognized as learned from Sam, Paulie lifted Annie in his arms and moved towards the door. "Grace, can you run ahead and start my car?" he asked between quick but sure steps.

Sam met them at the hospital; Sarah had never been so relieved to see his solemn face. "I came as quickly as I could," he told Sarah through the open car window once Paulie's car had pulled up to the curb. "Can she walk?"

Wordlessly, Sarah shook her head, glancing down at the pallid face of the girl whose head rested on her shoulder. *Lord, have mercy...*

"Right," Sam turned and jogged back into the hospital, just a few feet away. Sarah heard him call, "Stretcher, please!"

In just a moment, he was back at the car, and behind him came a couple of young men, outfitted in white, bearing a stretcher. With no fuss at all, the capable orderlies moved Annie from the backseat of the car onto the stretcher. "Can I go with them?" Sarah asked Sam. Her heart reached out towards Annie... and towards the grandbaby that she carried.

Sam spared her a quick smile. "You'll need to stay in the waiting room, dear. I'll make sure that I get you any updates as soon as I can." With that promise, he dropped a kiss to her cheek and hurried after the stretcher, leaving Sarah, Grace, and Paulie to follow at a brisk walk.

Ben burst through the doors of the hospital, his panicked heart fairly bursting in his chest.

Mama looked up as he entered the waiting room. "Ben," she spoke his name aloud, rising to her feet.

"What happened?" Ben forced the words out of his mouth. "Paulie said that she... she collapsed?"

His mother's eyes went toward the window, where Paulie faced them, his usual smile absent, his hand holding Grace's. "Yes." Mama seemed to struggle to swallow. "It was sudden, wasn't it, Grace? She seemed fine all morning. Quiet, more than usual, but I thought that it was because of the kerfuffle of this morning. But she must've felt unwell and said nothing."

Ben ground his teeth. He was such a fool. "She said she wanted to talk to me before I left. I wonder if she felt sick even then, and was gonna tell me, and I just didn't have the time for her." He didn't stop himself from laying a fist to the wall. Why did he have to be such a blockhead sometimes?

Mama's hand came to his shoulder. "Ben, you can't

blame yourself."

Out of respect for Mama, Ben stayed silent, but he knew that, yes, he could blame himself. He swallowed before he spoke again. "Is it the... the... baby?" He almost couldn't form the words.

Mama dropped her eyes from his. "We haven't heard anything much. Paulie called you as soon as we arrived here. Sam did come out once to tell us that it appears that Annie's life is not in danger."

*Appears*... That was no guarantee, though, was it?

He felt a small hand on his shoulder. *Grace.* "We've been praying for Annie, Ben, and for the baby."

Nodding, he sank into a chair, his legs unable to support him any longer. How could it be, this child that he had not wanted, this child who at first it seemed like a terrible reminder of his past, this child whose existence had driven a wedge between him and Betty, how could it be that his heart was struck as though with a knife at the thought of losing it now? And Annie... what of her? *Help, Lord.*

Time seemed to stand still, or not to exist at all. The clock meant nothing as the light of morning grew brighter and then as the sun reached noon. Still, Sam did not come.

And Ben's mind continued begging, pleading, asking with an odd kind of numbness, *Oh Lord, let the baby be all right. Let Annie be all right.* And then... *But help me to trust You even if they ain't.*

"Ben," Sam's voice jolted Ben's eyes open. He had not been sleeping, but the world had become too much for him to take in, so he had closed his eyes to shut it out.

He leapt to his feet to face Sam, who looked officially doctor-like in his white coat. Ben opened his mouth, but the question in his heart couldn't find a voice.

"Annie is all right." Sam laid a hand to Ben's shoulder.

A weight lifted from Ben's chest, but he could not gain breath again until he asked, "And... And the baby?"

Sam's tired face relaxed into a huge grin. "The babies are both doing fine, too. They're both very small, so we're keeping an eye on them – and a couple of hot water bottles around them, too."

There was a long moment of stunned silence. Ben's mind worked to understand what Sam was saying.

"Congratulations, Ben." Sam extended his hand to shake Ben's. "You are the father of twins: a little boy and a little girl. We had to deliver them by Caesarean section, and I truly thank God that this hospital finally got the equipment that is needed to do that kind of surgery adequately."

Stunned, Ben couldn't even respond enough to raise his hand to meet Sam's, so instead, Sam gathered him in a hearty embrace. "You are a blessed man, Ben Picoletti."

All around Ben, excitement prevailed: Grace's outburst of delight, along with Paulie's slap on the back, and Mama's whispered, "Oh, thank You, Lord."

When Sam released Ben, Ben stammered, "Can... Can I see Annie now?"

Sam hesitated for a moment, but then he said, "She's not yet fully awake, but you can come and see her if you are quiet. The surgery that she had undergone is not a pleasant one, and the recovery from it will not be pleasant either."

Through a haze of pain, Annie recognized Ben's voice. She felt too physically wounded to open her eyes or to respond in any way, but she heard his voice, nonetheless, and it comforted her. "Annie, ya just rest. Everything is all right. We have a little son and a little daughter."

And then she felt, soft as a brush of wind on her skin at the ocean, the brush of his lips against her forehead. "Rest, sweetheart. Just rest."

When Paulie pulled the car into the driveway on River Avenue that afternoon, Sarah saw that the postal flag was up. *Taylor must not have had a chance to collect the mail yet.*

"Do you want me to get the mail, Mother?" Paulie asked as he parked the car.

"No, I'll get it. It'll do me good to stretch my legs a little." Sarah opened the door, not waiting for Paulie to come around. She pulled her wool coat closed against the chilly December wind and headed back down the driveway on foot, lighthearted with the news of her new grandchildren – and to know that Annie, dear to her now, would also be all right.

Reaching the mailbox, she pushed the flag down and opened the box. A single envelope lay inside. She began to tuck it into her purse to look at later, but something about its appearance caught her eye. She peered more closely at it.

It was an envelope from her husband's home office; she could tell that from the embossed design on the flap. Her eyes traveled it over as she flipped it in her hands. No stamp. What in the world? And no address. Someone had simply written *Ben* in a rough hand.

Sarah's heart clenched in her chest, though she didn't know why it should.

"We gave her something to sleep," the nurse's whisper came to Ben's ear, jolting him out of the tired vigil that he kept at Annie's side. "She won't wake up for quite a while."

Ben nodded wordlessly. He was too exhausted emotionally to answer. Earlier, he had seen his children. *My children!* For the first time, Ben had felt such a unique love come over him, totally unexpected, welling from deep within him. It crashed over his soul as he stood gazing through the glass at his two very little children – a boy and a girl side-by-side in those little cubicle things that the hospitals put them in in the nursery. *How great is the love the Father has lavished on us...* In becoming a father himself, Ben had been drawn suddenly deeper in comprehending the fatherhood of God.

His hands had clenched by his side as he had tried to keep the tears from rolling down his cheeks. But the effort had been in vain. He had stood there, silently weeping as he stared at this great gift that God had given him. A gift against which he had revolted, a gift over which he had grieved. "But Ya knew better, Lord," he murmured, wiping his eyes. "Thank You."

And now, in this lamp-lit hospital room, he stared at Annie, the woman who was to be his wife. Her face was pale, even more so than it normally was, the freckles standing out starkly across her cheeks. He reached out a hand and smoothed her hair back from her face. She stirred but did not awaken.

"You should go home and get some rest, Mr. Picoletti," the nurse interrupted his thoughts again, and the rustling sound that she made as she put sheets away in a closet roused him more fully from his stupor.

"No, I wanna stay for the night." His voice sounded gravelly to himself.

"Why don't you go home and at least get some fresh clothes, Ben?" He turned to see Sam had entered the room.

Ben opened his mouth to protest, but Sam held up a hand. "Like the nurse said, Annie will sleep for a long while yet. She won't even know you're gone. If you want to sleep here, they'll get a cot ready for you for when you return. But at least go home for a few minutes, change, and eat something."

Ben deliberated on this for a long moment, his eyes flickering over Annie's face. "All right," he finally agreed and rose from his chair.

Sarah was relieved to see Ben walk in the door. Despite the terror of the day, followed by the joy that had attended the birth of the twins and the news of Annie's safety, Sarah had been unable to rest since she had laid eyes on that envelope with Ben's name on it. Why, she couldn't say, but it bothered her.

Ben frowned when he saw her hovering in the library's doorway. "Mama, you should've gone to sleep. It's after eleven o'clock." He took off his hat and coat and hung them on the peg in the entryway.

Sarah fingered the envelope in her pocket, hesitating for just a moment. "Are you back for the night?"

Ben shook his head, turning reddened eyes to her. "Naw, just to change. Then I'm heading back to Annie. Sam said that I should just stop here instead of going to my own house. He said ya'd want some news, and…" He smiled a little sheepishly. "He said that I could get some grub while I was here, too."

A smile broke through Sarah's tension. "Sure, that'd be fine." Her thumb rubbed the edge of the envelope, hidden still in her pocket. "How's Annie?"

"She's doing fine," Ben answered, moving towards the stair. "They gave her some strong medicines, I guess, so she's sleeping. They said they'd put a cot out for me so's I could stay in the room, too."

Sarah nodded. "That's good. I called the Clouds and let them know, so they could put it on the prayer chain."

Ben's jaw tightened. "Thanks, Mama." He plodded up the stairs. "I've just gotta get changed."

Sarah couldn't wait any longer. "Ben," she said pulling the envelope from her pocket, "this was in the mailbox today with your name on it. No stamp," she added.

Ben paused on the staircase. His brow wrinkled as he looked down at the envelope in Sarah's hands. "What is that?"

Sarah shook her head. "I don't know." She held it out to him.

He came back down the rest of the stairs slowly, as if he was quickly running out of steam. He took the letter in his hands and turned it over. When he looked up at Sarah, his frown turned into a smile — *as if he senses my unease.* "Well, guess there's only one way to find out what it is. Let's open it."

Sarah trembled as he ripped open the flap of the envelope.

The smile dropped off her son's face as his eyes scanned the words on the paper he'd withdrawn. "What is this?" His voice hardened. "What is this?" he repeated.

With a sinking heart, Sarah reached out a hand to take the letter from him. Wordlessly, he handed it to her. She scanned the lines quickly:

*Ben,*

*I thought that you should know: Annie's baby ain't yours. I know this, and she knows this, and now you know it, too. Right after you left Annie for another girl, she took up... Well, I guess I should say, he took up with her. Bousquet's son, I mean. You know, the one who used to come home from college on weekends and flirt with all the maids. Annie had always paid him no mind before, while she was with you, but I guess he was too irresistible in the end.*

*Have a great life, Benji-boy, and thanks for the dough.*

*Aldo*

*P.S. Tell Annie for me: Remember what I told you — no one double-crosses me. She had what was coming to her.*

Numbness stole over Sarah like fog over the ocean waves. She stared at the letter, unable to comprehend it. "But... it can't be true?" she said aloud.

The look on Ben's face nearly broke her heart: utter betrayal. "She always did like Bousquet's son. He did like to flirt with her," Ben muttered, his face reddening.

Anxiety rose in Sarah's heart. "Ben, you don't know if this Aldo is telling the truth. He may be doing this just to get to you. He maybe..."

But Ben was shaking his head. "Annie was trying to tell me somethin' this morning, and I put her off – I had to get to work. I dunno what he has against her except whatever money she owed him, but..." Ben swallowed hard, and Sarah saw tears in his eyes. "Aldo is telling the truth, Mama. I know it."

Sarah opened her mouth, but she didn't know what to say. At last, she said the only thing that she could. "You have to talk to Annie. You have to hear what she has to say before you make a judgment."

Stiffly, Ben nodded and headed for the stairs. Then he turned back and took the letter from Sarah's hand. He shoved it into his pocket; it seemed to Sarah that he would have liked to tear the letter in two. She knew that she wanted to.

"I've gotta go change," he stated and pounded up the stairs.

How could Annie have done this to him? Just when he was beginning to feel tenderly toward her? Anger burned in Ben's heart, kindled by hurt.

He ran his fingers through his hair, his nails scraping his scalp, and stared at himself in the guest-room mirror. "I'm so confused, Lord. What am I supposed to do?" he said aloud.

Yet deep inside, he knew what to do.
*Trust Me.*
*But I'm so hurt, Lord...*
*Trust Me.*

And what about those babies – two nameless babies in the hospital? The sight of them had overwhelmed Ben's heart with love. Yet they weren't even his. What a cruel joke. Was that what it was? Had she been playing a joke on him all this time?

His stomach churned. His heart hurt so badly that his legs turned to putty. He sank onto the bed, head in his hands.

"That's what she wanted to tell me this morning," he suddenly realized, the spoken thought loud in the empty room.

*She did mean to tell me the truth, finally.* Knowing this helped him to push back the bitterness that rose within him to meet the hurt that Annie had done him.

*And yet it still hurts. So badly.* He slowly unbuttoned his shirt with one hand, his movements mechanical. *How could she betray me like this? How could she use me like this? Oh, God, how can I forgive her?*

Silently, he sat, head in his hands, shirt half-done-up, his eyes burning with tears of anger, tears of pain. If he had not begun to feel tenderly toward Annie, this betrayal would not have injured him so; he knew that. If his heart had not softened toward her, the arrow of this lie could not have punctured it and drawn blood.

*And such were some of you...*

He thought of the cross. He thought of his own sins, so freely yet not cheaply forgiven by Christ. There were so many of them: the more conspicuous ones in the past – fornication, drunkenness, lying, theft, and others – followed by the quieter but still terrible ones he struggled with in the present – hatred, lust, selfishness, and the list went on.

And then he thought also of that day that he had

gone to his own father's grave, had knelt by the stone marker, had not only forgiven his father from the heart for the things that had been done to him by that man, but he had also asked forgiveness of Papa in turn.

*All have sinned… All is grace.*

The tears rose to his eyes – tears of thankfulness this time – washing away the ones of anger and hurt. Oh, how he himself had needed Christ's forgiveness! Sometimes, Ben looked at himself – not just at his life and how God had worked the circumstances together so that he had a good job, a secure housing situation, and a loving family – but he took a hard look at *himself,* and he saw that he was a new man, a different person. Annie had seen that, too, when she'd first come. He had seen her looking at him, he had seen the wonder in her eyes when he had responded in ways that he would never have responded in days past.

Now he thought of Annie lying in that hospital bed with her two babies in the nursery down the hall, and it was as if he'd been a horse wearing blinders. Now they'd been removed.

She, too, had been forgiven by God. And what God has forgiven in heaven, men must forgive on earth…

Ben didn't know what this would all mean for him and for Annie, this new revelation that had come through Aldo's hand, the hand of one who sought to destroy; but he did know this: that God would work all things together for the good of those who loved Him, who were the called according to His purpose.

He buried his head in his hands. A sense of peace came over him as he let the words fall from his lips in willing surrender, "Heavenly Father, I trust You. Ya haven't let me down yet, and I believe You won't let me down now."

# Chapter Twenty

Betty kept her head down, dodging the snowflakes as she half-ran up the walkway to her front door, careful not to slip on the wet stones. "Mother, I'm home," she called out as she pushed open the door. *Finally.* It had been a long day. The parents of one of her students were interested in purchasing a brand-new piano, and the best place to shop for that was Providence. They'd asked Betty if she'd be willing to accompany them and to give her opinion on the instruments as they considered which to buy. Though she'd had to rearrange some of her to-dos, Betty had found herself agreeing to help them out. Now, she gave a final wave to the departing car through the open door and felt the fatigue of the day settle on her along with satisfaction that the Carmichaels had found an instrument that Betty felt would work well for them.

Clicking the door shut behind her, she unwound her scarf and removed her coat and hat. She laid her slightly-soggy mittens on the radiator to dry before finding her way into the kitchen, where Mother usually was.

Sure enough, Mother stood at the sink, finishing up the last of the dinner dishes.

"Hi, Mother." Betty stepped toward the stove, where she reached for the tea kettle.

Mother started. "Oh, Betty. I didn't hear you come in. Must have been lost in my thoughts." She nodded toward the kettle. "That water should still be hot. I just made tea for your father a few minutes ago."

"Oh, good." Betty reached into the cupboard near the stove and found her favorite teacup. Dropping a few dried mint leaves into a square of cheesecloth, she twisted it closed before adding it to the cup. The fragrance of mint wafted up, pleasant to her, as she poured water over the cheesecloth bag.

Mother was quiet – unusually so. Especially if Daddy had been in his study for a while, Mother loved to chatter away with Betty whenever she walked into her kitchen. Betty studied her for a moment. Had something happened? Mother and Daddy didn't often argue, but Mother could be quieter if they had disagreed about something important. Should she ask?

But Mother didn't give her a chance. "Betty." She turned abruptly from the sink, wiping her hands on her apron front.

Betty tensed. This was Mother's way – confrontational, take-the-pig-by-the-ears. She swallowed a large sip of tea. *Too hot.* She winced as the liquid burned its way down her esophagus. "Yes?" she managed at last.

Mother studied her for a brief moment. "Betty, I

received a telephone call from Sarah Giorgi today. She said that Annie gave birth to her babies today. It was an emergency Caesarean section. They asked for prayer because Annie has a long road to recovery and the babies are quite tiny."

"Babies?"

"Twins. She gave birth to twins, a boy and a girl."

Betty sensed the approach of self-pity – shadowy, pathetic, and weakening. She closed her eyes to it. *Let it be unto me according to thy word.* His word, not hers.

"All right." She paused, aware of Mother's concerned gaze. "I'll pray for them all. Let them know that if they call, won't you?"

A gentle smile lifted Mother's lips. "I will, Apple Betty. I will do that."

Through the glass, Sarah stared at the newborn babies, so innocent-looking in their white wrappings, Such tiny heads! They were so small, especially compared to her own babies, who had all registered at nine or ten pounds. But Sam told her that the twins had appeared to be a little early – perhaps three or even four weeks. "If they'd come any earlier," he'd said, "they may have been in trouble. So thank the Lord that they came when they did." He'd then grumbled quietly, "I wish this hospital would invest in an incubator."

And she did praise the Lord that they'd come when they did. That was not what made her want to weep.

Rather, it was the thought that these two little infants, whom she had welcomed into her heart almost from the moment Annie told them that she carried Ben's children, really had no natural place in her heart, or ought not. She ought not even know that they existed. If it had not been for Annie's deceit, Sarah's life would've gone on just as it had always gone on. Perhaps she would be preparing for Ben and Betty's wedding right now, rather than standing in a warm hospital hallway, staring at two small persons unrelated to her in any way.

Her heart tore at the thought. In her heart, in her mind, she had already been calling them part of her family. She had already welcomed Annie into her own heart, just as much as she had welcomed her into her home. After Annie's surrender to Christ, which Ben had told Sarah about, she must've desired to tell the truth to all concerned. But she had not had the chance to do it. Vaguely, Sarah wondered if it would have made a difference if Annie had told about her deception instead of Aldo.

But what did that matter in the end? The truth was the truth. And now, all of them – Ben and Sarah and Sam and everyone else involved – would have to make a decision about what their response would be to that truth.

*Ben won't marry Annie now.* Sarah was as certain of that as she was of her own birthday. She had seen how he had struggled over giving up Betty, how he had determined to commit to Annie in order that he might take care of her and their child. To love her, even. But the fact remained that he had done all of that because he believed that Annie carried his child and that he had a responsibility to her because of it.

That responsibility didn't truly exist. While feeling bewildered, perhaps even betrayed by Annie's long deception, at the same time, Sarah's own heart went out to her. What would Annie do now? She didn't seem to have any family, and Sarah guessed that, whoever he was, Bousquet's son was not interested in taking on the responsibility of two children and a wife, or even just providing for two children.

*She's alone then. They're fatherless.* And Sarah stared at the babies, wondering not only what would become of their mother, but also what would become of them. *I feel so helpless.* She swallowed. *Oh, Lord, You are a Father to the fatherless, a protector of those with no husband…*

When Annie opened her eyes, she knew that the medication-induced fog had lifted. Slowly, she turned her head towards the light that streamed in from the window of her private room and grimaced. Even moving her head dizzied her.

But the light was beautiful. Light had never seemed so beautiful to her as it did as she'd returned from the tunnel of pain and darkness she had experienced.

*I am the Light of the world.*

Where had that come from? From a long-forgotten Sunday-School verse or a sermon she had heard years ago? She didn't know where she had first heard it, certainly not recently, but Annie did know this one thing: that it was true. Jesus was the Light of the world. He had brought light into her darkness, and even in the midst of the pain and fear that the last many hours had brought her, she had known that He was with her. Jesus was with her.

She took a shallow breath. Breathing any deeper than that brought a surge of pain all across her midsection, extending even into her limbs. What had happened exactly? Had she lost the babies? At the thought, a dark dread came over her. Perhaps it was for the best if she had. *Then I wouldn't need to tell…*

*No.* Regardless of what happened with the babies, Ben must be told the truth. As soon as possible.

"Annie," Ben's voice broke into her thoughts. With extreme caution, she moved her head against the tide of pain toward the source of the sound. He stood in the doorway, relief evident on his face. The sight of him drew Annie's heart like a deer to the waterbrooks.

Yet she resisted the pull. *I can't. I have to let him go.*

"You're awake." He walked across the room, quietness in his step, so unlike the Ben of the past. That Ben had been all wildness, a fool rushing in where angels feared to tread.

Annie tried to force a smile to her face to welcome him. But she couldn't do it; the pain proved triumphant. She swallowed past her parched throat and tried to say something, but found the words stuck.

Ben didn't seem to notice but came to her side, sat in the chair there, and reached for her hands, lying limp on top of the bed covers. No strength remained in her to squeeze his hand back, but his grasp gave her the sense of protection and of comfort that she craved.

"Everyone has been praying for you," started Ben, as if he wasn't sure what to say.

Annie opened her mouth to try to speak again. She wanted to ask what had happened, for she could not remember past her collapse in the Giorgis' house. How had she found herself in the hospital, in searing pain, coming out of the medicine-induced sleep? And the baby she carried? Was it all right?

Her dry throat prevented her from speaking, though, and Ben didn't notice. "You're going to be all right, Annie," he assured her, his rough hand brushing back the hair from her eyes. A feeling of being cherished washed over Annie, as she had never felt in all her life. If Jesus Christ could do such a work in a man like Ben Picoletti, she wondered what could He do in her? *Will Ya do such a thing in me?*

She swallowed harder in an effort to get Ben to understand that she needed some water. At last, he seemed to make the connection. "You need a drink?"

She nodded as vigorously as she could. A glass of water sat on the bedside table. He placed it to her lips, holding one hand behind her head for support. At first, as she started to swallow the water, her throat felt as though knives cut into it, but then, slowly, it quenched her thirst.

At last, she leaned back and Ben put the now half-empty glass of water back on the bedside table.

"What happened?" she croaked.

Ben's brow furrowed in surprise. "Oh, Annie, don'tcha know?"

Her heart caved. Her baby was dead; that must be what he meant. *It is just what you deserved…*

"What do ya remember?" Ben's question interrupted the dark thought.

She wished that he would just tell her the truth outright. "I… I remember fallin' next to the bed at home – I mean, at your parents' house." She paused. The memory faded from that point on. "And then… nothing. Nothin' until now."

Ben's eyes widened. "Wow. Well, you've been through a whole lot since then. Maybe it's good that ya don't remember nothin'." He leaned back in his chair but still kept hold of Annie's hand. "When ya collapsed, Paulie brought ya here to the hospital with Grace and my mother. Your blood pressure was real low, and you'd fainted, but you also went into early labor, Sam says, but you couldn't deliver the babies. There were... problems somehow; I don't understand. You better ask the doc about that if ya wanna know."

He paused a moment. "We were in the waiting room, not sure what was going on, and then Dr. Giorgi came out and told us that you'd... that they'd opened ya up and gotten the babies out. Not just one baby, Annie, but two." And here, his lips broke into a smile.

So that was why she was in so much pain. She'd heard about those operations – Caesareans, they called them – but never had expected to experience one herself. But this thought was overtaken by the rest of what Ben had said: *Two. Two!* God had given her not one child, but two. *Two gifts from God.* Now joy flooded her, just as the sunlight that came in her window, enlightening the room.

Tears rose to her eyes. "I wanna see them." The urgency to see and touch her children overcame her.

A smile softened Ben's exhausted face. "And ya will," he said, "but they don't want ya to move much just yet. They hafta bring 'em here to you."

In a moment, Ben had gone to get Sam. The anticipation of seeing the babies drained her, and she let her eyes close. Just a moment of rest. Just a moment. While she waited for Ben...

When she opened them again, it was dark, except for

a little light. She turned her head and saw Sarah sitting there. The older woman smiled at Annie, but it seemed to Annie that the expression was a little troubled.

"You slept for a long time, dear," Sarah broke the silence, reaching forward to touch Annie's shoulder. Her hand felt gentle as always, but Annie sensed stiffness in her action.

In her life, Annie had cultivated the ability to read people; with the way she grew up, it had proved a useful skill.

"What's wrong?" The question came out without softening.

Sarah attempted to make her smile wider, but she didn't meet Annie's eyes. "Wrong?"

"What's wrong?" Panic trickled into her heart. She struggled a little so that she could raise her head. But then the sharp pain skewered her abdomen and shot down her limbs, and she fell back against the pillow, having raised herself only an inch or two to begin with. "Something's wrong. They never brought 'em to see me." The knowledge sparked through her mind. "The babies... The babies are..." And before she had even seen them!

But Sarah was shaking her head firmly. "No, no, the babies are fine, Annie. They're beautiful." And Annie heard the catch in the older woman's voice. Inwardly, she cringed. How would Sarah take it when she found out that those children were not of her blood at all? How would she take it when she found out that Annie had deceived the entire Picoletti-Giorgi family? Sarah was a woman so loyal to her own; Annie had found this out, had even exploited it at times. It was the reason why Sarah had so welcomed Annie into their home – because she knew that Annie carried her son's children.

Fear clutched Annie's chest, making her physical pain even worse. Like a riderless horse, her thoughts raced around her mind. What about this hospital room? And her stay here? The surgery to deliver the babies? All of that cost money – money that she would have been entitled to use as the mother of Ben's children and his wife-to-be.

*But I'm not.*

What would she do? What would she do? *Oh, God, I am so afraid.*

As a single mother of two infants, with no wedding ring on her finger to imply a widowed status, how would she find work? No one would want to employ her. No one reputable, that was. Sure, maybe once she got her figure back, she could find a job in a shady diner, or maybe she could scrape by and get some kind of unskilled work if she hid the fact that she had two children… She had no education and no training, except for housekeeping. Sure, she'd finished most of high school, through tenth grade. Most folks didn't go farther than that unless they had plans to go on to college. And while Annie had loved school, no one had ever encouraged her toward college, that was for sure. And the classes had been increasingly difficult for her in high school, especially with no one cheering her on at home to press through them.

The reality of her situation weighed on her now as she lay there, unable to move due to the pain, her whole heart already absorbed with love for the two children that she had not yet seen, yet also crushed because she knew that she couldn't care for them, could never provide them with the kind of life that she wanted to. *I will have to give them up.*

In her distress, her heart cried out simply to God. *Help me.* She knew that He had saved her and rescued her from sure death – not of her physical life but of her soul. She had been dying day by day and had not known it until that night at the Christmas pageant, or at least had not seen it clearly. But then, God had reached down to her when she was totally helpless. He had forgiven her through His Son; He had given His Son for her...

If He had done all of that for her, would He not now show her the way? *I need to believe in Ya.* A small peace settled over her as she began to ask Him what she should do. It was a new thing for her, this asking a dependable Father, for she had never known one, but it was a joyful thing to put herself so completely in His loving hands.

## Chapter
## Twenty-One

Ben waited a full day to return to the hospital. He knew that when he went, Annie would have to talk. And he had been turning it over in his mind what he should say and what he should do. He also knew that he needed to resist seeing the children; the last thing he needed was to become yet more confused by increasing the tenderness he already felt toward the little, helpless ones.

He had given his promise to Annie to marry her, to care for her children, but it was a promise made under false pretenses, so Ben no longer thought that it bound him. He had wanted to ask the advice of Reverend Cloud, but he felt that in this situation, due to Betty's involvement in his own life, he could not do that. So he'd spent the day fasting, a new practice for him, but one that he had read about in the Scriptures, seeking to hear God's voice speaking to his heart.

Would Annie even want to marry him, if he did go through with his promise? Yes, he was sure that she would. He would have to be blind to the way that the world worked to not know that an unmarried woman with children would have a very difficult time indeed in this life.

And yet, was it fair to expect Ben to take up the slack? He thought of Bousquet's son – of how that young man had tucked tail and ran from his responsibilities – and he grew angry. Yet he also knew that he himself would have tried to do the same exact thing perhaps half a year ago. How easily these children could have been Ben's own!

"What do I do?" he asked aloud as he walked through the hospital doors and up to the reception desk. "What do I do, Lord?"

"I'm sorry, sir. I didn't hear you." The receptionist looked up from some paperwork to meet his eyes.

Ben shoved his hands into his pockets. "Oh, I... I'm here to see..." He hesitated. Was she still that to him? "I'm here to see my fiancée," he finally finished. "Annie."

A flutter of curious disapproval passed over the receptionist's face. Though Chetham had grown enough in the past years to now boast this little hospital, the town was still much too small to keep such things as a fiancée who gave birth before the wedding under one's hat. But the woman said nothing except, "You can go on up. She's been transferred to Room 203."

Ben nodded. "Thanks." He took the stairs two at-a-time to the second level of the hospital. His steps slowed as he approached Annie's room. He didn't think anyone else would be here now. He had passed Mama on her way into the house. She had been at the hospital this morning and had said that Annie had still not revealed anything that had been in Aldo's letter.

That confused Ben a little. Mama had been very close with Annie. If Annie had not told Mama, would she tell him? Or would he have to confront her with the letter that Aldo had given him? Even now, it weighed on him, crumpled inside his pocket. Ben's insides curdled at the thought of showing it to Annie, of reading it to her. He wished he could burn it, forget all about it... and yet the truth in it freed him to marry Betty, didn't it?

All too soon, the doorway stood before him. Maybe she would be asleep, he half-hoped as he put his knuckles to the door and gave a little rap.

But she was not. "Come in," her weak voice called out.

*Oh, Lord God, give me your wisdom!* Arming himself with all the courage that he could muster, Ben took a deep breath and moved through the door.

Sarah stood before the hospital nursery, looking through the glass. The two red faces of Annie's infant twins filled her vision. She closed her eyes so that she could listen — so that she could speak to her Lord without the distraction of the outside world.

*Is it wrong, Lord, this idea that I have? This desire?*

It had come to her last night. She had woken up, slipped from between the warm sheets, filled with a strong sense of what ought to be done about the situation with Annie and her babies. Sam had continued to sleep peacefully, but Sarah had found herself fully awake. She had prayed long and hard throughout the night with no answer. Was this idea that had come into her brain in the darkness merely her own imagination combining with the secret wishes of her heart?

*Trust in the Lord with all your heart...*

*He will give you the desires of Your heart...*

She opened her eyes and looked again at the two swaddled babies. Her heart yearned for them. Certainly, they had a mother in Annie. She knew that the young woman, though inexperienced and alone, would do her very best, would love the children with all her heart. Yet she also knew that Annie had little support, other than the Giorgis. And Ben would not marry Annie now. How could he, when his promise had been founded on a lie? Yes, Annie would love these children, but love without the means to back it up... Well, Sarah knew how that went. The memory of baby David – her last child – filled her mind. And of her youngest daughter, Evelyn, whom Sarah had given away to her own sister to raise due to her hard situation with her first and now-deceased husband Charlie.

*If this is Your will, oh Lord, then show me. I don't want to do this only out of my own yearnings, but because it is for the best for all. I don't want to take things into my own hands, trying to fix things. You take it, Lord, and work it together without my needing to fight for it.*

She stood there for a few minutes longer and then turned, about to head back to Annie's room to say goodbye for the day. She was halted, however, by the appearance of her husband, coming toward her in his white coat, stethoscope around his neck, a serious and somewhat startled expression on his face.

"Is everything all right?" Sarah blurted out. "Is Annie...?"

"Everything's fine," Sam assured her, placing his

hand on hers. "I've had this... idea, I suppose you could call it, floating around in my brain all day, and, well, I have the urge to look at the babies again." He turned, his arm moving to loop around Sarah's shoulders, and together, they gazed through the nursery glass.

"Sarah," Sam broke the silence.

"Yes?"

"This is going to sound crazy, but what would you think of..." He shook his head, as if he himself couldn't believe what he was going to say. "I've been thinking, and Annie will have a hard row to hoe, what with the twins and trying to work, needing a place to live, and..."

He paused and Sarah felt as though her heart might pound out of her chest in anticipation. "What if we helped her get back on her feet? But long-term. And not just that, but what if we... what if we took her into our family, almost as if she were our own daughter?" He put up a hand. "I know it sounds impractical and ridiculous – but do you think it's possible?"

Numbness settled over Sarah. Could it be...? Was he really saying this? The fulfillment of, and more than the fulfillment of, what she'd thought and prayed about?

Sam took her shoulders in his hands, gently moving her to face him. He offered her a half-smile. "I know, I know. It's absurd. And Ben would have to agree; I don't want to make him uncomfortable at all. But perhaps we can at least pray about it? I don't know how to describe it, but I feel such a love and protectiveness towards these children, toward Annie, even, despite everything that's happened. Despite the letter from that man."

He softly laughed, shaking his head. "I know that it sounds – well, just plain crazy, especially since I was the one so against Annie when she first came here. God has been doing a work in my heart, though. That's the only way that I can explain it, Sarah."

Sarah stared at him, unable to speak.

"At least, let's pray about it?" he said, and then winked before going on, "but if God gives you the encouragement to commit me to Butler, well, just say the word."

"Yes." She couldn't get more than that single word off her tongue for the shock, but she knew she had to get at least that one out.

Sam stared at her for a second. "What? You do want to commit me to Butler?"

"Yes. I mean, no, I'm saying yes to the rest of it, Sam."

"Sarah," Sam looked at her intently, "we shouldn't take this lightly. We should pray about it. We should…"

"Yes. Yes. Yes!" She nearly shouted as she threw her arms around Sam's neck. A moment later, he returned the embrace, lifting her off the ground.

"Yes, yes, yes," she whispered again into his ear, for once heedless of the stares of Sam's colleagues passing by them.

Sam put her down and held her at arms-length. "Sarah, it's a big responsibility, and Annie might not –"

Sarah wiped tears from her eyes, but nothing could wipe away the joy that flooded her soul, filling her. "Sam, I already have prayed about it – all last night. When you came up just now, I was standing here at the nursery, talking with the Lord about it. And then you walked up and said it, too. I'm sure it is of Him. I never dreamed…"

Sam searched her face for a long moment, then his own lips rose in a smile. "We still have to ask Annie, you know. After all that's happened, she may not want to stay in Chetham at all."

Sarah nodded, but she did not doubt that Annie would say yes. For if God could change Sam's heart, why could He not change Annie's?

When Ben took a seat beside her bed, Annie couldn't wait – didn't want to wait – any longer to tell him the truth. *Better to get it over with, Annie.* How would his tenderness toward her change, how much would she lose, in the telling, though? *It don't matter. I gotta tell him the truth – at last.*

"Ben, I gotta tell ya somethin' – somethin' that'll shock ya," she blurted before she could chicken out.

Before she could go on, though, Ben looked her right in the eyes. "The babies ain't mine, are they, Ansy?"

The breath left her lungs in a whoosh. "But how didja know?" Annie looked at him in shock, raising herself on her elbows. The movement stabbed her with pain, so she let herself fall back against the pillow.

"Aldo left a letter," Ben told her, covering her hand with his.

"I was gonna tell ya –" Annie tried to say.

But Ben interrupted her, and she marveled at how grace gentled his voice. "I know."

Silence stretched between them for a long moment, then both spoke at once. "But our marriage–"

Each stopped, awkwardly smiled, and then Ben said, "You first."

"I can't marry ya now, Ben. It wouldn't be right." Annie let the words find their way out of her mouth, and in place of them sorrowful peace nestled in her heart. "I know that you'd be an honorable man or whatever, and still come through, maybe, but I just can't do that to ya or to Betty."

Ben sat there silently, his eyes cast down, his hands still on hers. At last he looked up. "What about you? Whatcha gonna do?"

When he didn't protest her announcement, Annie knew then that she had made the right decision. Maybe Ben had only been waiting for her to release him from his promise. And yet how hard it was to let go of this man with whom she had only truly fallen in love after she had accepted his proposal. She tried to turn her mind toward the question he had asked. "I don't know," she admitted, her spirit lamed. "I don't have any family…"

"We're your family," Ben interrupted her.

She tried to smile and shook her head. "No, you're not. You've got Betty, and it wouldn't be fair, after everything that's happened."

"We're your family," Ben said again, with firmness in his voice, a firmness that told Annie that he would not be argued with. "You're part of the family of God, Annie. You're my sister in Christ. And of course I'm gonna take care of my own sister, ain't I?"

She saw Ben with new eyes. *A sister. He, my brother. The family of God.* Was it true? If it was, perhaps she was not as alone as she thought.

The telephone rang, and Betty's eyes darted up from her book. She waited for it to ring a second time, reluctant to put down this latest Grace Livingston Hill novel. But when no one else appeared to answer the incessant ringing, Betty sighed, put aside her book, and strode into the hall to pick up the receiver.

"Clouds' residence," she spoke into the mouthpiece, trying not to let her impatience show.

There was silence for just a second, long enough to make Betty wonder, and then, "Betty? It's me, Ben."

She heard excitement in his voice. Her own heart sank, straight down into her saddle-shoes. *I will be calm. I want to handle this right, Lord.* "Yes?" Her hands clutched the receiver so tightly that her fingernails dug into her palm on the other side.

"Listen, Betty. I've got something to talk to ya about. Are ya home right now?"

"Yes, but my parents aren't home." Her parents generally didn't allow male visitors to come to the house if Betty was unchaperoned. She sucked in a deep breath. "Ben, congratulations on–"

Ben interrupted her. "Okay, if ya can't see me at your house, how about meeting me at the diner?"

At the diner? It was thoroughly known throughout Chetham, or at least throughout Ben and Betty's circles that she and Ben had broken up. What would folks say if they saw her with him at the diner? "I'm not sure that's such a good idea. What will folks say?" she asked bluntly. Betty did not want to be plagued by gossip without need for it.

But Ben laughed, joy ringing in the sound. "Oh Betty. You got nothin' to worry about." He paused for a second. "Look, please meet me at the diner. I'll bring Cliff. He can sit in the booth across from us. Will that help?"

She had half-a-mind to tell him no and to put down

the phone and go back to her book, but something inside her told her that she should say yes.

That she should accept this gift. That she should trust in her God and not in her own plans, her own self, her own wisdom.

"Yes, Ben. I'll be there in twenty minutes."

# Chapter Twenty-Two

The diner was empty at this time of the afternoon: the lunch crowd had left, while the three-o-clock coffee-break folks had not yet arrived. From the radio, Bing Crosby's mellow voice crooned "Silent Night," the words occasionally interrupted by the energetic clattering as Sally organized forks, knives, and spoons behind the countertop.

As Betty stepped into the diner, she felt its maple-scented, cozy warmth as an embrace. She let her eyes adjust to the lower lighting, taking the opportunity to look around to see if Ben and Cliff had arrived yet. No, she didn't think they had...

*There.* In the booth beside the window. Just as her eyes touched on him, his own lifted. He scrambled up, his mouth breaking into a grin, one that seemed to hold his whole heart.

She intended to walk toward him, but he appeared unwilling – or unable – to wait even that long. Half running across the diner, he caught her hands in his and brought them, paired, to meet his lips.

For once, Betty didn't feel embarrassed or irritated by Ben's spontaneous display of affection. Instead, peace settled into her heart – accompanied by bewilderment. "Ben. Ben, what does this mean? What's going on?" She heard the questions come out of her own mouth.

He dropped her hands and cupped her face, drawing her gaze to meet his own. "Will ya marry me, Betty, my sweet Betty?"

"But… what about Annie? The…The babies… I…"

Her words fainted in her throat as he shook his head. "They're not my children, Betty. Annie broke off our engagement this morning. She… She became a believer, and she told me the truth."

*Son of God, love's pure light…*

He swallowed. "So, if ya will have me – despite all my past – I promise that I will love ya, Betty, and be true to ya before the Lord Jesus Christ." He paused. "I spoke with your father already, so all's I have left to do is ask – Will ya… Will ya marry me, Betty, despite it all?"

*Radiant beams from Thy holy face,*
*With the dawn of redeeming grace…*

The final vestige of clouds lifted from Betty's heart. "Yes, Ben, I will."

"Wha… Ya mean… Do ya…?" Ben's eyes searched her face, as though he couldn't believe what she'd said.

With gentle hands, she cupped his face as he had done to hers moments before. "Yes," she whispered again, delighting in the joy that swept over them both. "I will marry you."

At that, Ben gave a whoop that brought a clatter of silverware from Sally, such as Betty had never heard before and never likely would again. She found herself lifted off the ground as he clutched her in his arms and hugged her tightly.

Her face half-smushed in his shoulder, Betty freed herself enough to murmur in his ear, "I love you, Ben Picoletti."

### Three Months Later

The wet winds of March whipped around them as Sam led Sarah and Annie down the brick pathway. "It's not much to look at right now." He smiled apologetically over his shoulder. "But wait until springtime really arrives. The crocuses and tulips will be blanketing the ground out here. It will be much prettier then."

Prettier? How could it be prettier than it was now? Cuddling Peter closer against her body, Annie took in the cottage before them with tear-glazed eyes. Sure, a little snow still lay in sloppy piles against the foundation – the last of winter's strength – and the windows stared out dark, absent of any company save her own. But it was her home – a place where she could continue to build her life on the sure foundation she had in Jesus Christ, a secure place where she could raise Peter and his sister Dora. She still couldn't believe that Sarah and Sam had so generously offered her the small, unused gardener's cottage at the back of their property – rent-free.

Her glance caught on the cheery yellow curtains

flouncing across the windows, and her mouth lifted in a smile. "The curtains look so good!" she said aloud to Sarah as they paused on the path.

Sarah returned her smile. "You did a wonderful job with them. Emmeline says that she hopes you have time to sew more; she knows a number of people who could use new ones." Her hand moved to pat the back of baby Dora, nestled against her woolen coat. "But I told her that I wasn't sure that you'd have time, what with your secretarial course beginning next month."

Annie's heart thudded a couple of times at the mention of the course. She'd been away from any kind of classroom for more than two years. Would she be able to pick up the material? What if she failed?

"You're going to do fine," Sarah assured her.

Annie gave her a sheepish smile. How had Sarah known exactly what Annie had been thinking? "I sure am grateful that you're willin' to take the babies on the days I have classes."

At her words, Sarah's face broke into a wide grin. "It's a joy, Annie, a real joy. You have no idea how much. Maybe someday I'll tell you all about it. I'll only say, He has satisfied my mouth with good things."

Annie couldn't help the curiosity from showing on her face, but before she could ask anything else of Sarah, Sam called to them from the freshly-painted door, "Are you slowpokes coming?"

"Men. Always in a hurry." Sarah winked and picked up her pace.

"I don't know why you're rushing us, Sam Giorgi," she said as they arrived at the door and Sam handed Annie the key, taking baby Peter from her.

"Nothing in there but an empty house," went on

Sarah.

Annie drew in a deep breath and plunged the key into the lock. She pushed open the door. *Home.*

"Surprise!"

Amid the many voices all laughing and shouting, the lights flicked on in the dark cottage. Well over a dozen people crowded the small front room, smiling and reaching out to hug Annie.

"What – What is this?" she managed to ask as Bertha Cloud squeezed her.

"It's a housewarming party, of course!" This came from Paulie, who grinned and pulled her into a hard hug around the shoulders.

She gazed up at him and then around at Emmeline and Geoff, Henry and Bertha, Betty and Ben, Cliff, Sarah, Sam, and even Sarah's older daughter Louisa with her children. "But why? Why for me?" She was nobody to them, not really!

"Because you're loved by us all, Annie dear, and we wanted to help make this house a real home for you and your children," said Sarah. Around her, the others nodded.

Annie couldn't help the tears that flooded her eyes, falling down her cheeks. What a gift she had been given by them all – undeserved, unearned – a true reflection of the perfect gift given to her and to all those who heed His call of salvation.

*Thanks, Lord. Thanks for leading me home.*

*Dear friend,*

Thank you for taking the time to read *Each Perfect Gift*. It's my prayerful hope that God will use the story of Ben, Betty, and Annie to enrich your relationship with Him through His Son, Jesus Christ, the greatest Perfect Gift. If you don't know Him as your Savior and friend, won't you come to Him today, in simple faith, as Annie did?

If you've enjoyed this story, you'll want to read the trilogy *A Time of Grace*, which gave birth to *Each Perfect Gift*:

*The Fragrance of Geraniums*

*All Our Empty Places*

*A Love to Come Home To*

And, if you love historical fiction that tells the story of real people who walked with God, you may also enjoy:

*A Holy Passion: A Novel of David Brainerd and Jerusha Edwards*

Finally, if you've enjoyed this novel, would you let a friend know so that they also might be blessed by it? You can do this personally or by leaving a review on Amazon or Goodreads. Thank you!

Please feel free to drop by my "squirrel-nest"; book-loving friends are always welcome to say hello:

Facebook - @AliciaGRuggieri

Website & Blog – www.aliciagruggieri.com

I look forward to meeting you!


Grace and peace through the Cross of Jesus Christ,

*Alicia G. Ruggieri*

## *My great thanks go to...*

My dear Mama-Bee, who nurtured a love for books in her children from a young age and whose prayers follow me daily.

My sisters, Londie and Rebekah, and my fellow-author and friend Anita, who are enthusiastic first-readers and give me so-needed suggestions for the plots of every story I write. I couldn't do it without you, ladies!

My husband, Alex, who encourages and sees the value of storytelling and who prays for me and those who read my books.

Ann, Carolyn, and Christina, who became Word Detectives when I needed final weed-pulling in the manuscript. What a blessing that was!

My wonderful street team members – God has blessed me through the way you help me out with character names, sharing news, and most especially, praying for me. Thank you!

My church family, many of whom pray for my writing and for the message of the Gospel to spread through it – a great encouragement.

Those who read and share these stories – May they bless you!

And to my Savior and Lord Jesus Christ, who seeks and saves those who are lost (Luke 19:10)